"If you're not wait...

Lucas's eyes shot ope... Mac, but the blonde s... his table looked like a stranger.

The woman wore a bright red skirt, barely the length of a dinner napkin. It fit her like a second skin and seemed to stop where her legs began. Lucas's mouth went dry. Was she wearing anything beneath it?

"You like?" She whirled in front of him, causing the skirt to inch up even higher.

Lucas dragged his eyes from the miraculous legs up her body. Beneath the stretchy fabric of her tank top, he could see the outline of her perfect breasts, beaded with excitement. Her blond hair was mussed, as if some man had just run his hands through it several times. And her eyes—they were huge, heavy-lidded...but there was no mistaking that golden-brown color.

"Mac, what in hell are you doing?"

In a flash, she slid in beside him in the back of the booth. "Shh." She gave him a slow wink. "You're mistaken. I'm not Mac. I'm Sally. And you're...John. We're complete strangers." She slipped a finger beneath his shirt, popping the first button free of its hole, then moving on to the next. "Feel like getting lucky, John?"

Blaze™

Dear Reader,

Is seduction a science or an art?

The brilliant Dr. MacKenzie Lloyd firmly believes it's a science and that all she has to do to keep her future husband from straying is to become skilled in pleasing a man in bed. Her plan for acquiring that expertise is the same three-step process that has brought her so much success in the lab.

Step 1: gather data on male sexual fantasies

Step 2: formulate some theories

Step 3: put those theories into practice, practice, practice!

But when Mac starts to practice her techniques on sexy CEO Lucas Wainwright, her plan hits a few unforeseen snags....

I love writing books about women who have the courage to take risks. And writing my first Blaze novel has allowed me to do just that. It's also been about the most fun a girl can have—unless, of course, she decides to try some of Mac's research out for herself....

I'd love to know what you think about my first Blaze book. You can write to me at P.O. Box 718, Fayetteville, NY 13066, or visit my Web site at www.carasummers.com.

Enjoy,

Cara Summers

Books by Cara Summers

HARLEQUIN TEMPTATION

813—OTHERWISE ENGAGED
860—MOONSTRUCK IN MANHATTAN

INTENT TO SEDUCE

Cara Summers

HARLEQUIN®

TORONTO • NEW YORK • LONDON
AMSTERDAM • PARIS • SYDNEY • HAMBURG
STOCKHOLM • ATHENS • TOKYO • MILAN • MADRID
PRAGUE • WARSAW • BUDAPEST • AUCKLAND

To my sister-in-law and friend, Julie Oliver Fulgenzi—
the risk-taker who married my brother. Thanks for always
being there and for being the voice of reason. I love you.

ISBN 0-373-79042-2

INTENT TO SEDUCE

Visit us at www.eHarlequin.com

Printed in U.S.A.

1

"LET ME GET THIS STRAIGHT," Sophie said. "You're planning to ask some man to offer himself up as a sex object so that you can practice on him?"

"*Sex object* isn't exactly the word I would have chosen." MacKenzie Lloyd kept her gaze locked on her best friend. Just as long as she didn't look down at the ground, the bubbles of panic rolling around in her stomach were going to subside. "I've conducted all these surveys on techniques and collected all this narrative data on male sexual fantasies. The next step is to test its validity in the field. What I need now is a research companion."

Sophie rolled her eyes. "Okay, nix *sex object*. We'll go with *research companion*. But I got the *practice* part right. You're not quibbling over semantics there."

Sophie was clearly upset. Mac could tell by the way she slapped her wineglass down and began to tap her fingers on the wide-planked floor of the tree house. They were seated just outside the doorway on a narrow platform. Only a small, flimsy railing separated them from a drop to the ground thirty feet below. If she let herself think about that…

Biting down on her lip, she fought against the sudden spin of dizziness that whipped through her. She would have been just fine if she hadn't glanced down on her climb-up-the-rope ladder. It had been the laughter from the tennis courts that had distracted her. The sound floated up again, bright, rich and infectious, but this time she resisted the temptation to look to her left beyond the hedge of forsythia bushes where four Wainrights were playing.

Tomorrow was Sophie Wainright's birthday, and the entire clan had gathered to celebrate it. Family was important to the Wainrights. It was something Mac had always admired about them—and envied.

What she intended to do was the best chance she had of creating and preserving that kind of family for herself.

"I know what I'm doing, Sophie."

"Do you?"

"I've been very thorough in my research, and I've learned so much."

Sophie rolled her eyes. "Some research. You've interviewed hookers and madams."

"Madame Gervais does not refer to herself as a madam. She runs a very exclusive finishing school for female companions. It's really more like a matchmaking service. Most of the girls she's trained have married the men she's introduced them to. They're really very bright women. The only difference between them and me is that they were very beautiful and very skilled at pleasuring a man in bed."

"And they shared all their secrets with you?"

Mac studied her friend. In addition to the worry in Sophie's eyes, she saw curiosity. Leaning a little closer, she said, "Pretty much. Did you know that if you wrap a string of pearls around a man's erection during fellatio, you can get amazing results?"

"Pearls?"

"You can use a silk tie—or better still, a wispy silk scarf—but pearls are the best. You wrap them around several times, then draw them slowly up the entire length, and then down again. Men love it."

"I don't doubt it. It's just that I...I don't like the idea of you wrapping your pearls around a stranger." Pausing, Sophie shook her head with a rueful sigh. "I should have known the minute you suggested coming up in this tree house that you were going to spring something on me. You dragged me up to the roof of my shop the night before you tried that last experiment in your lab—the one that gave you a breakthrough.''

Mac tightened her grip on her knees and kept her eyes fixed on Sophie. ''I figure if I can face my fear of heights, I can succeed at all the other things that scare me.''

Sophie pointed a finger at her. ''There. You *are* nervous about inviting some strange man to be your boy toy. And you should be.'' Then swearing softly, Sophie picked up Mac's wineglass and handed it to her. ''Here. Take a drink of this. You're white as a sheet.''

Mac took a careful sip.

''Why don't we get you out of here? I'll call Lucas. Between us, we can get you down the rope ladder.''

''I'm fine.''

Sophie studied her over the rim of her glass. ''I wish I could be sure of that. This field-testing thing you're planning…it's not you.''

''You're wrong. It *is* me. That's the beauty of it. I'm not good at dating or relationships, but I'm excellent at doing research and then devising a way to put the results to work. If I approach keeping a husband that way, I know I can do it.''

''But you don't even have a husband yet. Shouldn't that be your first step?''

''That's the plan that most people follow and over fifty percent of all marriages fail. Research shows that the number one cause of divorce is infidelity. Usually it's the man who strays—just as soon as routine sets in. I saw that happen to my parents, and my plan is designed to prevent it.''

Sophie gazed helplessly at Mac. ''You're making it sound so logical, and it's not! Sex and relationships aren't something that you can map out and predict like something in your lab. Shit happens. Take it from someone who's been out there in the trenches.''

Leaning forward, Mac took Sophie's hands in hers. ''I'm

sorry I'm laying all of this on you right now when you've just broken up with Bradley.''

Sophie shrugged impatiently. "Bradley Davis is history. But he's a good example of what I'm talking about. When it comes to a relationship, there are no guarantees. And the only man I've ever been able to predict is my brother. He never gets involved emotionally in his relationships. He runs them the same way he runs Wainright Enterprises. And he thinks he has the right to run mine that way too.''

Mac didn't say anything for a moment. Although more than a month had gone by, she knew Sophie still resented that Lucas had uncovered information on Bradley Davis that had caused her to break off her engagement. "The one thing that you can always depend on is that Lucas loves you, and he cares about what happens to you.''

"He's smothering me. Ever since he took over Wainright Enterprises, he's decided that he can run all of our lives. He's even having me followed. But…'' Sophie stopped, shook her head and then narrowed her eyes at Mac. "Oh no you don't. You're not going to change the subject. I want to know what I can say to convince you to drop this whole idea.''

"Nothing.''

Sophie slumped back against the wall of the tree house. "There's got to be something I can do.''

"You don't have to worry. I've taken every possible safety precaution.''

"I'd feel a lot happier about this if you were going to try out your research on someone you knew. What about that representative from the biotech company that's been wining and dining you lately?''

Mac made a face. "Vince Smith is panting over my research not me. All he talks about is how brilliant I am, what wonderful lab facilities they could provide for me if I would just sign over exclusive rights to anything I might discover.''

Taking a sip of her wine, Mac pushed the thought of the

man out of her mind. The truth was she wasn't good at dating. It probably had something to do with the fact that she'd started college at fourteen. The men she'd met had treated her like a kid sister. If they'd called her, it was to get help on some assignment they were having trouble with. And then, later, in graduate school, her two forays into the realm of romance had been disasters. "Men just don't seem to think of me in a sexual way."

"And they won't until you start to think of yourself that way."

"Now you sound just like Madame Gervais. In fact, she thinks field testing my research will increase my self-confidence."

Tilting her head to the side, Sophie studied Mac for a moment. "Maybe I'll have to revise my opinion of her. Is she the one who talked you into lightening your hair?"

Mac tucked a loose strand back into the bun she wore at the back of her neck. "Yes, and she took me shopping for a new wardrobe."

Sophie's eyes widened. "Why aren't you wearing it?"

"I bought most of the clothes for the field testing I'm going to do. I don't feel quite myself in them. When I put them on, I feel like I can do things Dr. MacKenzie Lloyd would never do."

Sophie paused with her wineglass halfway to her lips. "Oh? More stuff like the pearl trick?"

"Yes, and other kinds of things too. When Madame Gervais and I shopped for the clothes, we chose pieces that would facilitate some popular male fantasies."

Sophie studied her friend over the rim of her glass. "Okay, I'm hooked. How about filling me in a little more on the specifics of this research of yours?"

"I started out by reading a number of anthropological and sociological texts."

"Let's just fast-forward to the good stuff."

Mac grinned at her. "It's always good to have a sound theoretical background."

"Mac…"

"There's so much. You have no idea how many books have been written on sex. Or what's available online. There's this one woman who makes her living giving all-day seminars on how to…pleasure the penis."

Sophie choked on her wine. "All-day seminars?"

Mac nodded. "I went to one. We worked on plastic models."

"And you're actually going to field-test that on a complete stranger?"

"I'm trying to think of a fantasy I can fit it into."

Setting down her glass, Sophie said, "And these fantasies—what exactly are they like?"

"Well, there was one I found very interesting. It involved male bondage."

"Handcuffs, silk neckties—that kind of stuff?"

Mac shook her head. "Plastic wrap."

"Let me guess. You meet him at the door wearing nothing but?"

"Nope. It's the one where I wrap him up in it like a mummy. Of course, I would leave his nose free. And his toes." She smiled at Sophie. "And one other part."

"Something you could wrap your pearls around."

"Exactly. A blindfold is optional, but I've heard it doubles the pleasure."

"I'll bet. In these fantasies—is turnabout fair play?"

Mac blinked, then smiled slowly. "I think that depends on how well round one goes."

They were both laughing when the ringing of Sophie's cell phone interrupted them. Mac could tell by the expression on Sophie's face it was someone she was happy to hear from. When she moved inside the door of the tree house for privacy, Mac decided it was a new beau calling. Sophie just naturally attracted men.

Pressing her back against the wooden frame of the doorway, she reminded herself not to look down. Sophie's laugh drifted out to her, low and intimate. She was definitely talking to a new beau.

Very carefully, Mac shifted her gaze in the direction of the tennis courts. This time there was no onslaught of panic. Though her view was partially blocked by trees, she recognized Sophie's two stepbrothers, the ''step-twins'' as she called them. Nicholas and Nathaniel were both in college now. They lived with their Aunt Jan. The estate was their home, but it was owned by Sophie's older brother Lucas Wainright, the final member of the foursome.

Tall and lean, with a swimmer's athletic build, Lucas looked very much at ease as he rushed forward to the net and killed his stepbrother's serve. According to Sophie, Lucas was good at everything he put his hand to—sports, as well as the family business. Four years ago when his father had died, he'd taken over and ruthlessly dragged Wainright Enterprises back from the edge of bankruptcy.

The first and only time Mac had met him, he'd reminded her of a fallen angel, incredibly good-looking on the surface with danger lurking just beneath. But that first impression of danger had been softened somewhat by the fact that he'd spent most of the day hidden behind a camera snapping pictures of the grand opening of Sophie's antique shop.

According to Sophie, Lucas regarded his duties as the head of the Wainright family every bit as seriously as he took his financial obligations. As a result, he'd turned into a total dictator and an interfering ogre.

The man on the tennis court did not resemble an ogre. She let her gaze linger on the dark hair and the tanned skin stretched taut over what she was sure were hard muscles. His hand had certainly been hard when he'd shaken hers that day. She'd felt something too—a little jolt. Whatever it was, it had made her very aware of him for the rest of the party.

''Who's winning?'' Sophie asked as she joined her on the edge of the platform.

''Looks like Lucas and your aunt.''

"Who would have thought?" she muttered. "Not that I begrudge Aunt Jan the victory, but I would give a lot to see Lucas taken down a peg or two."

Mac turned to study Sophie. "You never told me what he did to make you break things off with Bradley."

"He had him followed. Turns out the man I thought was the love of my life was cheating on me. There were some very compromising photos, thanks to the Shadow."

"Shadow?"

"That's what I call the super spy who heads up Wainright Enterprises' security. I managed to get a pretty good look at him once. But he doesn't like to be seen. He's there, and then he's not. Anyway, he checked into Bradley's finances. Lucas made me read the report so that I would have no doubt that old Brad was obviously only interested in me for my money."

Mac covered Sophie's hand with hers. "Lucas loves you, Soph."

"I love him, too, but he sees everyone I date, especially anyone I get serious about, as a threat to the company. The worst of it is he's probably right. I've decided that the next man I decide to go out with is not going to know that I'm a Wainright. And I'm going to make very sure that no one—not even the Shadow—knows who I'm seeing."

Mac put her arms around her friend and just held her. For a moment, neither of them said a word.

"Okay," Sophie said as she drew back. "Enough of my problems. I think we ought to come up with a solution for yours."

"You're not going to talk me out of it."

"I know better than to waste my breath. Besides, the more I think about it, the more I can see that this field-testing plan of yours might have some merit. In fact, it could even be fun if you did it with someone you could trust. There's got to be someone I know—"

"Hey, you two!"

The sudden shout had Mac glancing down through the

branches before she could stop to think. Lucas was striding toward them across the lawn. "C'mon down out of that tree. Aunt Jan and I have defeated the step-twins and we're ready for our next challengers."

For just a moment, Mac's gaze locked with Lucas's, and she experienced that same instant jolt of awareness she'd felt before. Then a wave of dizziness slammed into her and she squeezed her eyes shut.

"That's it!" Sophie whispered in Mac's ear. "I don't know why I didn't think of it sooner. Lucas is the answer! You can practice your research on him!"

Lucas? No. Mac shook her head, and a second, more potent, wave of dizziness hit her. Her hand shot out to the railing. It gripped nothing but air.

As she pitched forward, fear fisted in her throat, leaves scraped her face, and one image formed in her mind—the earth below racing toward her. Then arms clamped around her like a steel vise, pressing her against something hard and solid and warm before she hit the ground and lost her breath in a whoosh.

"Mac!"

Sophie's voice was almost drowned out by the beating of her heart. As she struggled for breath, Mac became aware of the very male body beneath her.

"You can open your eyes now. You're safe."

The moment she did, she saw that Lucas's eyes were just as dark as she remembered—the deep blue of the sea.

"Are you all right?"

Mac said nothing. She couldn't. He was holding her so tightly, molding her body to his from breast to thigh. An icy flame was searing her nerve endings and sensitizing her body to every plane and angle of his. For the first time in her life, words, thoughts, logic, deserted her, washed away by a flood of sensations. The warmth of his breath on her lips. The pressure of each one of his fingers on her back. The swell of her hips. His body growing rock hard beneath her. She watched awareness fill his eyes as her body melted in reaction.

"Just what I've been waiting to see all my life—my brother knocked off his feet by a woman! I think it's an omen of things to come."

Omen of things to come. Sophie's words and the memory of what she'd suggested—practicing her research on Lucas—penetrated the haze filling Mac's mind. She broke free of the paralysis that had gripped her, and shifting off Lucas, she scrambled to her feet.

Sophie grabbed her arm and pulled her toward the tennis courts as she tossed over her shoulder, "C'mon, bro. Prepare to meet your match..."

2

LUCAS LEANED BACK in his chair and listened to the steady ticking of his grandfather's clock. It was the only sound that marred the tense silence in the room as he studied the two men seated on the other side of his desk.

Both of them were self-contained. Both were very intelligent. And he wouldn't relish going up against either one of them in a dark alley.

It was ironic that in spite of their many similarities, the two men were the complete antithesis of each other.

The younger was his best friend, the man he'd recently hired to head up security at Wainright Enterprises. He'd known T. J. McGuire since they'd served together in the Gulf War. Tracker was the name the flight crew had given T.J. because he'd been a hell of a lot better at finding their targets than both the high-tech radar systems and so-called "smart" missiles.

It had taken Lucas four years to convince his friend to come and work for Wainright Enterprises. He'd needed someone he could trust, and Tracker was that kind of man. Beneath the black-Irish good looks and the accompanying charm lay the strength and the loyalty of a Celtic warrior. Lucas ranked loyalty right up there next to competence when it came to his employees—and his friends.

The older man with the mane of white wavy hair and the impeccably tailored suit was not a friend. Nor could he be trusted. Doing business with Vincent Falcone had been one of the biggest mistakes his father had made. It had taken Lucas four years to find the money and the right opportunity to buy Vincent Falcone out of Wainright Enterprises.

Still, he didn't want the man as an enemy.

A rustle of paper broke the silence as Vincent turned over the final page of the contract. Glancing up, he met Lucas's eyes squarely. "If I sign this, I will own Lansing Biotech outright. Wainright Enterprises gives up any right it may have had in the past to patents or future research results. You're being very generous."

"I want the break between us to be fair but clean. This deal severs all connections between your various other businesses and mine."

"Ah yes, there is that. And the fact that I will no longer sit on the board of Wainright Enterprises."

"That's correct."

The older man smiled slowly. "You've done a thorough job of systematically cutting me out for the past four years. I admire your technique. And today, inviting me here to your home to end our business relationship over a drink…" Pausing, he glanced around the room. "It's a nice touch. Very classy. Your grandfather would be proud of you."

Lucas was careful to keep his expression impassive. He hadn't wanted to invite Falcone to the Wainright estate. He'd never lived here himself. It was the place his father had lived with his last three wives. If it hadn't been for Sophie's birthday celebration, he would have worked as he usually did on the weekends and the contract would have been signed at his D.C. office.

"I would have enjoyed meeting your sister. I hear she is very beautiful."

Lucas didn't let his gaze waver, and for a moment neither man spoke.

With a slow smile, the older man raised a hand. "Another time perhaps. If I could borrow your pen?"

Lucas picked up a pen and handed it to him without a word.

Seconds later, Falcone rose and placed the signed contract on Lucas's desk. "It's a shame that you felt it necessary to terminate our business connections."

"You have certain interests that I do not want Wainright Enterprises involved in."

"Your father was not so particular."

Saying nothing, Lucas rose from his chair and, after a moment, Vincent Falcone continued, "The connection between our families is still close. Like this." Raising his hands, he clasped them together tightly. "For that reason, our paths will cross again."

"It's very unlikely," Lucas said as the man turned away and allowed Tracker to escort him from the room. The moment the door closed, he sat down in his chair. It had gone smoothly. Too smoothly, perhaps? Closing his eyes, he began to run the entire event over in his mind, turning over every word, every nuance in his mind. He stopped only when he heard Tracker reenter the room.

"Nice job, boss."

"It was too easy."

Tracker's eyebrows shot up. "The four years of work and sacrifices that went into accomplishing this weren't easy. And you chose the right time to make your move. Vincent Falcone has troubles of his own right now. There are factions in his other, less legitimate business interests who require his attention."

"I don't like that he mentioned Sophie's name. He's quite capable of exacting some kind of revenge for this on my family." Rising, Lucas moved to the window, but he didn't focus on the sweep of lawn that ended at the tennis courts. "I have a feeling that Falcone is plotting something."

When Tracker didn't reply, Lucas turned to face him. "You think I'm overreacting, don't you?"

Tracker grinned. "You're not going to get me to say that, boss. You're worried about your little sister. It could be because you've been going through a rough time with her.

But in my experience, a man had better pay attention to his hunches or they'll come back to bite him.''

"I don't like that you saw her with Falcone's son.''

"Sophie only met Sonny once for a casual drink in a Georgetown watering hole. She hasn't seen him since.''

Lucas shook his head. "She knows nothing about the Falcone family and certainly nothing about the fact that my father was doing business with them. But if I try to warn Sophie off, she might take it in her head to get really serious about him. She's in rebellion mode right now.''

"And you even end up with a black eye this time,'' Tracker said.

Lucas rubbed his jaw, where his sister had landed him a pretty decent right cross. "You may be right about that. Sophie got past you last time.''

"She's got some good moves. And she was pretty upset about that information you dug up on Bradley Davis.'' Tracker's grin widened as he moved to the small built-in refrigerator near the windows. Opening it, he took out two beers, twisted off the caps and handed one to Lucas. "She's smart too. I think she may suspect she's being followed. She tried some evasive tactics the other day when she left her shop.''

"Did she lose the tail?'' Lucas asked with a frown.

Tracker nodded. "For about a half hour. My man picked her up coming out of a restaurant. I have two men on her now. Another two are keeping tabs on Sonny Falcone.''

"Good. I'll feel a lot better when she's down in the Keys with me. I'll send the plane for Sophie on Wednesday. She claims she can't get away before then. And I didn't want to push.'' He rubbed his jaw again. "Once you're sure she's on my plane, you can devote all your attention to both Falcones.''

"You want me to continue to keep tabs on your aunt and stepbrothers?''

"For the time being.'' Lucas frowned as he turned and led the way through the open French doors to the balcony.

Beyond a row of flowering shrubs, an Olympic-size pool gleamed in the late-afternoon sun. His younger siblings were engaged in an intense water-polo match with their aunt, and at the far end of the pool he spotted Sophie seated on the edge of a chaise lounge talking to MacKenzie Lloyd.

"I think you ought to put someone on Dr. Lloyd. She's been Sophie's best friend for years. They live about three blocks apart in Georgetown. Falcone may try to use her to get to Sophie."

"I'll get right on it, boss. You want me to run a background check on Dr. Lloyd?"

Lucas considered for a moment. He'd been thinking of MacKenzie Lloyd off and on quite a bit in the last few hours. When she'd fallen out of that tree into his arms, she'd called up the memory he had of the little waif in jeans and a T-shirt whom he'd met at the opening of Sophie's shop two years ago.

There'd been something about her that day that had caught his attention. At first, he'd thought he'd imagined the tug of desire that he'd felt. But each time he'd found her framed in the viewfinder of his camera, the pull had grown stronger. Later, he'd studied the photos he'd taken, trying to put his finger on just what it was that had drawn him.

She wasn't anything like the women he usually dated. His taste ran to tall, leggy brunettes and blondes. She was small, and she wore her red hair pulled back into a bun. But her eyes… Even in the representation on film, they were the incredible color of golden amber.

Today her hair had seemed lighter and looser—a reddish-gold explosion of color as he'd stared up at her in the tree. His body had reacted to her the moment he'd seen her, hardening, tightening. And when she'd been lying on top of him…for a moment he'd forgotten everything—where they were, who was watching. If Sophie hadn't spoken, he might have rolled her beneath him and taken her right there beneath the branches of the elm tree. Frowning, he pushed away the image.

It had been years since he'd been tempted to be that reckless with a woman. He'd put it out of his mind during the tennis game, chalked it up to putting in too much overtime on the Falcone deal.

Then she'd beaten him.

Oh, Sophie had made some good plays, but Lucas was fully aware that it was Dr. Lloyd's careful, methodical style that had been his downfall. It was almost as though she could predict exactly what he would do next. And that was…he searched for a word…intriguing.

"Boss?" Tracker cleared his throat loudly.

"What?" Lucas asked, turning to him.

"Do you want me to run a background check on the doc?"

Once again, Lucas hesitated. On some gut level, he knew that he should steer clear of his sister's best friend. It wasn't merely the strength of the physical attraction he felt that had the warning bells going off in his mind. She was Sophie's friend. He kept his dating life separate from his family. To pursue a relationship with MacKenzie Lloyd would foster expectations that he would never fulfill.

Relationship? He frowned at the direction his thoughts had taken. Who was she that she could affect him this way?

Experience had taught him that ignorance was seldom bliss, and knowledge was always power. "Yeah. I want to know everything about her."

"MacKenzie, you've got to listen to reason."

Mac opened a bag of carrots and for a moment allowed herself to picture dumping the whole bag over Gil Stafford's head. Then stifling the image, she selected one carrot and began to shred it on a grater. She hoped feeding Wilbur, her pet lab rat, would soothe her temper. Gil was her department chair and he had ten years' seniority on her.

That and the fact that she worked in a lab that adjoined his had made him think he could give her advice.

"If you'd just listened to me earlier and signed a contract to turn the results of your research over to that biotech company, you would have prevented this break-in."

Mac shoved down the little skip of fear that she'd been experiencing ever since she'd arrived at the university and learned that her lab had been broken into sometime on Sunday. The intruder had gotten away, but not before he'd broken into her office safe.

"They would have made sure that there were better security measures taken around here. And I still don't understand why you turned down the money. Even if you don't want it for yourself, think of all the equipment it would have provided."

As Gil continued to pontificate, he strode toward the window. Mac privately thought the man should have gone into politics instead of science. Not only could he talk nonstop, but he had the tall, rangy build of an athlete and a very photogenic face. With the sunlight turning his blond hair into a halo, he looked like one of the good archangels.

The antithesis of what Lucas looked like with his dark hair and those midnight-blue eyes.

Lucas again. She hadn't been able to block him out of her mind since Sophie had first suggested she use him for her research. The idea had been enough to put her off her serve in the first two sets of the tennis match. After that she'd focused all her concentration on the game. Beating Lucas had been a challenging and exhilarating experience. And the moment they'd won, Sophie had started making her case.

It was a good one. Everything that Sophie had said made perfect sense on a logical and theoretical level.

It was just that every time she thought of actually trying out her research on Lucas, she felt the same funny quaking in her stomach that she got whenever something was about to go wrong in her lab. No matter how hard she tried, she couldn't seem to forget what it had felt like to be pressed against him, to feel his body react to hers, especially a certain unmistakable part of his body. A vivid image slipped into her mind of looping a long strand of pearls around and around—

"Are you listening to anything I say?"

Mac dropped the grater as she struggled to gather her thoughts. "Gil, I know you mean well." She was almost sure of it. But he was giving her a headache. Glancing down at the carrots, she considered dumping them on his head, after all.

"Am I interrupting?"

Mac looked up in surprise to see Sophie hurrying toward her. "Who told you?"

"Who told me what?"

"Someone broke in here last night."

"They did? Are you all right?" Sophie enveloped Mac in a hug.

"I'm fine."

"What about Wilbur?" Sophie flicked a glance at the small white rat running circles in his cage.

Mac couldn't prevent a smile. "I thought you couldn't stand Wilbur."

Gil cleared his throat, and the moment Sophie turned, shot her his best smile. "I'm Gil Stafford. I'm the chair of the biology department and I work in the lab next to MacKenzie's."

"My friend, Sophie Wainright." Mac completed the introductions as the two shook hands.

"Perhaps you can talk some sense into her, Ms. Wainright," Gil said. "The research she's doing has been getting a lot of attention. It was only a matter of time until this happened."

Sophie turned to Mac with a frown. "Were they after your research?"

"The police certainly suspect it," Gil said as he glanced

around the room "And it clearly wasn't vandals. Nothing's been touched except the safe."

"No harm's been done," Mac said as she watched Wilbur attack the grated carrots she'd shoved into his tray. "Wilbur's appetite hasn't been affected. And I don't keep any of my records here in the office anyway."

"I still don't like it." Turning, Sophie paced down the length of the lab and then whirled around. "Lucas could send the Shadow over. On a personal level, I can't stand him, but he's good at what he does."

"Not necessary," Mac said. "The university is going to install a high-tech security system. They've even given me a few days off while they work on it."

"That's wonderful. That means you can get started right away on your..." Sophie's voice trailed off as she glanced at Gil.

He was frowning at her. "The university doesn't have the funds to install a proper security system. And the research she's doing is much too valuable. I was just trying to explain that to MacKenzie."

Beaming a smile at him, Sophie moved toward him and placed a hand on his arm. "Would you mind terribly if Mac and I have some time alone? A little girl talk does wonders for the nerves."

"No. Of course not." A little uncertain, Gil glanced from one woman to the other. "I'll be right next door if you need me, MacKenzie."

Sophie waited until the door closed behind Gil Stafford. "*MacKenzie?* No one calls you that."

"He means well." Mac glanced at the bag of carrots again.

"You weren't thinking of asking him to be your research...guinea pig, were you?"

Mac stared at Sophie. "Gil?"

"Good. Because I've come here on a mission—to convince you that Lucas is your man."

Mac held up both hands. "Sophie, I just don't—"

"I know you, Mac. You've been considering it, weighing the pros and cons. And the pros are winning. He's the perfect man for the job. Why not admit it?"

Picking up another carrot, Mac began to grate. "It's just that I'd planned on doing everything with a stranger."

Sophie moved closer and took the grater away, then shoved it out of reach. "I'm going to be brutally honest with you. That's what best friends are for, right? You're not going to hate me for saying this?"

Mac couldn't prevent her lips from curving. They'd always been able to be honest with each other. It was what had made their friendship last for so long. "I'm not going to hate you."

"Okay." Sophie reached for Mac's hand and gave it a squeeze. "I don't think you're going to be able to go through with your plan if you choose a stranger."

"You think I'm a coward."

"No!" Sophie's reply was quick and vehement. "You are one of the bravest people I know. But I've known you for a long time, and you're very…hesitant when it comes to relationships with the opposite sex."

"*Resistant* might be a more accurate word," Mac said.

Sophie grinned. "You know, one of the most endearing things about you is your ability to be brutally honest about yourself. Most of us sail through life telling ourselves whopping-big lies."

Mac frowned in puzzlement. "What's the point of doing that?"

"We think it helps. But to get back to you, this resistance you have to pursuing relationships with the opposite sex is the reason I think you might be much more successful with your plan if you choose someone you already know. I don't think you're going to be able to…let's say, *implement* these fantasies with a complete stranger. Plus, your ultimate goal is to use them on your husband. And he won't be a stranger. Isn't it best in a scientific experiment to try and reproduce all the circumstances to the best of your ability?"

"You really do listen when I rattle on about my work."

Sophie grinned at her. "Of course I do. And I'm right, aren't I—on both counts?"

Mac was very much afraid that she was. One of her own biggest fears was the idea of using her newfound knowledge on a stranger. Still… "Lucas wouldn't…I mean, he doesn't think of me that way."

Sophie's eyebrows shot up. "Well, there you go. Lucas represents the kind of challenge I think you should be looking for. Someone who would put your research to a true test. These men that your…*contacts* in the sex industry will put you in touch with are bound to be easy marks, don't you think? After all, they're eager enough to be paying for sex. Some of them might even be married and have started to wander, so to speak. And if your plan is all geared toward keeping a husband from straying in spite of his genetic mapping, then surely you ought to be able to seduce my brother."

Sophie had a point. Lucas Wainright would certainly offer her a challenge. And if she wasn't up to it, then she might as well forget her whole plan.

"Mac—" Sophie took her hands "—do this for me. I don't know if I can stand to think of you putting this research project into action with someone else. I know that Lucas, in spite of his many flaws, will be kind to you."

One glance at the concern in her friend's eyes, and Mac knew she was going to agree. She was about to, when Sophie continued, "And the truth is, you could do me a big favor at the same time."

"What?" Mac asked.

"On Wednesday, Lucas has made arrangements for me to join him at his hideaway cabin on one of the Keys. You know what they say about timing being everything! I want you to go in my place. I've never been there, but it seems to me that an isolated island in the Keys would be the perfect setting for you to put your plan into action. It will be just you and Lucas—hot, sunny days, palm trees, the ocean pounding on a sandy beach, warm, tropical nights. Just imagine it, Mac.''

It sounded just a little bit too good to be true. She studied Sophie. ''Why don't you want to go with him?''

''Because—'' Sophie began to pace again ''—every time I look at Lucas right now, I think of Bradley. My feelings are very raw, and having Lucas lecture me for a week on my abominable taste in men is the last thing I need. But he's adamant that I join him. I think he feels guilty and he wants to *bond* with me.''

''What will you be doing while I'm down in the Keys seducing Lucas?'' There. She'd actually said it aloud. Putting your fear into words was supposed to be half the battle.

Pacing back from the window, Sophie leaned against the counter. ''I need to be by myself for a while. And I've found this great spa in North Carolina where I can hike in the mountains and ride and meditate. It's run entirely by women for women. When I read the brochure, it sounded like heaven to me. It's exactly what I need. Lucas is right about one thing. I do seem to attract men who are only interested in using me. An all-women retreat ought to at least protect me for a while.''

''Lucas won't be happy about the switch,'' Mac pointed out.

Sophie patted Mac's hand. ''If your research is as good as you say it is, he'll adjust. And I'll call him from the spa so that he'll know that I'm perfectly safe. Believe me, Lucas and I could both use a break from each other.''

Mac drew in a deep breath. She'd never been able to refuse Sophie anything.

''Do this for me. Please.''

''Okay.''

''Great!'' Sophie beamed a smile at her. ''C'mon, the first thing I want to see is the wardrobe that Madame Gervais helped you select. Then we're going to shop for some additional pieces that will be appropriate for a holiday in the Keys. Have you ever worn a wig?''

''No. Why would I?''

''The better to create fantasies with, my dear. I'll explain everything while we shop.''

3

_____

"Is THERE ANYTHING I can get you before we take off, Ms. Wainright?"

Mac smiled at the young brunette, Captain Jill Roberts, who would fly her to Key West. "No thanks, I'm fine."

She hated that she had to lie to the woman, but Sophie's instructions were very explicit. Lucas's pilot had never met Sophie Wainright, and Mac was to keep up her impersonation until they had landed in the Keys. The blond wig was helping, and so were the clothes that Sophie had lent her.

No one could know that she was taking Sophie's place until she stepped off the plane in Key West. Sophie had been adamant about that because she was sure that Lucas was having her followed.

"The flight will take about two hours, and the galley is fully stocked."

"And Lucas is going to meet the plane?" Mac asked.

Captain Roberts smiled. "That's what he said. I spoke with him just as you were crossing the tarmac to come aboard, and I gave him the time I thought we would be touching down. That means I'd better get us airborne. If you want anything, the intercom button is right there on the armrest."

It was only as the captain disappeared into the cockpit that Mac allowed herself to relax a little. She felt as if she'd been caught up in a whirlwind ever since Sophie had breezed into her lab on Monday, but she had to admit that the plan was really working. It had been at Sophie's insistence that they'd switched identities.

The initial step had gone like clockwork thanks to a sudden summer storm that still held D.C. in its grip. Sophie had worn her red rain poncho, hood up, when she'd opened the antique shop at nine, and Mac had worn a bright yellow one, hood down, when she'd arrived fifteen minutes later. Once inside, they'd gone into the back room and changed clothes. As a final touch to their disguises, Sophie had donned a reddish-blond wig tied back into a bun, and Mac had put on a blond one.

They'd gotten the wigs and had them cut and styled on Monday when they'd gone shopping. The fact that they were almost identical in size and shape had helped. Friends in college had always remarked that they could have passed for sisters. Still, Mac had been amazed at just how much she resembled Sophie once she was wearing the blond wig. When they'd emerged from the shop, their hoods up and umbrellas open to hail separate cabs, she was sure that anyone watching "Sophie" would have been bound to follow "Mac," and vice versa.

Mac prayed that the rest of their plan would go as smoothly. Just the thought of facing Lucas Wainright and admitting that she'd purposely switched places with his sister had the butterflies dive-bombing around in her stomach. But it was much easier to concentrate on that first hurdle than the one that would come after, when she told him why she'd really taken Sophie's place.

"We've been cleared for takeoff, Ms. Wainright."

Mac jumped at the sound of Jill Roberts's voice pouring out of a nearby speaker.

"I'll let you know when you can move around the cabin, but if you have any concerns or questions, don't hesitate to use the intercom button."

Mac found her gaze riveted to the button for several moments after the plane's engine roared to life. All she had to do was press it and she could call the whole thing off.

The plane vibrated, then moved forward.

Mac gripped her hands together. Whatever second

thoughts she was having, she couldn't let Sophie down. Things had gone too far.

Leaning back in her seat, she took a deep breath and held it for the length of time that it took the plane to make its mad rush down the runway.

There was no need to panic. Years of experience in the lab had taught her that any project became simpler and much less inhibiting if she could just break it down into steps and take them one at a time. All she had to do was view her coming fieldwork in that light. Flying down to Key West to meet Lucas was just the first step. Telling Lucas about her plan would be the next—and a big one it would be.

The moment she felt the plane leave the ground, she let out the breath she was holding and took in another one. In her mind, she tried to picture herself taking the third step— making love to Lucas Wainright.

Every time she let herself think about that, a very vivid image of Lucas, totally naked, filled her mind. She could almost feel what it would be like to run her hands over the smooth tanned skin on his shoulders, down his chest to his waist and below. Of course, she'd fantasized about touching a man before. And that all-day seminar had certainly given her fantasies a lot of fuel. But never before had her hands tingled with anticipation. As she glanced down at them, grasped tightly in her lap, the realization streamed through her. She wanted to touch Lucas. Not just any man. She wanted to press her fingers against his hardness, to test his strength.

She could still recall how lean, how hard those muscles had felt through the thin cotton of his polo shirt. His whole body had been so hard. Even his hands. When she concentrated, she could still feel the pressure of each finger—on her back and, lower, on her hip. And there was that incredible stab of heat, the melting of muscle and bone.

She was still searching for a word to describe what she'd felt. *Hunger* was too mild a word for that needy, restless ache that had threatened to consume her. More than anything, she'd wanted him to—

"Ms. Wainright?"

Mac started as the voice flowed out of the speaker. Then, unclenching her hands, she pressed the button on the armrest. "Yes?"

"We've reached our cruising altitude. You can wander around the cabin or use your cell phone. Make yourself at home."

"Thanks."

Reaching into her bag, Mac took out her phone. She was about to press a button to speed-dial Sophie when she realized that it wasn't her phone. It was the color of white mother-of-pearl. Hers was black. A quick search of her bag confirmed her suspicion. When they'd switched outfits in the back of Sophie's shop, they'd switched the identical purses they'd bought too. After punching in her own number, she listened to it ring.

"Mac?" Sophie asked. "Where are you?"

"I'm in the air."

"Lucky you. I'm still on the ground, but we should be moving away from the gate soon. I take it everything went smoothly."

"Everything except that I have your purse."

"Yeah. I figured that out when I grabbed the phone. But it shouldn't be a problem. You have my permission to use my credit cards. I doubt that I'll need yours at the spa."

"Go ahead and use them if you have to."

"We're lucky that's the only thing that's gone wrong. I can't believe we've pulled this off."

"I hate to rain on your parade, but there's still the possibility that Lucas will send me packing and show up at your spa."

"They don't allow men on the premises. Besides, he's going to be much too busy engaging in those sexual fantasies you're going to create for him."

What if he doesn't? What if he refuses to—

"You're having second thoughts, aren't you?"

"No...well, maybe a few." Mac sighed.

"Stick to your first answer. And don't let my brother intimidate you. He's a man. And in spite of his numerous and infuriating faults, he's fair. The moment he realizes we've made a switch, he'll get me on my cell phone and lecture me. I'll make sure he knows this was all my idea—and then I'll suggest he have one of his hotshot security people check out the spa. Uh-oh. We're starting to pull away from the gate. Just remember that when Lucas finds out I'm perfectly safe, he'll calm right down. The rest is up to you."

For a few minutes after Sophie broke the connection, Mac stared straight in front of her. It *was* up to her. She was used to that kind of pressure in her lab. She could handle it there.

And she would handle it once she got to Key West. In the meantime, she was going to find something else to think about. An idea bloomed in her mind and she pushed the button on her armrest.

"What can I do for you, Ms. Wainright?"

"First, you can call me Sophie."

"Only if you agree to call me Jill."

"Do you ever fly with a copilot?"

Jill's laugh flowed into the cabin. "Frequently. In fact, when I fly with Mr. Wainright, I usually sit in the copilot's seat. He prefers to be in charge."

"A top gun?"

"You got it."

"Could I come up there with you? I'd love to learn about flying."

"Sure thing. I'd love the company."

"Where's Sophie?" Lucas bit out the words as he glanced from MacKenzie Lloyd to the pilot of his private jet. Somehow he'd managed to keep his voice low and controlled—a sharp contrast to the feelings coursing through him. The first thing he'd felt when Mac had walked down the short flight of steps from the plane was pleasure. It had sprung to life so quickly that he'd barely had time to recognize it before he'd discovered that his sister was not with her. Then the fear had struck.

"Sophie's perfectly safe," Mac said. "She's at a spa in North Carolina. I...we switched places."

Lucas shifted his gaze to Jill Roberts who had descended the short flight of steps directly behind Mac. "Are you involved in this deception?"

Mac stepped in front of his pilot. "No. I told her the truth just as we landed. Before that, I was wearing a blond wig, and she believed I was Sophie. Please don't blame Captain Roberts. Sophie said you'd be fair."

Ruthlessly shoving his hands into the pockets of his shorts, Lucas narrowed his eyes. It was a look he'd honed to perfection when dealing with employees who'd displeased him. He kept Mac pinned with it while he considered what she'd said.

It would have been easy enough to fool his pilot. She hadn't worked for Wainright Enterprises that long, and he seldom used his private jet to transport family. He'd done it this time to ensure that Sophie arrived safely. And he was also blaming Mac for something he was almost certain his sister was behind. "I want to talk to Sophie."

"Of course." Instead of withering under his glance, Mac efficiently punched numbers into her cell phone, then handed it to him.

He listened to two rings.

"Lucas?"

His sister's voice had some of his fear fading. "Where in hell are you?"

"Didn't Mac tell you? I'm on my way to the Serenity Spa in Serenity, North Carolina."

"Hold on." Lucas cut her off, then directed his gaze at Mac and his pilot. "You two wait right here. We're not finished.'' Turning, he strode to the privacy and shade offered by a nearby hangar.

"Where exactly is this spa?"

"I told you, Serenity, North Carolina—about an hour's drive from Charlotte. I'll be quite safe. The place is run by women for women. No chance of any fortune hunters here—although you might argue the prices they charge puts them in that category. I'll give you their phone number and their Web site address. You can have one of your security men check it out."

"I intend to. They can do it in person when they pick you up and bring you here."

"Not a good idea, bro. I told you before, I won't have you running my life. You promised you'd back off for a while."

"And in return you agreed to spend some time with me down here in the Keys."

"You had me followed. That isn't backing off. And it's something I won't put up with."

Lucas sighed. "Soph, there's something I haven't told you. It's why I wanted you to come down here for a while. We need to talk."

"Talk is the last thing I need right now. I'm sorry. I know I agreed to come there, but I…just couldn't."

The quick change in her tone from anger to contrition pulled at him.

"I love you, Lucas. And I know that you did what you thought was best for the family. But being with you right now is only going to make me think of how lousy I am at choosing men. I really need to be alone."

It was the catch in her voice that had the pain shooting through him. He couldn't help recalling the scene in his office when he'd forced her to look at the evidence Tracker had gathered on Bradley Davis. It would be a long time before he could forget the words she'd hurled at him. They'd hurt much more than the right cross she'd managed to land on his chin. She'd accused him of having ice water in his veins, of being a ruthless dictator, of caring only about Wainright Enterprises.

What else could he expect her to say? He was prepared to go to almost any length to protect the company his grandfather had built and his father had almost destroyed. He stared past the low-slung buildings that formed the small private airport. The air was stifling, not even a hint of a breeze stirred the palms. If Sophie had a built-in homing device that seemed to attract fortune hunters, she'd inherited that gene directly from their father. His last and fifth divorce had come close to destroying Wainright Enterprises.

He'd tried to tell himself that Sophie would have been hurt even more if she'd gone ahead and married Bradley Davis. But that certainty hadn't helped a bit when she'd broken down and sobbed in his office.

"Please let me do this, Lucas. The spa has excellent security, and you can call the desk each day to check on me. You can even send one of your security people up here—as long as he's willing to camp in the woods. No males are allowed on the grounds."

For a moment Lucas said nothing as he ran the risks through his mind. A spa that was off-limits to men sounded secure, especially if he had Tracker assign one of his people to keep an eye on the place. While she was there, Sophie should be safe from any plot that Vincent Falcone might be hatching. Lucas drew in a deep breath. "As long as what you're telling me about this Serenity Spa is the truth."

"Check it out. I'm at the Charlotte airport now. Their van will be picking me up any minute. And whatever you do, don't blame Mac for this. I talked her into it. I can be very persuasive when I set my mind to it."

Lucas's lips curved in a smile. "Tell me about it. Don't worry, I'll have your friend back in D.C. by midafternoon."

"Oh, I don't think you should do that. She has a little problem she's depending on you to help her with, and I assured her that you were the perfect man for the job."

"What does she want me to do?" Lucas asked, glancing toward his plane. Mac had moved to the shade cast by one of the wings and was motioning his pilot to join her. Shaking her head, Captain Roberts stayed where she was. Evidently his order to stay put hadn't intimidated the doc. Courage had always appealed to him.

"I'm going to let Mac tell you that. But she may need a little encouragement. And I don't suppose you were very welcoming when you saw she wasn't me."

No, he hadn't been welcoming, Lucas thought as he studied Dr. MacKenzie Lloyd. Part of that had been due to the fact that for the past four days he hadn't been able to get her out of his mind.

In the linen slacks and blouse, she looked prim, innocent and untouchable. It had never been those qualities that had drawn him to a woman before. Perhaps it was that detached way she had of summing up her opponent in a tennis match and then calmly going in for the kill. It was a skill she'd probably picked up in her lab work. But wherever she'd come by that single-minded determination, he couldn't help but admire it. Nor could he help but view it as a challenge.

"I'm depending on you to be fair, Lucas. Don't blame her for something that's not her fault."

Wasn't that exactly what he'd been doing—blaming her for that quick skip of delight he'd felt when she'd gotten off the plane?

"Mac doesn't have anyone else to turn to for advice. Her parents always lecture rather than listen."

"Ouch." Lucas winced. It was an accusation Sophie had hurled at him more than once.

"Please, Lucas. I'm asking a favor here. At least take her out to the island and hear her out."

Take her out to the island? Whatever second thoughts he might have had about the wisdom of doing that had to be dismissed. Sophie so rarely asked for favors. "All right. But at least give me a clue. What kind of problem?"

"It's personal. And she needs help from a man. That's all I can tell you."

Personal? Did it have to do with a boyfriend? An ex-lover? The possibility had him frowning. "I'll do what I can. In the meantime, I'm going to be checking in on you at that spa."

"I can't always promise to be available on my cell phone. They make you check them at the desk. But you can always have one of your security people pitch a tent on one of the hillsides and keep tabs on me that way."

Lucas sighed at the trace of bitterness he heard in her voice. "I love you, Soph."

"Ditto, bro. Enjoy."

As soon as Sophie ended the call, Lucas took out his own cell phone and pressed the number that would get him through to Tracker.

"What's up, boss?"

"Sophie tricked you."

"I followed her myself until she got on your private plane." There was a slight pause, and then he continued. "The raincoats. When she and Dr. Lloyd came out of her shop, they both had their hoods up and their umbrellas open…and I followed the blonde, just as she wanted me to. Damn! Let me check with the man I had tailing Dr. Lloyd."

"I can tell you where Sophie says she is—the Serenity Spa in Serenity, North Carolina. They don't allow men on the premises. She claimed she was calling me from the Charlotte airport. She says she wants some time alone, but I want you to make sure she's there."

"I'll check the flight manifests right after I check with Dr. Lloyd's tail. Am I right in assuming that the good doctor is with you?"

"Yeah. Sophie says she has a problem, so I may have another job for you."

"I'll be in touch."

SOPHIE ENDED her conversation with her brother, then crossed her fingers in the hope that Lucas had bought her story. Of course, he'd check out every detail. She knew from experience just how thorough he was.

However, she'd been thorough too. She glanced at her watch. The first thing Lucas would do would be to check out the flight manifests and see if an S. Wainright had indeed flown from National Airport to Charleston that day. He would find that she had. Hopefully, he wouldn't find it too suspicious that an M. Lloyd had also made the same flight. She was banking on the fact that he would relax once he found that Sophie Wainright had checked into the Serenity Spa. Hannah Parker, the out-of-work actress she'd hired to do just that should be arriving at the spa any minute, and once that final crucial step had been taken and Lucas had verified it, she should be free.

For the next week, she wasn't going to be Sophie Wainright. Instead, she would be MacKenzie Lloyd, a burned-out research biologist who was taking a little break from her lab.

She'd begun to formulate the plan when she and Mac had talked in the tree house on Sunday, but the details hadn't all fallen into place until Mac had finally agreed to trade places with her. Of course, she hadn't told Mac everything.

She knew her best friend too well to believe that she could lie to Lucas for an entire week. So she hadn't admitted to her that she'd switched purses on purpose. Nor had she confided to Mac that she never intended to go to the Serenity Spa.

Stifling the impulse to get up and pace, Sophie leaned back in her chair and scanned the occupants of the airport lounge. At nearly two in the afternoon, the lunch crowd had thinned to a few businessmen at the bar who were nursing beers as they talked nonstop into their cell phones. They'd been there when she'd entered, so she didn't think they were following her. And she doubted that the couple with four kids at a nearby table were being paid to keep tabs on her.

For a second, her gaze locked with one of the men at the bar. She was quick to glance away, then let out the breath she was holding when she saw him slide off his stool and leave in the direction of the departing flights.

Paranoia—that's what it was, pure and simple. If she wasn't careful, she'd turn into Lucas, forever afraid that everyone he met was trying to threaten Wainright Enterprises.

She couldn't, she wouldn't live her life that way.

Forcing herself to relax, Sophie took a sip of bottled water. Not that she hadn't borrowed a page from her brother's paranoia handbook. In making her plans for switching identities with Mac, she'd followed Lucas's number-one rule: Never underestimate the enemy.

Even after they'd each hailed their separate taxis in front of her shop, she'd made herself assume that she still had a tail. Though she couldn't think of a single reason why Lucas would be having Mac followed, she wasn't ever going to underestimate him again. That was why she'd waited to switch identities with Hannah Parker until they'd both entered the first available ladies' room at the airport in Charlotte.

It had been almost too simple to walk into adjoining stalls and then pass her poncho and a bag containing her identification, sunglasses and a duplicate of the red wig she was wearing to Hannah. Just in case Lucas *had* assigned someone to follow Mac, Hannah couldn't turn into the blond Sophie Wainright until she was safely in the van to the Serenity Spa.

For the space of about fifteen minutes, there had been two fake MacKenzie Lloyds in the Charlotte airport.

Sophie took another quick look around the lounge. No one was paying her the least bit of attention. She drummed her fingers on the table, then jumped when her cell phone rang. Grabbing it, she put it to her ear. "Yes?"

"It's Hannah. I just wanted to let you know. I'm all checked into the spa. You should see the room."

"Did everything go all right?"

"Like clockwork. The woman behind the desk told me that my brother had called. She was going to call him back and let him know I'd arrived safely."

"Have a great week," Sophie said as she ended the call. Then she lifted her bottled water in a toast to herself. "I'm free at last."

MAC GRIPPED the windshield of the boat tightly as Lucas let out the throttle and the *Adventurer* raced over the choppy water. She'd felt a certain kinship with the boat the moment she'd spotted the name. Together, they were racing off into the unknown.

With the wind whipping against her face, she concentrated on enjoying the feel of bright afternoon sun and the occasional salty spray against her cheeks. It wasn't hard. She would have enjoyed it even more though, if it hadn't been for the man standing only a few feet away at the helm of the boat.

Even when he wasn't looking at her or speaking to her, Lucas was a hard man to ignore. He projected...*something* that went beyond simple good looks. And it was mesmerizing. She'd barely taken her eyes off him as he'd gone about the task of casting off the boat, then steering it quickly and surely away from the marina toward the open sea.

She risked a sideways glance at him. Perhaps it was the mixture of competence and control that had her gawking like a teenager. No, she thought, it was more than that. There was also that hint of danger about Lucas that lurked just below the very civilized surface. She'd seen it in his eyes when he'd first realized that Sophie wasn't on board the plane—something hot, dangerous and lethal. It fascinated her.

And she was gawking again. Tearing her eyes away, she

looked back at the marina that was fast becoming a spec on the shoreline behind them. A small plane lifted and soared out over the water as it climbed steadily into the sky. Jill Roberts was heading back to D.C. Only when it disappeared did she allow herself to look at Lucas again. He stood there, totally impassive, as if he were alone on the boat.

Clearly, he was still annoyed. He'd spoken only two words to her since he'd gotten off the phone with Sophie. Once Jill had disappeared into the plane, Lucas had turned to her, his expression neutral, and said, "This way."

His tone had been so cool she'd nearly shivered in spite of the hot southern Florida heat. They'd walked down to the small marina where he'd tied his boat. The moment she saw it, anxiety mixed with anticipation. It was her day for firsts, it seemed—her first time sitting in the cockpit of a plane and now her first time on a boat…to be topped off by her first time propositioning a man.

She glanced at him again. He stood completely at ease, his hands on the wheel, his feet planted apart, totally in control of the engine that roared beneath them. There was no sign now of the predator she'd glimpsed earlier. But it was still there, lurking. And it was touching off something in her. She pressed a hand against her stomach. The warm melting sensation that seemed to be centered there had nothing to do with the fact that the boat was beginning to bump more frequently into waves.

"Nervous?" Lucas had to shout the question.

"A little," she shouted back. "This is my first time on a boat."

"You're kidding."

She shook her head.

"How old are you?"

"Twenty-six."

"I can't imagine it. What did your family do on vacations?"

"They didn't take me with them."

"What about later?" Lucas asked. "You live in D.C. and you never went out on the water?"

"Too busy, I guess." She moved toward him then, carefully maintaining her grip on the side of the boat as she did. "Is it easy to steer?"

"For me it is. I've been doing it most of my life."

Suddenly, the boat struck a wave that lifted her feet right off the deck. The moment they smacked down, she felt them lift again, her stomach with them. The laugh escaped the moment she felt the boat solidly under her again.

The sound of Lucas's laughter mingling with hers had her turning toward him.

"You have the makings of a good sailor, Doc. Would you like to take a turn behind the wheel?"

At her nod, he stepped back and she slipped in front of him. Once her hands were on the wheel, he covered them with his. "Feet apart. Hands steady."

Lucas continued to talk, words of encouragement, but Mac's mind couldn't take it in. Just the sound of his voice in her ear was having the strangest effect on her breathing. And there were other sensations pouring through her. Instead of the salty air, it was Lucas's scent she inhaled. He smelled like sun and sweat and something else that she couldn't quite place. She could feel him too. His chest when it brushed against her back was like iron, and the hands trapping hers on the wheel were sure and firm, the palms surprisingly rough. For a moment, she closed her eyes and imagined what it might be like to have those hard hands pressed against other parts of her body.

Another wave had him shifting closer. His hands tightened on hers, pulling the wheel to the right. An arrow of heat shot through her, and her heart began to beat hard and fast, just as it had when she'd been lying on top of him.

"I'd better take over."

"Yes," she thought. Oh, yes.

"Doc, are you all right?"

Her eyes shot open as he turned her around to face him. "I'm…fine," she managed to say.

"You look a little weak in the knees. Why don't you sit down? You can see the island off there to your right."

Very carefully, Mac made it to the cushioned seat that ran along the side of the boat. Just as soon as Lucas wasn't actually touching her, some of her strength returned. It also helped that she wasn't looking at him.

Fascinating, she thought as she focused her attention on a tiny speck some distance away in the water. Her reaction the first time he'd held her hadn't been an aberration. Lucas Wainright could definitely turn her mind and body to mush.

And she liked it.

However, it would add complications to her research. How was she supposed to keep her mind on creating male sexual fantasies if Lucas could scatter her thoughts and melt her into a puddle whenever he touched her?

Narrowing her eyes, she watched the speck become larger. It was a problem she'd have to solve.

4

WHEN SHE STEPPED OUT onto the dock, Mac's eyes were first drawn to the white sand beach that stretched in both directions until it curved out of sight. Waves broke against it, then drew back to attack again in a steady rhythm. Fifty yards ahead, palm trees shaded a squat box of a cabin with a covered porch. Almost covered, she amended when she saw the ladder tipped against it, a pile of shingles stacked on its sloping roof.

Lucas grabbed her suitcase and climbed out of the boat. "I hope you're not expecting anything fancy. Every time I come down here I try to make a few improvements, but it's pretty rustic."

"It's lovely." Pausing as she stepped off the dock, she looked at the sweep of shore again. "I've never seen a beach that wasn't thronged with people. You must love it here."

He looked at her for a moment. "I do. None of the rest of my family does. They call this place Lucas's Folly."

It was impossible to imagine the confident man striding in front of her up the path to the cabin as being capable of folly. She found her gaze riveted on his broad shoulders. Beneath the thin polo shirt he was wearing, she could see the easy, sure movement of muscles as he swung her suitcase in rhythm with his stride. She'd learned in her research that from a psychological standpoint, a woman who was attracted to a man's muscular shoulders was probably looking for a strong emotional bond.

That was the last thing she wanted with Lucas Wainright,

she reminded herself. If her plan was going to work at all, he was just someone she would practice on. A guinea pig.

She forced her gaze down the length of his back to his waist and below…. Suddenly, her mouth went dry as dust. He had what Madame Gervais would definitely call in her Parisian French a…

As she watched him climb the porch steps, the foreign words escaped her. "Great buns" was the only description she could think of in English. His cutoff jeans fit over his backside like a second skin, leaving very little to the imagination…just enough to make her wonder what his skin would feel like beneath that denim. Soft and smooth…firm and hard? Would it feel as hot as her own skin was beginning to feel?

The urge to find out was so sudden, so strong that Mac stopped dead in her tracks. If she hadn't, she was sure she would have reached out and actually placed the palm of her hand on Lucas's butt.

She made herself take a deep breath and let it out. In spite of the heat, the air felt cool compared to the fire that had started to burn in her body. What in the world was the matter with her? She'd never before found herself mesmerized by a man's *derriere*—that was the French word. According to Madame Gervais, women who were attracted to that particular body part were lusty adventurers who were looking for similar qualities in a man.

The thought of herself as a "lusty adventurer" nearly made her laugh. Still, it might be evidence that she did have a sensual side to her nature, after all.

It was only as Lucas opened the door of the cabin and glanced back over his shoulder that she realized she was staring at that part of his anatomy.

"Are you all right?" Lucas asked.

"Fine." She moved quickly up the steps and into the cabin. The air was stuffy and even warmer than outside. Or perhaps it was her own inner temperature rising because she was standing close to Lucas again. Close enough to touch.

Pushing the thought out of her mind, she focused her full attention on the small, tidy interior of the room. Though the darkness contrasted sharply with the glaring brightness outside, she noted that the room was minimally furnished with a couch, a coffee table, a desk and a chair. At one end, a wooden counter with two stools tucked beneath its wide ledge framed a space for a tiny kitchen. There was no clutter, nothing to suggest that the place was occupied except for the laptop computer and thick, sturdy briefcase that sat on the desk.

It was then that she noticed the framed photographs that nearly covered the wall above. Curious, she moved closer to get a better look. Most of the pictures were snapshots of Sophie and her younger brothers, the step-twins. Nicholas and Nathaniel's high-school graduation, Sophie's graduation from college. She'd met Sophie five years ago when she'd been doing postdoctoral work and Sophie had been finishing her undergraduate degree. They'd been fast friends ever since.

Her gaze shifted to a shot of the opening of Sophie's antique shop in Georgetown. And there were others that captured less formal occasions—Sophie and the step-twins beneath a Christmas tree, a teenage Sophie standing by a red convertible dangling the keys from her fingers. There were twenty pictures in all, a sort of family album/mural, except that there were no parents in any of them. And no sign of Lucas.

Her attention was caught and held by the last photo in the bottom row. She was in it, standing next to Sophie. Lucas had snapped a victory picture after she and Sophie had beaten him at tennis.

Something moved through her then. Envy? Longing? Lifting her hand, she ran her fingers over the frame. The pictures were concrete evidence of something she already knew. Lucas Wainright valued his family.

"You played a great game. I'd be glad to make you a copy of the photo, if you'd like."

"Thanks." As she turned, she nearly bumped into him.

He handed her a bottle of water. "You'd better drink it all. In this kind of heat, it's easy to become dehydrated."

She took a long swallow, then watched as Lucas drained his bottle. She was close enough to see a drip of water run from the corner of his mouth to his chin, and then down the long column of his throat. In her mind, she imagined what it might be like to trace its path with her finger, to feel the coolness of the water, the heat of his skin underneath.

"Penny for your thoughts."

Mac reined them in. This was the second time in almost as many minutes that she'd fantasized about touching Lucas Wainright.

"Sophie says you have a problem you'd like my help with."

Her nerves slithered into a knot in her stomach, and she felt the bottle slip from her fingers.

Lucas caught it before it hit the floor and handed it back to her. "That bad, huh?"

Before she could reply, he took her arm and led her out to the porch. "Why don't you sit down. You can finish that water while I fix some sandwiches. We'll talk about it over lunch."

In the doorway, he turned back to her. "You can stay here as long as you want. If it helps any, Sophie was pretty sure I could help. And I'm certainly willing to do anything I can."

WAS HE GOING CRAZY? Lucas spread slices of bread out on the counter. Standing on that boat with her body so close to his had turned his brain to mush and another part of his anatomy into something hard, erect and ready to go.

Except it wasn't going anywhere. Taking a calming breath, he slapped slices of ham, then cheese on the bread.

MacKenzie Lloyd was his sister's best friend, and he could not, would not, get involved with her. He'd vowed a long time ago to keep his relationships with women entirely separate from his family. He never dated anyone in his family's social circle, and he never brought any of his women friends home. It was just one of the methods he used to ensure that the women in his life never nurtured the false expectation that he would marry them. His other method was to be totally honest with them up front.

What was he thinking when he'd invited MacKenzie Lloyd to stay as long as she wanted?

Dumb question. He reached into the small refrigerator for mustard and spread it liberally on the ham. He hadn't been thinking at all. His mind had been too busy remembering the way her scent had wrapped itself around him, the way her hair, whipped back by the wind, had felt against his chin. And once he'd led her into the cabin, his mind had taken the leap from memory to fantasy, and had totally immersed itself in imagining what it would be like to make love with Dr. MacKenzie Lloyd.

Even as she'd settled herself on the steps, the image had slipped into his mind of sitting right down beside her and slipping her out of that neat little blouse, then the slacks. He'd been wondering just what it was that she wore beneath that cool-looking linen. Thin, white, practical cotton—the kind that schoolgirls wore—was what he'd pictured. Once he'd discarded that, he could spend the entire afternoon pleasuring her until she was spent and limp beneath him. And then he could begin again.

Bending down, he grabbed two beers from the cooler. He couldn't recall another woman who'd aroused such erotic fantasies in him. And she'd yet to give him any indication that the attraction he felt was mutual.

Was that what fascinated him? That cool, seemingly unflappable image that she projected? Certainly, he was curious about what lay beneath the surface. He'd already discovered that she wasn't as serious as she seemed. It had been pure, innocent enjoyment he'd seen in her eyes when that wave had lifted her right up off the deck of the boat.

And her laugh. Just recalling the sound of it had him wanting to surprise another one out of her.

Maybe she wasn't as indifferent to him as she appeared to be. He could think of several interesting ways to test that theory.

And he'd be a fool to put any of them to the test. Slapping the sandwiches onto a plate, he snagged the beers with his free hand and walked back out onto the porch.

She wasn't there.

"Mac!"

He was off the steps and scanning the beach when she said, "I'm up here."

Fear shot through him when he saw her perched on the sloping roof of the porch. "What the hell are you doing? You're afraid of heights."

"I'm also a coward. This is my way of summoning up some Dutch courage so that I can tell you why I'm here. But you may have to eat without me. I'm not sure I can get down."

Whatever else she was, MacKenzie Lloyd wasn't a coward. And what in the world had her so frightened that she'd climb onto a roof to screw up her courage? Tucking the bottles under his arm, he started up the ladder. "We'll eat up there then. I don't relish the thought of being flattened again if you decide to jump."

He had the pleasure of seeing her lips curve in a ghost of a smile as he settled himself beside her and distributed the sandwiches and beer. "Is it helping? To sit up here, I mean?"

"My stomach is still in a knot. But watching the water helps."

"Take a drink of the beer."

She glanced at it dubiously. "It'll make me want to take a nap."

"That's allowed. In fact, with the sun at its hottest, it's a very smart plan."

Damn tempting too. Lucas pushed away the image of lying down next to her on the narrow cot in his bedroom. He was trying not to think about the fact that he'd have to carry her down the ladder, but his body was already reacting to the possibility.

"Plan. Yes, that's what I wanted to talk to you about." She took a quick sip from the bottle, and when some beer dripped onto her wrist, she touched her tongue to it.

Lucas felt the hot lick of desire and took a long swallow of his own beer. "Sophie said you had a problem."

"That's because she didn't approve of my plan."

"She wants me to handle it."

"Exactly." Holding the bottle tightly in two hands, she kept her eyes on the sea. "I should begin by giving you some background. I want a family someday. For me that means kids and marriage. Not in that order, of course." She shot him a sideways glance. "I'm not one of those women who wants to raise children in a single-parent household. I know from experience that it can make for an unhappy childhood, so I want to avoid it at all costs. That's why I want to be prepared. A good plan is everything in the lab." She glanced at him briefly. "It must be the same way in a business deal."

"Yes," Lucas said. "But I'm not sure I'm following you."

Mac took another swallow of beer. "What are your feelings about divorce?"

Lucas's eyes narrowed. "I want to avoid it at all costs. That's why I'll never marry."

She nodded, then drank more beer. Lucas watched her lick the moisture from her lips as she lowered the bottle and turned to face him. "I want to avoid it too. We just differ in out approaches to the problem. I want to get married and my research is designed to make sure my marriage lasts forever."

Bells began to ring in Lucas's head—the ones that always warned him about women who were thinking about weddings. "I don't intend to get married. Ever."

"Of course you don't. You already have a family. I only had one until I was five. That's when my father's eye started to wander." She took another long swallow of beer, then glanced at the bottle. "You know, you were right about this. It is relaxing me."

"Maybe too much," Lucas muttered. "Have you had anything to eat today, Doc?"

"No. I never eat before I fly." She tipped the bottle up again and drank thirstily. "It's been ages since I've had beer. I didn't think I liked it, but I do."

"You were talking about wandering eyes." His own sure weren't wandering. They were glued to MacKenzie Lloyd's mouth as she licked the last trace of beer from her lips.

"First it's the eyes, and then it's the whole body. Did you know that infidelity is the number-one cause of divorce? And the number-one reason for one of the partners to stray is that monogamy usually leads to monotony? Hopefully, my plan will prevent that."

"How?"

"By making sure that my husband *never* gets bored in bed." Pausing, she rubbed the bottle against her cheek. "It's getting really warm up here."

"Tell me about it."

"I'm trying. I've done all this research on how to please a man in bed. Most of the data I've compiled is on male sexual fantasies. Did you know that the number-one fantasy of men is to make love with two women at once?"

"I think I read that somewhere."

When she turned to study him, he had the fleeting sensation of being put on a slide.

"Is that *your* favorite?" she finally asked.

"Not at the present moment."

"I haven't figured out exactly how to create that one,

but I have a lot of other ones I'd like to try out. Are you going to finish your beer?''

Before he could reply, she plucked his bottle from his hand and replaced it with her empty one. Then she took a long swallow.

"Maybe you'd better spell out exactly how it is that I can help you."

As she turned to face him, she slid a little toward the end of the roof.

He gripped her arm. "Careful."

"There's a time in every research project when you have to put your theories to the test in the lab. I'm at that point right now. I feel like I'm bursting with research, and if I don't put some of it to use, I just might explode. Do you ever get that feeling?"

"Yeah."

"I feel that way in the lab too—and it's so exciting. That's why I need a man right now. I have to have someone to practice on. And Sophie suggested you."

Lucas's mouth went dry as dust. "You..." He cleared his throat. "You can't be serious."

"But I am. I tried to explain to Sophie. This is the exact procedure I follow in the lab. Theories always have to be tested. But you shouldn't feel pressured. I can certainly find someone else to test my research on. I have a friend in Paris who has several volunteers lined up. But Sophie insisted that I ask you first."

Lucas stared at her. It had to be the beer. He removed his bottle from her hand. "Let me make sure I have this straight. You're asking me to become your lover so that you can field-test your research on me?"

"Exactly. And it won't go any further than that. I promise that I'm not out to trap you into marriage. Sophie said you would be worried about that. This is strictly a no-strings arrangement. I've been on the Pill for three months, and I've always practiced safe sex, not that I've had to worry about it lately. What about you?"

Lucas stared at her, incredulous.

"Is there anything in your sexual history I should be concerned about," she asked.

"No, I'm a very careful man."

Mac nodded. "Of course, you could still use a condom as an extra precaution…"

"Of course. And if I agree to the arrangement…?"

"There are some particular male sexual fantasies that I want to try out. If you're willing." She took his bottle back and emptied it.

As her proposition swam around in his mind, Lucas watched a thin trickle of beer run down her throat. He imagined the bitter taste it would have, along with the sweeter, warmer flavor of her skin. But if he gave in to the temptation of leaning forward and following the path of the beer with his tongue, he wouldn't stop there. He would have to kiss her. And if he did, he wouldn't stop there either.

He felt as if he was fighting against a riptide that was carrying him farther and farther from shore, from his sanity. Even as the battle went on in his mind, he was leaning forward. Then the shingles moved beneath him.

"You're slipping." Mac grabbed his arm, and then she was sliding too.

In the instant it took him to realize that they were both going over the edge, he wrapped his arms around her and held her close. If he'd been alone, he would have simply tucked his arms in and rolled. As it was, the moment his feet hit the ground, he twisted and fell backward to take the brunt of the impact. It took his breath away.

As soon as he could, he loosened his grip on her. "Are you all right?"

She raised her head and looked down at him. "Fine. What about you?"

For a moment he didn't respond. All he could focus on was the way sunlight brought out the fiery glints in her hair and the way the amber flecks had brightened in her eyes.

The way her body had softened until it fit perfectly against his.

He couldn't recall ever wanting a woman this much. "About your plan…"

"Oh," she said, her eyes suddenly narrowing. "Do you want to…? That would be great. If you'd like to get started…" She pushed against him. "I'll get the questionnaire."

"Questionnaire?"

"So I can tell which fantasies are your favorites."

He was thinking of carrying her down the beach to the small inlet where the palms touched overhead. There, he could make love to her until she couldn't think of anything, of anyone but him.

And the doc was thinking of paperwork!

"It won't take long. Once I know exactly what you like to fantasize about, I can run them through this program I created on my laptop."

"Wait a minute." When she tried to rise, he grabbed her wrist and sat up with her. The frantic skipping of her pulse against his thumb told him she wasn't anywhere near as cool as her voice had sounded.

Oh, she was excited all right. But was it about making love with him, or was it because she was thinking of her questionnaires and programs? "I stopped indulging in fantasies when I was twelve. I much prefer reality."

"Oh…are you saying you don't want to? I told Sophie that you don't think of me that way."

"I think of you that way." He couldn't stop himself from thinking of her that way.

"Then…" She moistened her lips. "You'll do it?"

The strength of his desire to agree had him releasing her wrist carefully. He had to think, to weigh the possible outcomes. And he couldn't think at all when she was sitting on his lap, her mouth only a breath away. "I never make snap decisions in business. I'm sure you never do in the lab."

"No, of course not."

"Then I suggest we take twenty-four hours to think it over before either of us jumps into anything. Agreed?"

"Agreed."

He saw something flicker in her eyes, but he wasn't sure whether it was relief or disappointment. Then to his complete astonishment, she settled her head on his shoulder and yawned.

"I feel so much better now that I've told you why I came here."

Better wasn't exactly the way he would choose to describe the mix of emotions moving through him. Desire, he could handle. But there was something unsettling about the warmth that was also spreading through him, solid and sure. And it shouldn't feel so damn right to have her sitting on his lap. He should be setting her away from him, but he hadn't been able to prevent his arms from moving around her.

And then he didn't move at all. For a few moments he allowed himself to simply sit and hold her. The silence was broken only by the sound of waves rushing onto the shore and the cry of a gull overhead.

Who in the hell was Dr. MacKenzie Lloyd? Was she the cool, unflappable scientist? Or was she the sensual woman who'd just offered to practice her sex research on him? And which one was having this effect on him?

Glancing down, he saw that her eyes were shut, her breathing even. She was asleep. Lucas frowned. Was she so indifferent to him that, one minute, she could tell him that she wanted to create sexual fantasies for him and then, the next, calmly doze off?

There was a part of him that wanted to wake her with a kiss. To catapult her from slumber to wakefulness by arousing in her at least some of the feelings that were tormenting him. He wondered if this was what that prince had felt when he'd fought his way into the castle and come upon Sleeping Beauty.

He'd always privately thought the poor guy had gotten more trouble than he'd bargained for when he'd kissed that beauty awake.

And Lucas Wainright hadn't gotten to where he was without looking before he leaped.

Twenty-four hours. He repeated the number to himself several times as he rose to his feet and carried Mac into the cabin. By the time he settled her on the bed and retreated from the cabin down to the beach, he wasn't sure whether it was a caution or a promise.

5

WHEN SHE WOKE the next morning, the first thing Mac was aware of was the heat. Her entire body seemed to be on fire. Pushing herself into a sitting position, she felt a trickle of sweat run down her neck.

One quick glance around the room reminded her of where she was. Lucas's cabin. Then her eyes widened as the memory of just what she'd been dreaming about flooded into her mind. She'd been making love to Lucas, or more precisely, he'd been making love to her—touching her with those clever, callused hands. There hadn't been one part of her body that they'd left unexplored. She'd barely been able to breathe, let alone move. Even now, as she thought of the way those long, hard fingers had stroked her—down the length of her arms, her legs and then slowly, torturously up the inner side of her thigh—she could feel tiny little flames licking along her skin.

Mac sat up and scooted to the edge of the bed. She'd just had a fantasy! The one thing she'd discovered in her research was that she had a very dull fantasy life. Obviously, that was changing. Madame Gervais had insisted that she had a sensual side to her nature. Lucas Wainright seemed to be helping her discover it.

Pushing herself off the bed, Mac moved to the window, but even the breeze making its way into the room felt warm on her skin. No wonder. The sun was already quite high in the sky. A quick glance at her watch told her it was eleven o'clock. Another four hours to wait until Lucas would announce his decision.

What would it be?

Nothing in the way he'd acted the day before had given her the slightest clue. From the moment that she'd awakened from her nap, he'd been polite and attentive, encouraging her to walk along the beach while he fished in a lagoon for their dinner.

After they'd eaten, he'd taken her on a tour of the island. He'd even slept on the boat so that she could have the one narrow bed in the cabin.

In short, he'd been the perfect host. Other than that one terse statement—"I think about you that way"—he hadn't done one thing to indicate that he might be interested in becoming her…boy toy.

Moving toward the dresser, Mac gazed at her reflection. Better to face the facts. MacKenzie Lloyd was not a woman that most men had lustful thoughts about. Even with a new hair color and a head full of research, what did she really have to appeal to a man like Lucas Wainright?

The muffled ring of a cell phone had her moving quickly to the main room where she located her bag and fished it out. "Hello?"

"It's Sophie. If Lucas is there, pretend I'm someone from the university."

"He's not here." And she wasn't sure where he was. Mac went to the door of the cabin and spotted him on the deck of the boat polishing brass with a white cloth.

"Good. Whatever you do, don't tell him I called. As far as he knows, I had to check my cell phone in at the desk of the spa. The one thing that would spoil my week in paradise would be to have him calling me every day to check up on me."

"You're enjoying the spa?"

"It's heaven. For the first time in months I feel absolutely free. I wish you could see the view I have from my balcony. There are at least three air balloons suspended in the sky. They look like giant lollipops. I have to go up in one while I'm here. Wait…Mac, can you hold on a minute?

I ordered something from room service. They're at the door.''

In the background, Mac could hear voices, the sound of Sophie's laugh, then a deeper one. On the boat, Lucas continued to polish brass with sure, steady strokes. Odd that she'd never before pictured him as a man who would like to do any kind of work with his hands. It explained why they'd felt so hard when they'd settled over hers on the wheel of the boat. The memory had a sliver of heat shooting through her.

"You still there?" Sophie asked.

"Yes," Mac replied.

"Tell me how your plan's progressing."

"I asked him."

"Asked him what?" Sophie prompted. "Give me the details."

As she told Sophie what had happened, Mac once again replayed everything in her mind. Her stomach plummeted farther. "I don't think it was my most persuasive presentation."

"Surely he didn't turn you down?"

Mac smiled at the disbelief in her friend's voice. "Not exactly. He wants us both to think about it for twenty-four hours."

There was a great deal of exasperation in Sophie's sigh. "That is *so* typically Lucas. He's probably having one of his security people do a thorough background check on you to see if you're any threat to Wainright Enterprises. My advice is don't wait."

"What do you mean?"

"Seduce him into agreeing. That research of yours is worthless if you don't have the guts to use it."

"I don't know—"

"He who hesitates is lost. Picture yourself five years after you walk down the aisle with your future bridegroom. You're in your kitchen feeding two screaming kids and you're afraid your husband's eye is about to wander. Are you going to wait for *him* to make the first move?''

"No," Mac said softly.

"But? I hear a *but* in that sentence."

"I just imagined he might be a little more enthusiastic."

Sophie laughed. "Enthusiasm is contagious. Starting out by asking him to fill out a questionnaire was not your best move. As foreplay, it wouldn't rate very high on *my* list."

"Oh...I didn't think of that."

"I warned you that this plan of yours was not going to be like your usual experiments. You can't approach it like a job. Besides, it should be fun! And people are not like your docile little lab animals, Mac. Sometimes they need a little extra push."

The moment Lucas turned and glanced in her direction, Mac felt the impact of his gaze ripple through her. So what if his hormones weren't as stimulated as hers were. So what if he was just being kind to his kid sister's best friend. Didn't she have the kind of knowledge to change all that?

"Sometimes they need a big push," Sophie added.

Mac couldn't think of a man she'd rather push than Lucas. Slowly, she smiled as one of the fantasies from her research unfolded itself in her mind. "Thanks, Soph. I'm going to take your advice."

"You go, girl! And have some fun!"

SOPHIE HUNG UP her phone with a satisfied smile and glanced out at the view from her balcony. Covered in lush grapevines, the hillside rolled down to the valley below. There, the neat rows in the vineyards were crisscrossed by narrow roads until hills rose sharply again.

Napa Valley, California, was as far away from D.C., the Florida Keys and North Carolina as she could get without actually leaving the country. And since she'd never been here before, she doubted that Lucas would think of it. Her lips curved in a smile. Not that she expected him to be thinking about her at all for the next week. Mac should be able to handle that.

And she was going to handle the rest. For the next week, no one would know she was Sophie Wainright, least of all the man she'd agreed to meet today for lunch. When she'd first met him in that small café on Capitol Hill three weeks ago, she'd told him she was Susan Walker. The initials matched her own, but that was all that linked her to Sophie Wainright.

It was on the way home from that first meeting that she'd discovered she was being followed. Now she pushed herself away from the railing and began to pace back and forth along the length of her balcony. Just the thought of it made her furious.

Well, she'd made sure that no one had followed her here. Not once since she'd gotten off the plane in San Francisco had she had that prickling sensation at the back of her neck that had warned her before. Not even Mac knew where she was coming to spend time with the man who only knew her as Susan Walker. A man who wasn't just interested in her because she was Sophie Wainright.

Pausing, she leaned on the balcony railing to watch one of the air balloons make a soft landing on the valley floor. Then she smiled. Lucas would have a lot of trouble finding her even if he did discover that she wasn't in that dreadful spa. A bonus to switching identities with Mac was that she'd been able to make all her plane and hotel reservations in Mac's name.

Reaching for the coffee that room service had just delivered, she raised her cup in another toast. "To real freedom, at last."

THE MOMENT THAT Mac turned and strode back into the cabin, Lucas frowned and went back to polishing the brass trim that edged the deck of the *Adventurer.* Performing repetitious physical tasks always helped him to think and to put things in perspective. But he was no closer to sorting out what he was going to do about MacKenzie Lloyd's proposition than he'd been yesterday when he'd left her in his bedroom.

Could the doc possibly be as honest and disingenuous as she seemed? Gut instinct told him she was.

But experience told him that women usually had a hidden financial agenda.

That was the one lesson he'd learned from watching his father bounce through five marriages. He'd been ten when his mother had walked out for good. His father had reacted by marrying again on the rebound. It had been up to Lucas to help Sophie negotiate the emotional trauma. It wasn't until marriage three or four that he'd become aware of the financial toll that his father's behavior was taking on the company his grandfather had founded. By the time wife number five had departed, Wainright Enterprises had been deeply in debt. Not even Sophie knew how close they had come to losing everything.

When he'd taken over the company, he'd made a vow to himself never to make the same mistake his father had. He would never marry because he already had a family—Sophie and the stepbrothers his father had left behind.

MacKenzie Lloyd had seemed to understand and accept that. But maybe it had been the beer. Either way, she'd made him an offer he was finding it very difficult to refuse. The whole idea of researching men's fantasies and then offering to make them into a reality for some lucky guy was…almost irresistible.

When his cell phone rang, he put down his cloth and pulled it out of his pocket. "Yeah?"

"As far as I can tell, Sophie Wainright is somewhere in this damn spa," Tracker said.

"As far as you can tell?"

"I'm about fifty yards from the gates right now. The guard on duty says Sophie Wainright registered about three o'clock yesterday afternoon, but the people who run this place are a bunch of amazons who clearly have an aversion to men. If you have a Y chromosome, you can't set foot on their sacred ground. I'd feel more certain if I could get in there and see for myself.''

''A little paranoid, are we?'' Lucas asked.

''I'd prefer to think I'm being thorough,'' Tracker said. ''I don't like that she pulled that switch on me, and I'd like to make sure she hasn't pulled another one.''

''Your pride is wounded.''

There was a slight pause at the other end. Tracker's drawl when it came was laced with humor. ''Could be that. Could be the challenge too. I haven't figured a way in yet.''

Lucas grinned. ''I told you your policy on not hiring women would come back to bite you.''

''No way, boss. I only hire people I can trust, and I don't trust the female of the species.''

Lucas's grin faded. ''Should I be worried about Sophie?''

''Not yet. If I thought she might be in danger, I'd go in there, grab her and get her out. And if you're worried about Falcone, he and his son have both flown to California. I've got a man on each of them. If there's any problem, I can be at the airport in an hour. Unless you want me out there right now.''

Lucas considered it for a moment. ''No. As long as you've got Falcone covered, you can indulge yourself with the challenge of getting into that all-female spa.''

''Go ahead. Rub it in. What about the little doc? You find out what her problem is?''

''Yeah.''

''You want me to do something about it?''

''No.'' The sharpness of his own tone surprised Lucas.

''You want me to butt out.''

''Yes. No,'' Lucas said on a sigh. Tracker was a man he'd trust with his life and the only man he'd ever trusted with details of his business deals. ''I think I'm going to have to tackle it myself.''

''It's personal, I take it.''

The delight in his friend's voice had him frowning. "It's complicated. And…it's confidential."

"Goes without saying."

Lucas kept his gaze on the cabin as he tried to think of the best way to summarize Mac's plan. Finally he began, "Long story short. She's done some research on how to keep a man pleased…" His frown deepened. "No, *pleasured* is a better word. In bed. So far all her data has come from books and interviews, and now she wants to put it…into practice."

"On you."

"Or on some other volunteer."

There was a beat of silence at the other end of the phone. Then Tracker said, "What's the problem?"

"Maybe it sounds too good to be true."

Tracker laughed. "You got a point there. Your little scenario has just moved to the number-one spot on my favorite-fantasy list. If you turn her down, please mention my name as a backup."

"No."

Tracker gave an exaggerated sigh. "Hands off. I get the picture."

"It's not that." But Lucas was all too afraid that it was just that. For some reason, he didn't like the idea of Mac taking her proposal elsewhere. It was bad enough to picture her with some anonymous man that one of her research contacts fixed her up with. But when he pictured her with Tracker, it was even worse. Tracker appreciated certain things about women, but he didn't trust them. And it occurred to Lucas that he wanted very much to protect Mac from getting hurt.

"If you're worried about her being after your money, I think you're safe there. I ran a financial check on her. She has a trust fund of two million from her parents, but she seems to live on what she makes as a full professor at the university. And she may get an influx of money in the near future. Several biotech firms are very interested in the research she's doing. It's some very promising stuff on slowing the aging process at the cellular level. One of them has been wining and dining her recently. That's all I've got so far, but she sure doesn't fit the profile of a fortune hunter.''

''No, she doesn't.''

''One other thing,'' Tracker said. ''There was a break-in at her lab at the university. Must have happened when she was at your place on Sunday. According to campus security, there was no damage. Whoever it was got into the safe, but she told the police none of her research was stolen. She evidently keeps it elsewhere.''

''Who would be after her research?''

''I figured you'd want to know, so I put a man on it. I assumed that might be the problem she wanted your help with. Look, boss, I'm going to give you some unsolicited and probably unwanted advice.''

''Tracker…''

''No one works harder for your family than you do. Maybe it's time you relaxed and had a little fun. I say go for it.''

Tracker's laughter was still ringing in his ear when he cut the connection. He'd come to pretty much the same decision on his own. If the doc was determined to create fantasies, he might as well be on the receiving end. Hell, he'd come up with several of his own he'd like to try out. And when the time came for the fantasies to end…he'd just have to let her down very easy. It was the one thing besides business that he'd worked to develop a skill for. He knew how to say goodbye.

MAC CAREFULLY CONSIDERED the two bathing suits she'd packed. The one still lying on top of her suitcase was a black tank top with a matching thong. The one she was wearing was a whisper-thin piece of silky latex in a shimmering emerald green. It covered her like a second skin from her breasts to her thighs, and it did everything that Madame Gervais said it would—revealing practically everything and suggesting more. More importantly, it fit the particular fantasy she wanted to create.

Picking up a flowered piece of silk, she wrapped it around herself and tied it at the waist. Then she studied herself in the mirror and nodded.

Guilt-free sex with a beautiful, young island girl—that was the fantasy she'd chosen. She'd thought of it when she'd been talking to Sophie. It supposedly appealed to most men. Music from *South Pacific* hummed at the edges of her mind as she ran through the details in her mind. It would help if she could get Lucas to go into the water with her. Supposedly, men had very erotic fantasies about mermaids too. And since she didn't have the information that the questionnaire would have given her, a backup plan was a good idea.

Moving closer to the mirror, she ran her hands through her hair and studied herself more closely. Madame Gervais had told her that the right clothes could make all the difference. Mac was beginning to believe she was right. The outfit she was wearing did make her feel different, more confident.

When she stepped out that door, she was going to be a young girl who'd been born and raised in a village on this island. Lania was her name. And Lucas was a stranger who had been washed ashore by a storm. A dark handsome stranger she was strongly attracted to, a man whose touch she was beginning to crave. A man who would leave her soon, unless she convinced him to stay.

On impulse, she picked up the string of pearls she'd taken from her bag and fastened them around her neck. They fit well with the fantasy.

Turning, she headed toward the door of the cabin. She saw him even before she stepped out on the porch. He was hurrying up the path. In her mind, she pictured running to him across the sand. He would sweep her up into his arms and carry her down to a secluded section of the beach.

It was the water bottle she'd left on the top step that

shattered the image forming in her mind. Her foot snagged on it, and she made a grab for the post. It kept her from falling, but it also swayed ominously, rattling more loose shingles on the roof. Three of them showered to the ground and one landed on Lucas's shoulder as he reached her.

"Are you all right?" he asked, brushing it off.

"Are you?" It was his quick grin that made her smile, and suddenly they were both laughing. When she reached for the post again to steady herself, he grabbed her hand.

"Please. I don't want to be hit by any more falling debris."

She felt a fresh wave of laughter bubbling up.

When it finally subsided, she found she was standing on the bottom step, his hands were at her waist, steadying her, and her eyes were level with his. Laughter had lightened the color, but the blue was already deepening, and his gaze had become intent. Her body reacted instantly, every nerve ending snapping to attention the way they always seemed to when he was close.

Her gaze dropped to his mouth. His lips were wide, not thin…not too full either. It was hard to tell if they would be hard or soft, and she had a sudden, compelling need to find out. In her dream, he'd touched her—everywhere. But he hadn't kissed her. She leaned closer.

"Doc…" Lucas cleared his throat as he tightened his grip on her waist, once more steadying her. "I came back to the cabin to tell you that I don't need twenty-four hours. I've reached a decision."

A quick skip of panic moved through her. He was going to say no. To forestall him, she pressed her fingers against his mouth. "I've reached a decision too."

"Go ahead."

The movement of his lips against her fingers sent a wave of heat through her. "I was coming down to the beach to…"

"Yes?"

Another wave of heat shot through her. "I wanted

to…that is, I wondered if you…'' It was hard to keep her mind on the fantasy, hard to think of anything but the pressure, the heat of his mouth on her fingers. What would his lips feel like on hers? What would they taste like? At the same time that she struggled to keep her focus, she couldn't seem to prevent herself from moving closer. ''I have a fantasy in mind…''

''Yes.''

In the fantasy that filled her mind, he gripped her wrist to pull her hand away. Then his mouth crushed hers, strong arms lifted her, carrying her into the cabin, and then the full weight of his body pressed her into the mattress of that narrow cot. Even as a sharp spear of pleasure streaked through her, she struggled to rid her mind of the image. She was supposed to be creating *his* fantasy, not hers.

Struggling to concentrate, she said, ''My name is Lania. You're shipwrecked on my island. And every day I've come from the village to nurse you. To bring you food. There isn't a part of your body I haven't seen.'' She pictured it in her mind. ''There isn't a part of you I haven't touched.'' She could feel the smooth skin stretched taut over long bones, solid muscles. ''You've been growing stronger every day. You haven't noticed, but I've been watching you work on your boat. I know that you'll leave soon. But before you do…I want to—I need to—''

She wasn't sure what it was—the fantasy that her words were conjuring up in her mind or the heat that seemed to be steadily drawing her closer to him. But the need she felt to kiss him had twisted into something sharp and compelling inside her. She dragged her fingers away from his mouth, rubbing them over his bottom lip as she did.

''I just have to kiss you. I've been dreaming of doing this for so long.'' Framing his face with her hands, she touched her mouth to his. His lips were neither soft nor hard. ''Just right,'' she murmured.

''What?''

She drew back slightly but she didn't meet his eyes. She

couldn't seem to take her gaze from his lips. ''Not too hard. Not too soft. Your mouth feels just right. I was wondering…''

This time when she pressed her mouth to his, she couldn't seem to prevent her tongue from slipping between his lips. If she'd thought he'd tasted good a moment before, this was heaven. Not sweet really, and not any flavor that she could remember tasting before. It reminded her just a little of her favorite childhood candy—the dark chocolate that her father would always send her on her birthdays and that her mother would take away from her and hide. It always tasted so delicious, so forbidden when she found it.

But Lucas's taste was much more potent. It seemed to be spreading through her, clouding her mind—and she had to focus. She'd forgotten for a moment the fantasy. In just a minute—or two—she'd have to get back to it.

And she would…definitely…just as soon as she tasted him one more time. Withdrawing a little, she nipped at his bottom lip, then let her tongue probe deeper. The tip of it brushed the edge of his teeth, then met his tongue. In the space of a heartbeat, the flavor changed again to something very dark and very male. As it streamed through her, she tightened her hands on him and felt her toes curl on the edge of the step. In the space of a heartbeat, each sensation intensified—the rough wood of the porch beneath her bare feet, the burning warmth of his thighs pressed against hers. Beneath her hands, she felt the sharp line of cheekbones, the hard strength of his jaw.

She wanted more. She wanted him to touch her, to kiss her back. And he was just standing there, letting her do whatever she wanted. Suddenly chilled, she drew away and met his eyes.

''What's wrong?'' she asked.

''You stopped. Why?''

She blinked. ''You're not kissing me back. I should have

insisted that you fill out the questionnaire. Then I would have some idea—''

"Forget the questionnaire and kiss me again."

IT SEEMED LIKE an eternity to Lucas as he waited for her to bring her mouth to his again. He'd seen the confusion in her eyes and the hurt. He wanted to erase both. More than that, he wanted to ease her to the ground and run his hands over her, slowly, molding every inch of her until she felt as helpless as he did.

How could he possibly explain to her what he didn't understand himself? He hadn't touched her, he hadn't taken control of the kiss because he quite simply couldn't. Even now, he wasn't sure he could lift his arms.

Was it the fantasy that her words had conjured up? He'd imagined what it might be like to lie there, powerless, while she touched him—everywhere.

Or had it been the reality of her kiss—the softness of her lips and those tiny, tentative movements of her tongue as it glided over his? Perhaps it was the combination that had acted like a powerful drug on his system, pouring through him and trapping him in a world of sensations.

He wasn't sure of anything except that she'd weakened him. He'd never allowed a woman to do that to him before. And it wouldn't happen again. This time he intended to be in control of himself, but the moment her mouth brushed against his, a short, explosive fuse ignited. Any intention he had of keeping the pressure light and teasing was blown away. Feelings she'd stirred up with that first kiss tore through him in a series of explosions, and wave after wave of sensations rocked him.

He'd never been so aware of a woman before—the helpless hitch of her breath when he nipped at her bottom lip, the husky, pleading sound of her moan as he swallowed it, and her skin…it was on fire. He could feel the flames licking at his fingers as they moved down her throat over her breasts, burning him even through the thin material of the bathing suit. And her taste, the deep ripe flavor poured through him.

He'd sensed this raw passion in her before, simmering beneath the surface, waiting to break free. He could feel it now in the way her hands gripped him, in the way her mouth met each of his demands with one of her own.

Though the ocean was over fifty yards away, he could have sworn he was standing in it, feeling the push and pull of the water as it sucked the sand out from beneath his feet. He pulled her closer for balance and felt her breasts crush against the hard line of his chest. It wasn't enough.

Desperation clawed at him as he ran his hands over her. He knew he was being rough. And in some distant part of his mind, he knew he should slow down, be patient. But his hands seemed to be operating of their own accord, following one directive—he simply had to get her closer to him. Impatient with the bathing suit, he stripped it down to her waist and cupped her breast in his hand. It was as soft as rainwater. Liquid silk. He wanted to savor it, taste it, but she arched against him, calling his name.

He had to have more.

''Mac.'' He cupped his free hand under her hip. ''Scoot up. Wrap your legs around me.''

With a murmur of acceptance, approval, she did. Then, arching against him again, she began to move, rubbing against his hardness. What he'd thought were flames before couldn't compare to the searing heat that sliced through him now. He'd felt need before, but not this kind—unreasonable, unmanageable. Something inside him snapped with the same quick finality of a switch being pulled. Then he wasn't thinking at all.

Sinking to his knees, he managed to pull down the zipper of his jeans, push aside the thin protection of her suit, and then he was sinking into her. But it still wasn't enough. With a quick, savage movement of his hips he went deeper, stretching her, feeling her slick, hot core take all of him. Gripped fiercely inside her, he felt his climax begin to build. His hips began to move, thrusting harder and faster.

Swearing, he drove her, drove himself until the final release and the world went dark around him.

Shattered. That's what he felt like when sanity returned. He was lying on the rough boards of the porch beside Mac, but he had no idea how they'd gotten there. He couldn't move, could barely think.

And he was trembling. A small shiver of fear moved through him. Shame came next. He'd never before taken a woman with so little care. He wasn't even sure that she'd reached her climax. His own had been so quick, so consuming, and he'd been so totally lost in it.

Had he hurt her? He'd been close to violent, definitely out of control when he'd pushed into her. When he turned to look at her, he found wide amber eyes studying him intently. He had the uncomfortable feeling that he'd been smeared on a slide. He opened his mouth, but she spoke first. "That didn't go exactly as I'd planned."

The words were such a clear echo of the thoughts in his head that he blinked.

"I'm sorry."

She'd even stolen his apology. Suddenly, he frowned. "You don't have anything to be sorry about."

"I lost control. It wasn't supposed to end that quickly."

"No, it wasn't. But that was my fault."

"We were supposed to make it at least to the beach. I really wanted to get you in the water. Kissing underwater is supposed to be very erotic."

She was talking about the fantasy. Had she been kissing him or the sailor? And who had he just made love to?

She rubbed her fingers across her lips. "The way I react to your kiss is going to present a challenge that I didn't quite foresee." A fine line appeared on her forehead. "I'm going to have to make some adjustments to my plan."

It was the last thing he'd expected her to say. Whoever it was who'd been kissing him, it was definitely the doc who was talking to him now. And he wanted her even more than he had before.

"That is...." The frown line deepened. "I hope you're going to let me go ahead with my research."

Her lips were still swollen from his kisses. A pulse was still jackhammering at her throat, and yet he could hear the wheels turning in her head. "You're hard on a man's ego, Doc."

The corners of her mouth turned down slightly. "I don't mean to be. Next time I'll try to stay more focused on the fantasy."

"You do that, Doc." Next time he was going to make sure that she couldn't stay focused at all. With a quick grin, he said, "I may have to make some adjustments of my own."

For some perverse reason, derailing that one-track mind of hers was becoming his number-one desire. Perhaps it was the challenge she offered that was drawing him. He could swear that he was dealing with more than one woman—there was the doc and the island girl, Lania. And which one was the real MacKenzie Lloyd? One way or the other, he was going to figure her out.

"Before we go any further with this little experiment, I think we need a change of scene." He rose, then drew her to her feet. "Let's pack."

"Where are we going?" she asked as he ushered her into the cabin.

"Wainright Enterprises owns a resort hotel on Key West. It will provide us with a more romantic atmosphere."

"I don't need romance."

Lucas threw back his head and laughed. "I think I do. You'll just have to indulge me." Then, throwing an arm around her shoulders, he gave her a quick hug. "And you better start figuring out what to do when I kiss you again. I plan to do it again very soon."

6

TRACKER SWORE SOFTLY as he lowered his binoculars. The North Carolina mountains had too many damn trees, and he'd lost track of how many he'd climbed trying to get a good view of the guests at the Serenity Spa.

One problem was that the compound was spread out over a couple of square miles. A large building sat in the center on a hill. Fanning out from there were tennis courts, a glassed-in, Olympic-size swimming pool and acres of lawn set up for volleyball, badminton, croquet. One unpaved road connected the grounds to the highway a mile away. In the more than four hours since he'd had the place under surveillance, only two vehicles had used that road. One had been the spa van, the other a truck delivering fresh produce and bottled water to the main building.

Raising the binoculars, he focused them on the group of women who were gathering on one of the playing fields, watching to see if any of them walked with the confident, distinctive gait of the Princess. He'd dubbed Lucas's pampered and temperamental sister that the first time he'd seen her. His view was being hampered, not only by the branches of several trees, but also by the fact that the women were wearing what seemed to be the spa uniform—sweatpants and hooded jackets.

Huge gray clouds had settled like a lid over the mountains, and thunder growled overhead. As the hooded figures began to disperse, he shifted his gaze to the individual cabins, most of which were tucked away beneath the trees. The information he'd downloaded from the Serenity Spa Web site emphasized complete privacy. It promised clients a totally female environment, free from the "intrusion of any male vibrations."

Tracker couldn't prevent a grin. In the very near future, he was going to break their promise. He just hadn't figured out the best way to do it. If he forced his way in, the Princess would be furious. When the lady got all fired up, she reminded him of some warrior goddess about to wreak her vengeance on mere mortals.

She'd been mad as hell when she'd read the file he'd gathered on Bradley Davis. The heat of her anger had been aimed at her brother. And she'd taken him completely by surprise when she'd landed that right cross to her brother's chin. Just the memory had him grinning. Oh, she'd been quick as lightning. He couldn't help but admire her for it. And she was strong too. She might look as slender as a wand, but when he'd grabbed her, he'd had to put some effort into subduing her.

The Princess was smart too. No one he'd tailed had ever spotted him before. But she had. He could still recall the cold fury in her eyes when they'd met his in that Georgetown pub. He'd felt it like a blow in his gut.

He'd underestimated her. That had been his mistake—a moment of carelessness that he was paying for now, he thought as he shifted carefully on the branch to ease the sharp impressions the bark was leaving on his backside.

If she hadn't become aware that she was being tailed, she wouldn't have pulled that switch yesterday, and he'd know for sure if she was indeed escaping from "male vibrations" in one of those damn cabins.

A bird landed on a nearby branch, gave him a startled look and flew off.

"Good idea," he muttered as he started to lower himself to the ground. He'd hoped to study the women as they made their way to the main building for lunch, but the steady and insistent slap of rain meant that umbrellas would be out in full force.

After hitting the ground, he ran toward the main road. Time for plan B.

THE MOMENT LUCAS TURNED his attention to uncorking the champagne that had been waiting for them in the suite, Mac drew in a deep breath and slipped out onto the balcony. What she needed was a moment to plan and get back on track. He hadn't allowed her much time to do that on the boat trip to Key West. Instead, he'd seemed determined to distract her in any way he could.

Not that he'd kissed her again. He'd just taken every opportunity he could to touch her. A hand at her back as they'd walked down the dock, a firm grasp on her fingers as he'd helped her onto and off the boat, the brush of his body against hers as they'd stepped into the same slot of the revolving door that had spun them into the hotel lobby.

Each time he'd come in contact with her, her heart had made what felt like a somersault in her chest, and each and every nerve in her body had responded. So many images had filled her mind when the bellhop had given them a quick tour of the hotel suite. Every time he'd gestured to a different feature—from the oversize hot tub in the bathroom to the grand piano tucked into a corner of the sunken living room—she'd pictured Lucas making love to her in each spot.

Clearly, her ability to create sexual fantasies for herself was growing by leaps and bounds, and they all centered on Lucas Wainright. No other man had ever made love to her that way, with such intensity—as if he couldn't help himself. And she wanted him to do it again. And he would, just as soon as he followed her out onto the balcony. Just thinking about it was enough to make the muscles in her legs turn to water.

She had to get a grip. It would be so tempting to just give in to the spell that he seemed to weave around her. To enjoy it for however long it lasted.

As soon as he poured the champagne and followed her out here, she'd probably dissolve into a puddle at his feet.

No. If she allowed herself to give in to the temptation of what Lucas was offering, how could she fully field-test her research?

She had to focus on the fantasies. Resolutely, she walked to the railing of the balcony. A glance down at the man-made lagoon twisting like a turquoise snake around the hotel triggered a quick spurt of dizziness. The moment it passed, her gaze fixed on a waterfall tumbling over a small cave at the side of the lagoon. That definitely had possibilities. It would work for both the mermaid and the island-girl fantasies. The cave would also provide the perfect setting for making love in a semipublic place—another very popular male fantasy.

All she had to do was...

When the second wave of dizziness hit, Mac raised her eyes and concentrated on the view of the ocean stretching to the horizon. Taking a deep breath, she exhaled, then drew in another one. Her stomach settled, and her head cleared again.

The solution to keeping her plan on track was to get the jump on Lucas and draw him into a fantasy before he could totally mesmerize her as he had on his grandfather's island. Simple.

"What's wrong?"

She started, then turned. He was standing there studying her, and she felt the pull right down to where her toes curled in her sandals.

It was not going to be so simple.

"Tell me," he said, moving to the railing.

"Nothing. The room—everything—it's perfect."

"So perfect that you had to come out here to screw up your courage?" Taking her hand, he waited until she met his eyes.

"There's nothing wrong. No one has ever done anything

like this for me. Sophie said you would be kind. But I didn't expect you to be sweet too.''

''Sweet?''

The slightly disgruntled, slightly shocked look on his face made her smile. ''It'll be our little secret. I won't tell a soul.''

''Just tell *me*. What's wrong, Doc.''

She shrugged. ''I needed to come out here and think.''

''Ah,'' he murmured, his forehead clearing. ''Getting all your ducks lined up in a row?''

''Fear clears my mind. I know that might sound...'' The rest of her sentence trailed off when he lifted her hand to his lips. He kissed the palm of her hand, then the veins at her wrist. For a moment, she couldn't say a thing. She was too busy absorbing the little waves of fire and ice that radiated up her arm. ''You're trying to seduce me.''

''You got me, Doc. I'm busted.'' He began to kiss her fingers one by one as if they were a delicacy he'd been waiting all day to sample. ''I want to make up to you for what happened at the cabin.''

She blinked and stared at him. ''Why? I mean we both...I enjoyed it, really. It was my fault that I lost control.''

''I lost control too, and I want to make it up to you.''

''Wait.'' She pulled her hand away. ''It's not necessary for you to make anything up. I don't think I've explained the essentials of my plan quite clearly enough. It's my job to seduce you.''

He had her hand again, and she could feel a pull that went beyond the pressure of his fingers on hers.

''I'm not going to be able to create any fantasies if you keep distracting me,'' she continued weakly.

''What if I told you that I don't have any fantasies?'' His eyes never left hers as he drew her fingers to his mouth. ''I gave them up when I was a kid because I thought they were a waste of time. I much prefer reality. What I really want to do is to keep you in this suite and make love with you nonstop for the next three days.''

The images that his statement conjured up nearly melted her knees again. And it didn't help one bit that he was touching her again, drawing one finger along her jawline, then down her neck to the hollow of her throat. She had to clear it to speak. "Sophie was right on the button when she bragged about your negotiating skills. You're trying to make me an offer I can't refuse.''

His laugh erupted then, quick and infectious. The sound of it only added to the ribbons of heat spreading downward and upward from her center.

"I can never predict what you're going to say next. Maybe that's why you fascinate me, Doc.''

She fascinated him? She'd never fascinated anyone in her life. It had to be the proposal she'd made him. Either that or he'd liked the island-girl fantasy. "I have some fantasies in mind that may fascinate you even more.''

"I'd much rather spend some time with *you,* Doc. I've been wanting to touch you, really touch you, since you got off that plane yesterday morning. I don't know how much longer I can wait.''

She felt her heart stutter.

"Why don't you come inside and let me show you?''

She was halfway to the door when she finally found the strength to dig in her heels. "Wait. Do you hear the way we're talking?''

"I know I'd like to stop talking.''

"Just think about it. I said, 'I have some fantasies in mind for you.' You said, 'I want to touch you... Let me show you.' You see what that means, don't you?''

"We want each other?''

"More than that, we each want to be in charge. We're both control freaks, so to speak. Admit it. Don't you want to be in control when you're in a business deal?''

"You bet.''

"And I am always in control in the lab. I have to be.''

Lucas considered her for a minute. "What exactly are you saying, Doc?"

"We have a problem, and there's only one solution." She turned it over in her mind a few times, then said, "We'll have to take turns."

"Take turns?"

"Being in charge, calling the shots, whatever you want to call it. The first time we make love, I get to call the shots, create a fantasy, whatever I want. The next time, you're in charge. You can do whatever you want."

Lucas considered the idea for a moment. "How do you get to go first?"

She lifted her chin. "This whole thing was my idea. I flew all the way down here with the original proposition. And I just came up with a compromise so that two control freaks can work together. Clearly, I get to go first."

"How about we flip?" he asked, pulling a coin out of his pocket. Before she could agree or protest, the coin was spinning upward into the sunshine.

"Heads," she called as he snatched it out of the air. Holding her breath, she watched his fingers slowly open.

"Heads it is," Lucas said.

Mac beamed a triumphant smile at him. "I'm going to freshen up. I'll meet you down in the lounge in thirty minutes."

"The lounge?" His face looked as incredulous as when she'd called him sweet. "Why do we have to go to the lounge when we have a perfectly good suite?"

"My call. And the fantasy I have in mind requires a different setting."

SHE WAS DRIVING him crazy. That much he knew. But now Lucas was beginning to suspect she was doing it on purpose. A glance at his watch told him that thirty minutes had lengthened into forty-five. No, forty-six.

Had he actually begun to count the minutes?

He glanced around the spacious but crowded lounge.

Three TV sets hung from the ceiling over the bar, each one offering a muted version of a different sporting event. Other than that, the decor was rain forest, with moss dangling from the walls and ceiling, and exotic-looking plants bursting out of clay pots. Water dribbled steadily over rocks behind his booth and shot up in bright, colorful spouts from a pool twenty feet to the left of his table.

Directly ahead, beyond a wall of glass, the dimness gave way to light. Though the midday sun beat down mercilessly on the water, a few swimmers still sought relief from the heat in the coolness of the lagoon. Most guests were inside, enjoying the benefits of air-conditioning.

There was no sign of Mac anywhere. He lifted his beer, drained it, and thought of the perfectly good champagne he'd abandoned in the suite... And of what they could be doing right now. After what had happened at the cabin—he still couldn't figure it out. He'd never before desired a woman with that kind of intensity. And he'd never made love to a woman with less finesse.

He wanted to give Mac romance. There was a definite air of innocence about her that made him want to seduce her slowly—with champagne, soft music. When the bellhop had given them that whirlwind tour of the suite, he'd pictured undressing her and making love with her on that large, smooth bed. Then he would have carried her to the Jacuzzi where they would have finished the rest of the champagne and then made love again. Very slowly.

But she'd decided he was a control freak. No one else he'd dated had ever complained.

But then Mac was unlike anyone else he'd ever wanted to make love to.

He tapped his fingers on the table. Maybe it had been a mistake to bring her here. If they'd stayed at the cabin, he wouldn't be sitting alone in a bar, nursing a beer. They could be lying right now on that narrow bed.

Leaning against the back of the booth, he allowed the image to slip into his mind—those smooth legs wrapping around him, drawing him closer, trapping him. Right now he could be pushing into her heat, withdrawing and pushing in again. Deeper. He could almost feel her wet, silk heat closing around him.

"If you're not waiting for someone…"

Lucas's eyes shot open at the voice. It was Mac's. Perhaps a little huskier. But the blonde standing a few feet away from his table had to be a stranger. Still half caught up in the fantasy he'd fashioned in his mind, he blinked and tried to focus.

She wore a bright red skirt, barely the length of a dinner napkin. It fit her like a second skin and seemed to stop where her legs began. His throat went dry as his gaze moved down the length of them, then back up to where the skirt rode high on her thighs. Was she wearing anything beneath it?

"That outfit…" he began.

When she whirled in front of him, the skirt inched even higher.

"You like it?"

"Mac?" He dragged his gaze from the miraculous legs up her body to her…. He could see her nipples through the stretchy fabric of the tank top—perfect little buds. With great effort he managed to focus on her face. Her blond hair looked mussed, as if some man had just run his hands through it several times. And her eyes—they were huge, heavy-lidded…and there was no mistaking that golden-brown color.

"Mac, what in hell are you doing?"

In a flash she had slid in beside him in the back of the booth. "Shh." She gave him a slow wink. "You're mistaken. I'm not Mac. I'm Sally. And you're…" She paused to slip a finger beneath the button of his polo shirt and flick it free of its hole. "You're John."

"John?"

"My first of the day." Leaning closer, she lowered her voice. "We're complete strangers. We've never met before.

You saw me on the beach when you were docking your boat, and you've just invited me to join you in your very fancy hotel for a drink. I've never been in a place quite like this before."

Pausing, she glanced around, then dipped her finger into the water that ran over the rocks behind them. Slowly, she ran her damp finger along his jaw, then down his throat until she could unfasten the next button of his shirt.

"Mac—"

She leaned closer. "It's Sally. The fantasy will be more enjoyable if you let yourself get into it. Since you didn't want to fill out the questionnaire, I chose one of the most popular ones—sex with a perfect stranger."

She freed another button on his shirt.

"I'm hoping you'll like it. This too."

She set a package on the table. "I stopped in the gift shop and got you a surprise. Take a look and tell me what you think."

He was finding it difficult to think at all while he could feel the hard pebbles of her breasts brushing against his arm. But he found his gaze wandering to the bag. He couldn't remember the last time anyone had bought him a surprise. It had been sweet of Mac to think of it—except that it might not have been Mac but Sally who'd bought him the gift.

Her fingernail traced a line down the center of his chest, sending little ribbons of heat outward and downward. Then her fingers were on his belt, pulling it free. He clamped his fingers around her wrist. "Stop."

"You don't really want me to." Her free hand dropped to his thigh.

"We're in a public place." The ribbons of heat had burst into flames where her hand was resting. "Let's go."

"You're embarrassed. That's so cute."

"Cute?" He stared at her for a minute. All he could see was a mixture of amusement and excitement in her eyes. "You're enjoying this."

She leaned closer and dropped her voice to a whisper. "Because I'm *Sally*. Getting into these clothes really helped. I think you'd enjoy it too if you could get into the fantasy. In one survey, fifty-three percent of the men fantasized about having sex with a stranger they picked up in a bar. Thirty-five percent of those wanted the stranger to be a hooker. Have you ever had either of those fantasies?"

"No. I told you I don't have them."

"Never paid for sex?"

"No."

"A first-time John. My favorite," she said. He didn't think it was possible but she suddenly seemed closer. "Think about what I'd promised you we'd do when I persuaded you to invite me here." Her fingers traced a delicate pattern on his inner thigh as they moved higher.

"Doc, you can't." The words erupted on a moan.

"Want me to tell you what I promised to do?" The words were just a breath in his ear.

"Mr. Wainright, sir…"

Lucas turned to face a tall man wearing a conservatively cut suit with an insignia that marked him as a member of the hotel's staff.

"Is this lady bothering you?"

Immediately Lucas slipped an arm around Mac. "Not at all. This lady is my wife."

The man's glance slipped to Mac, then back to Lucas. "Your…I'm sorry, sir. I just thought…"

"You thought wrong."

"My apologies, Mr. Wainright. I…I'm sorry to have disturbed you. I hope you'll let me know what the staff can do to make your stay more pleasant." With a brief nod, the man turned and walked away.

The moment he was out of earshot, Mac spoke on a bubble of laughter. "'This lady is my wife!' How did you manage to say that with a straight face? I don't think he believed you."

"No, he didn't." Lucas kept his eyes on the man's retreating back until he was out of sight. "He was trying to do his job."

"He was going to throw me out, and you saved me. It was just like in *Pretty Woman* when Richard Gere brings Julia Roberts into that swanky Beverly Hills hotel. He doesn't let them throw her out either. Instead, he hires her for the whole week. Now *there's* a fantasy. How about it? Would you like to hire me for a week?"

Her hand was burning its way up his thigh again. Lucas covered it with his own, and when he turned to face her, he found that she was very close. It wasn't just her hair that was different. Her mouth was too—slicked with red the color of wild raspberries. It took all his willpower not to sample. "What I'd like to do can't be done here—" he tore his gaze from her lips "—unless you want to get us both thrown out. Let's take this to the room."

She smiled at him. "I'm not done yet."

Before he could prevent it, her hand slipped from beneath his to cover his erection.

"Ever fantasize about having sex in a public place?"

"Doc..." The word was barely audible. He couldn't breathe, didn't dare to move.

"I'm Sally, remember?"

Beneath the table, he grabbed her wrist and removed her hand very carefully. "This fantasy is over. We're getting out of here."

"Not until you kiss me. I've been dying for you to kiss me. I can't stop thinking about it."

Lucas gazed into her eyes. The teasing light was gone. In its place was something hot and needy. Was it Mac talking? Or Sally? And just who had brought him nearly to completion with her touch? At the moment that his mouth covered hers, he wasn't sure he cared.

7

KISS ME. The words had slipped out before she could prevent them. She hadn't meant to say them. But touching him, feeling the strength of his desire fill her hand had changed the fantasy into a desire so sharp she couldn't resist.

She hadn't even had time to blink before his mouth had crushed down on hers. The memory of their last kiss shattered as new sensations streamed through her. She welcomed the heat, the urgent demand, and wanted more.

The feelings racing through her were as exciting as the first time one of her theories had proven to be true in the lab. There was that breathless rush of pleasure, then the exhilaration that came with knowing that the results were just the beginning. That they could be taken to the next step and the next.

Touch me, she wanted to cry out. *Please touch me.*

And then he did. His hands were hard—and rough. One had clamped like a vise on the back of her neck. The other was running down her in a smooth, possessive stroke until it reached the top of her thigh. When he scraped his teeth over her bottom lip, a bolt of pleasure shot through her. She could feel everything—the soft give of the cushioned leather at her back, the hard line of his body pressing against her, and the beating of her own heart—so fast, so hard, she was sure it was going to pound its way right out of her chest.

And all the while, something inside her was beginning to boil like hot molten rock at the earth's center.

More. She arched toward him, and suddenly his hand was just where she wanted it to be. Right at the center of her heat.

"Excuse me."

The two words didn't register at first. All she was aware of was Lucas's abrupt withdrawal. First, he pulled his mouth from hers and then his hand. But he kept one arm around her as he turned.

"What is it?" Lucas's voice sounded like a snarl, and the perky little waitress took a quick step back from the table. At least he could talk. Mac's lips felt as if they were vibrating. She wondered if she could ever use them for forming words again.

"I'm sorry to interrupt," she said with a faltering attempt at a smile. "But my manager sent me over. There's a call for you at the main desk. He thought it might be important."

Mac could almost feel Lucas put a clamp on his anger. His voice was much milder when he said, "We'll take the bill."

"Thanks." She beamed a smile at him, then waited until he signed it and handed it back to her.

Mac didn't look at Lucas until the waitress left. He was studying her, and there was nothing on his face that gave away what he was thinking.

"You're trouble," he said.

She could have said the same about him and meant it. She didn't kid herself for one minute that she'd been successful at sustaining her fantasy for even a second after Lucas had begun to kiss her. One taste and Sally might just as well have been vaporized. She was the one who'd been kissing Lucas, wanting Lucas. And she hadn't wanted to stop.

He slid out of the booth and held out his hand. "We're getting out of here before we're arrested."

"I think I'm glad I'm with the owner of the hotel," Mac

said as she grabbed the bag that contained his present, then tucked her free hand in his.

Lucas's lips twitched. "I'm glad I *am* the owner of the hotel."

They were both laughing as they walked out of the lounge.

THE LOBBY WAS CROWDED. Some people were clustered in groups, others wove their way toward the bank of elevators or up a curving sweep of stairs to the second level. The sun streamed down on them from a skylight as they circled a fountain in the open atrium.

At any other time, Lucas might have taken a moment to just mingle and observe how smoothly the staff was running the place, but two things were on his mind—the woman beside him and the phone call waiting for him at the desk. No one knew he was here at the hotel. Even if Tracker had guessed, he would have called him on his cell phone. After he solved that problem, he would have to figure out what he was going to do about the doc.

If he could just predict what she might do or suggest next, he might be able to get a handle on that. Clearly, his first priority was to get her back upstairs to their suite before she got them both arrested.

"Lucas Wainright," he said to the well-groomed young man at the reception desk. "I was told there was a call for me."

"Yes, sir. Just one minute, Mr. Wainright."

While he waited, he glanced over to where Mac was leafing through one of the brochures stacked on a nearby table. She'd kicked off one of her high-heeled sandals, and he found himself wanting to slip her out of the other one.

Odd, but he'd never been particularly attracted to women who dressed in clothes that screamed casually available sex. He preferred his dates to wear elegant but conservative styles.

The outfit Mac was wearing was even more eye-catching

than it had been in the dimness of the lounge. As he watched, the gaze of more than one passerby locked on her. One man stumbled, nearly falling into the man ahead of him. Another lurched into the woman at his side. Yet the doc seemed totally unaware that she was causing traffic mishaps.

Instead, she was totally engrossed in the brochure. Clearly, he was looking at Dr. Lloyd. His eyes narrowed. But there was a Sally lurking inside her. And he was beginning to think he was fascinated by them both.

He planned to have both of them in his bed tonight.

He let his gaze wander down the length of her legs. She'd taken off both sandals now, and she was rubbing the back of one foot against the calf of her leg. Evidently, the doc wasn't in the habit of wearing hooker shoes.

Very soon, he intended to have her out of the rest of her hooker outfit too. The tank top would go first. First one strap, then the other. And then he would slide the fabric down slowly until he could cup her breasts in his hands. Then he would—

"Sir, I have your call ready."

Turning, Lucas picked up the receiver. "Wainright here."

"Are you enjoying your vacation?"

Lucas recognized Vincent Falcone's voice immediately. "Very much. Are you enjoying the wine country?"

Falcone's laugh sounded relaxed in his ear. "You've been keeping tabs on me, I see."

And you've been doing the same with me. Lucas didn't like it one bit, but he didn't say the words aloud. He said nothing at all. A long time ago, he'd learned that silence was often more effective than a direct question in getting the information he wanted. While he waited, he let his gaze sweep the lobby. Did Falcone have a tail on him even now? He noted that Mac was chatting with the bellhop who had shown them to their rooms. In a moment, the young man was going to drool all over his uniform.

"You're much harder to locate than I am," Falcone said. "I heard a rumor that you were off to the Keys. I thought naturally of the Wainright Casa Marina, but I didn't really expect my call to strike pay dirt."

Right. And pigs fly. "It hasn't. Our business relationship is terminated."

"That's why I called. I have something in my possession that will change the picture."

"You'll have to be more specific."

There was a sigh of regret on the other end of the line. "I'm afraid I can't. Phone calls can be tapped. Let's just say that fortune has dealt me a few cards I didn't hold before. One of them might grab your attention."

Lucas wanted to hang up the phone. But he couldn't afford to. He knew the kind of ruthlessness that Falcone was capable of. That was why he'd wanted his sister with him and not in some damn spa. "A meeting then?"

"Ah. I thought you'd never ask. Saturday at my vineyard in Napa."

"Saturday in my offices in D.C."

Falcone's laugh lacked both humor and warmth. "My dear Lucas, this time it's my turn to call the shots. Three o'clock on Saturday at my vineyard. If you're curious, you'll come to me. If not, well, that could be very unfortunate."

Lucas listened to the phone go dead in his ear. *Hell would freeze over first.* There wasn't anything that the man could possibly offer him to renew their business relationship. Vincent Falcone was a crook. Hell, it had taken him four long years to find a way out of doing business with the man that wouldn't violate any of the contracts his father had signed.

He'd bided his time, making sure that any joint ventures Wainright had with Falcone's companies steadily lost money. Then when the man had come to him wanting the capital to invest in Lansing, a biotech company, Lucas had all the ammunition he needed. He'd given the older man

Lansing as payment in full to buy him out of Wainright Enterprises.

Lucas reran Falcone's phone call over in his mind. He couldn't afford to underestimate him. A quick glance at his watch told him that it had been twenty-four hours since he'd talked to Tracker. Suddenly, he wanted to be very sure that Sophie was in that spa.

Pushing the numbers into his cell phone, he glanced over at Mac and stared. She'd perched herself on the table that held the brochures and crossed her legs. The skirt had inched about as high up her thighs as it could go. Three bellhops were now gathered around her, totally wrapped up in whatever she was saying, and the registration line had doubled.

Tracker wasn't picking up the call. Lucas disconnected it and punched the numbers in again. He hadn't taken his eyes off Mac.

"He wrote seventy percent of his works here—*A Fare-well to Arms, For Whom the Bell Tolls,*" she was saying. "Can you tell me how to get to his house?"

She was talking about Ernest Hemingway. Lucas couldn't prevent a smile.

"Sure thing. I read *The Old Man and the Sea,*" said the tallest of the three young men.

"I saw the movie once. I think," said another.

She was dressed like a tart, and she had three kids who were probably still in high school competing to admit they'd read Hemingway.

"My great-grandfather used to box with him on the front lawn."

"You're kidding," Mac said.

"No. There're pictures of him in the museum. You can see them if you go."

Clearly, being a descendant of someone who'd actually come into contact with Hemingway was much more impressive than merely reading his books. He might just have to tell her—Sally or the doc or both—that his own grand-father had fished with the novelist.

Lucas disconnected the second call and punched in the numbers again. The only time that Tracker didn't pick up a call was when he absolutely couldn't talk. Had he managed to get inside the spa? Each call he made would leave a message on Tracker's caller ID, and three calls in a row would let Tracker know that it was an emergency.

As the phone rang in his ear, Lucas saw one of his very able managers approaching. Obviously, the man didn't like that Mac had three of his bellhops enthralled—nor could he be too pleased that she was making a spectacle of herself, having captured the attention of most of the males waiting in the registration line. He'd taken two steps toward Mac, intending to remedy the situation, when Tracker picked up. "What's up?" he said.

"You're inside?" Lucas asked.

"Mr. Wainright?" The voice came at his elbow. "Sir, I hate to interrupt you."

"Hold on, Tracker," Lucas said as he turned to face the young manager. "What is it?"

"Do you think that Mrs. Wainright would be more comfortable in a chair? I'm having one brought down from the upper lobby."

A glance at the curving stairs told him that, indeed, a chair was making its way toward them. Lucas met the young man's eyes. "That's a very thoughtful idea, and I'm sure Mrs. Wainright will appreciate it. Her feet seem to be bothering her." Pausing, he glanced at the man's nametag. "Mr. Waldman, you're doing a nice job here."

Waldman nodded at him. "Thank you, sir."

"*Mrs.* Wainright?" Tracker asked in his ear.

"It's a long story."

"I've got time. My ride into the Serenity Spa won't be leaving for another hour. I'm being delivered with bottled water and organic produce, and I was in the middle of final negotiations with the driver when you called."

"Everything went well, I take it?"

Tracker laughed. "Piece of cake. I take it you're not at Lucas's Folly?"

That's debatable, Lucas thought. "No, I'm at the Wainright Casa Marina." He watched as the man scooped up Mac's high-heeled sandals, but she insisted on carrying the bag with his present in it herself. Waldman escorted her to the chair, and the bellhops were allowed to remain in attendance.

The only people who might be a tad disappointed were the men who were still waiting to register. Mac's skirt covered at least two inches more of her leg once she was seated in the chair, and they had to crane their necks to see her.

Waldman deserved a raise.

"You're at your Key West resort with a *Mrs.* Wainright. I'm assuming that's Mac. I'm also assuming that she's not really Mrs. Wainright because it does take time to get a license and so forth. But there are still a lot of gaps in your story, and I have at least another hour or so."

"I just got a call from Vincent Falcone."

Tracker was silent for a moment. "How did he get hold of your cell-phone number?"

"He didn't. He called me here at the hotel."

"I didn't even know you were there. How did he—"

"Exactly. No one could have known I was here unless—"

"He's having you followed." Tracker swore softly.

"He could have had Sophie followed too."

"I didn't see anyone, and I was looking." There was a pause. "But then I wasn't following Sophie. Maybe he believes she's with you."

Lucas sighed as he studied Mac. The waitress who'd served them in the lounge had just presented her with a drink. It looked like a Shirley Temple. She didn't look anything like the kind of woman who would be ordering a Shirley Temple. "He won't for very long. Right now Mac doesn't look anything like Sophie. She doesn't even look like Mac.''

"I'm sensing some more interesting gaps in the story. C'mon, boss. It's raining here and I'm stuck in the back of a delivery truck. I could use a good story."

"Falcone wants to meet the day after tomorrow at his place in Napa at 3:00 p.m. His exact words were 'Fortune has dealt me a few cards I didn't hold before. One of them might grab your attention.'"

"Cards as in plural."

"Yeah." One of the things that Lucas admired most about his friend was the way Tracker's razor-sharp mind always cut right to the quick.

"If—*when* I find Sophie, you want me to get her out of here?"

Lucas thought for a moment. "No. And I don't want you to cause any disturbance. I just want you to make sure no one can get to her there."

"Right. I'll be able to verify she's here by morning even if I have to search each one of those damn cabins. I'll also have a look at their security system."

"Have fun."

Tracker laughed. "You too, boss."

The moment that Lucas disconnected the call, he strode purposefully toward Mac. It was time to salvage his reputation and the reputation of his hotel by escorting "Sally" to his suite. The moment he reached her chair, she jumped up, his present still clutched tightly in her hand.

"Shall we go, Sally?" he asked.

Rising up on tiptoe, she said in a low voice, "I'm not Sally anymore."

"I was beginning to like that fantasy," Lucas said, taking her arm and guiding her toward the bank of elevators. "I especially liked the way it was bound to end."

Mac dug in her heels near the fountain. "My turn isn't over yet."

"I think it is."

She shook her head. "We haven't made love yet, and that was the deal. And I've got an even better fantasy in mind."

He studied her. Did he want to know? "What is it?"

She tapped one hand against the bag that contained his present. "It's right in here. You're going to love it."

8

___

"YOU'RE NOT REALLY GOING to make me wait until Saturday afternoon to see you again."

Sophie turned in the front seat of the convertible to smile at the man behind the wheel. Sonny Falcone had been surprised and delighted when Susan Walker had called to invite him to lunch. "I'm booked solid with clients until Saturday morning."

Susan Walker had a business trip that would coincide with a party his family was throwing at their vineyard. That was the story she'd given Sonny in D.C. When he'd invited her to attend the party, she'd agreed. But at some point during the time they'd spent together that afternoon, she'd decided she didn't want her time in Napa dominated by Sonny.

He'd taken her to a lovely place in the hills where they'd sipped wine on a veranda that offered an even more enchanting view than the one she had from her hotel room. Then they'd had a late lunch at a small inn. He'd been charming, but less than totally attentive to all the lies she was telling him about herself and her business.

He was a very handsome man with the kind of body that had fascinated Italian sculptors for centuries. Perhaps that was why he was so totally self-absorbed.

"It was my good fortune that your plane got in early," Sonny murmured.

"Mine too." He'd mentioned that four times now. It wasn't really his fault that he was...dull.

Taking her hand, he raised it to his lips.

Sophie waited, hopeful.

Nothing happened. His practiced, romantic gesture only confirmed what she'd been gradually discovering all afternoon. However smooth the moves, when this man touched her, she didn't respond at all.

"I had a really lovely time," Sonny said. Very gently, he leaned forward and pressed his lips to hers. The kiss was very soft, very warm—an expert caress of tongue and lips.

And it left her unmoved.

When she drew back, she kept a smile on her face. His eyes told her that he at least had enjoyed the kiss.

"Are you going to invite me in for a drink?"

"I can't," she said, taking care to inject regret into her tone. "Just as soon as I freshen up, I have to race to meet a client. After that I have to prepare for my presentation tomorrow. But I am so looking forward to relaxing on Saturday. The bulk of my business will be over by then."

He reached out and ran a gentle hand down her hair. "We'll relax together. The vineyard will be crowded, but I have a special treat for you. I remember what you said about wanting to go up in a hot-air balloon, and I have one reserved for us."

"I'll be looking forward to it." Sophie let herself out of the car. At the archway that led into the courtyard of the hotel, she turned and waved. But it wasn't until the doors of the lobby swung shut behind her that she let out a sigh of relief.

Or was it regret? No, she wasn't going to let herself think that way. Dwelling on the fact that she'd switched identities with Mac just so that she could anonymously date a man she wasn't attracted to was not going to be productive.

Squaring her shoulders, she strode across the lobby. Sonny wasn't the only man in the Napa Valley. She would just have to find someone else to date anonymously while she was here. Turning on her heel, she walked back to the small desk where the concierge stood, talking into a phone. The moment he hung up, she beamed a smile at him. "My business dinner has just been canceled. Can you recommend a place nearby where a single girl could have some fun?''

''Sure thing.'' The concierge placed a list in front of her, then began to run down it, adding to the information that was on the paper. By the time he finished, she had two possibilities in mind.

''Dr. Lloyd...''

The man had to call the name again before Sophie remembered to turn around. He was tall, blond, casually dressed and wearing the kind of sunglasses that reflected back a mirror image. He held a basket of flowers in his hand. ''I came in just as you were talking to the concierge. When I heard your name, I thought I might deliver these personally and save one of the bellhops a trip. You are Dr. Lloyd?''

''Yes,'' Sophie said, digging in her purse for a tip. She handed it to him in exchange for the basket. ''Thanks.''

''No problem. Enjoy the flowers.''

Sophie couldn't help but enjoy the scent. She had to hand it to Sonny Falcone. He had all the moves down pat. Maybe her lack of reaction to him was due to jet lag, and she'd feel differently on Saturday. It wasn't until she got to the top of the stairs that it struck her.

Sonny didn't know her as MacKenzie Lloyd. He couldn't have sent the flowers. Sitting down on the top step, she fished through the blossoms for a card.

There wasn't one.

WHAT IN THE WORLD was she going to come up with next? Lucas glanced down at the present in the hotel gift-shop bag Mac had been carrying around. To call the thin layer of latex he was wearing a bathing suit was a misnomer—unless you were an Olympic swimmer going for the minimum in aerodynamic resistance.

Turning his head and craning his neck, he attempted to

get a view of the back. The suit revealed as much there as it did in the front.

"Are you ready?"

At the sound of Mac's voice, Lucas poked his head out of the cabana. "This suit doesn't cover much..." Neither did hers. In fact, it left enough bare to have his breath clogging his lungs. The tank top fit tighter than a second skin, and it stopped well above her navel. His gaze drifted over her soft, silky-looking skin to the bottom of the suit—a thin triangle of cloth that barely covered her—

"You're embarrassed again," she said, the amusement clear in her eyes.

"And you're definitely not." Stepping out of the cabana, Lucas took a quick look around the pool area to see how many other men were feasting their eyes on her. The heat had driven most of the hotel guests inside where they were either drinking in the lounge or resting up so they could sample some of the nightlife that Key West had to offer. He and Mac were alone except for the young man behind the towel booth about fifty yards away.

When they'd arrived, he'd introduced himself as Yancey and waved them toward the cabana, all the while assuring them that he'd guard Mac's duffel bag with his life should they care to swim off to a more private part of the lagoon.

"Very nice suit," Mac said.

When Lucas glanced toward the towel booth, he saw that Yancey was giving him a three-fingered wave.

"I think Yancey likes you," Mac said. "In a totally sex-object sort of way."

Lucas looked at her. "That seems to be the story of my life lately."

"Are you ready to get started?"

For one moment, he was tempted to grab her wrist and drag her into the cabana. The fantasy filled his mind of how quickly he could have her out of that suit. God, he wanted to touch her—to run his hands over that skin at her waist, pale as moonlight, soft as rainwater. He wanted to taste it. The need ripped at him like a rusty claw as he whispered, "Come here, Doc."

She took a step forward, then stopped. "You want to make love to me in the cabana."

"You think?"

"That's amazing. At least fifty-five percent of the men interviewed fantasize about making love in a place where they might get caught. I thought the number was a little high. Is that one of your favorite fantasies too?"

Lucas never before would have lumped himself in with that fifty-five percent. He couldn't ever recall wanting to take the kind of risk that she was talking about. That he was thinking about. But he'd come very close to doing something in that lounge that might have gotten him arrested. Truth told, he was skating on pretty thin ice again.

It was high time he took another tack. Walking toward her, he stopped when their bodies were almost brushing. Then he pitched his voice low so that only she could hear him. "I don't want to get caught. I want to make love to you where no one and nothing can interrupt us. I want to take my time and touch every single part of you. Then I want to taste you. The cabana is way too dark. I want to see your eyes when I'm inside you. And I want to stay inside you for a long, long time."

Mac released the breath she was holding on a shudder. "You're trying to distract me."

"I'm trying to seduce you." Unable to resist for a moment longer, he touched her, just the tips of her hair. She'd taken the blond wig off. He much preferred the richness of her own color—a mix of gold and fire.

Her breath shuddered out again.

He pressed his advantage, taking a step closer and bringing his body into contact with hers. Only the thinnest scraps of latex separated his flesh from hers. He felt the soft give of her breasts against his chest. She had to feel his hardness pressing against her.

For a moment, neither of them moved.

Then she said, "It's still my turn."

"Come back to the room with me, Doc."

"I'm not Doc. I'm Fiona—at least, that's the closest approximation in English."

When she responded, her voice was barely a whisper, the sound erotic on the still air.

She eyed him provocatively. "Aren't you even a little bit curious about the fantasy I have in mind?"

Twin desires warred within him. A part of him wanted to haul her over his shoulder and cart her off to the room. Another part of him wanted to indulge her. Hell, a part of him was becoming very curious about what she'd come up with next.

"It won't take long," she murmured.

Unable to resist a moment longer, he lowered his head and nibbled along her jawline. Perhaps the room was too far away. But the cabana wasn't. "Come—"

"And we won't be in full view of the people in the lounge the way we would be in the cabana."

Lucas lifted his head and glanced over her shoulder. Hell, he'd forgotten that the lounge offered a panoramic view of this part of the lagoon. If he *had* dragged her into that cabana, they would have provided quite a sideshow for the hotel guests who were probably watching them even now.

"You're a damn good negotiator, Doc. If you ever get tired of working in that lab, I could use a mind like yours at Wainright Enterprises."

"You could?"

The quick leap of surprise and joy in her eyes sent a wave of feelings tumbling through him. It occurred to him that he would do a lot to see it there again. Often. "Absolutely."

"You really are—"

He put his fingers against her lips. "If you say *kind* or *sweet* again, you're going in the lagoon."

"Kind and sweet."

Before he could shove her, she twisted and dived into

the water. He had one clear view of smooth, white cheeks before they disappeared below the surface of the water. It wasn't a bikini bottom she was wearing—but a thong.

While they'd been negotiating, everyone in the lounge had been treated to the view.

She was driving him crazy, and he was going to put a stop to it. He followed her into the water.

MAC BROKE the surface for air at the same time that Lucas did. The water was cold, and she'd needed the shock of it. She couldn't have held her own much longer—not with his body, his mouth touching hers. Especially when she could see that wild, reckless gleam in his eye. For just a moment—one glorious moment—she'd seen that he wanted to carry her off. And she would have gone.

The thought alone had the heat moving through her again. She hadn't known she had the power to make a man look at her that way. Treading water, she twisted to face Lucas.

The wild, reckless look had disappeared.

"That bathing suit is indecent," he said. "Do you realize that everyone sitting in that lounge must have had their eyes glued to your...your..."

"Do you think so? I never thought I'd ever have the courage to wear it. And I was right. I didn't."

"You did wear it. You've got the damn thing on."

Mac shook her head. "No, Sally was the one who put it on, under those outrageous clothes. Just as soon as I decided to be her, I suddenly had the courage to put it on. I didn't even have to go out on that balcony again."

His gaze narrowed and he stared at her for a long moment. "Who the hell are you?"

His question was a cue if she'd ever heard one—and her chance to bring that look back into his eyes. Moving closer, she said, "I told you. I'm Fiona now, a mermaid, and I've just lured you into the water."

"You're a...mermaid?"

He didn't sound at all convinced. Or even interested. Beneath the surface, her legs tangled briefly with his. "In the survey, over forty percent of the men said they had erotic dreams about mermaids. I find that very curious, don't you?"

Underwater, he trapped one of her legs with his. "Not particularly."

"Well, I've given it some thought—from a scientific viewpoint."

"Ah, and you'd like to share your conclusions."

In a swift movement, he trapped her other leg.

A strange wave of helplessness moved through her.

"Mermaids are exotic, different, and the stories of them date back to primeval times. Part of their allure could stem from that." The feeling of helplessness was growing, she discovered. They were touching nowhere else—just where his legs trapped hers in a vise. But she was very much aware that his legs were stronger. Her heartbeat was accelerating, and it was getting more difficult to breathe. "Then there's the fact that man came out of the water and will always be lured back to his origins."

"Sounds like a lot of scientific mumbo jumbo to me, Doc. I think my reality's a lot better than your fantasy." Quite suddenly, her legs were free, but he had her hand and was pulling her toward the edge of the lagoon.

"Wait." What had she been thinking? She'd been spouting off her research, and he was seeing her as Mac. That was the problem. "That's not the real reason I think that men have erotic dreams about mermaids."

"I told you, Doc. I've never thought of making love to a mermaid."

She moved closer so that their bodies were just brushing beneath the water. "Think about it now. Just how would you do it?"

His gaze narrowed. "What do you mean?"

"How would you make love to a mermaid? Maybe you couldn't—I mean, in the normal way. Certain important parts of her body are…another species.'' Lifting her hand, she drew it across his shoulder, over his throat, and slowly down his chest to his waist. She let her fingers rest just where skin gave way to the thin material of his bathing suit. ''Right about here is where she changes. However, there are certain very specific ways in which she could pleasure you.''

''Yes.''

''Why don't you let me show you?''

For a moment, he said nothing, but she felt his grip tighten on her hand and saw the carefully guarded expression in his eyes change. This wasn't the recklessness she'd seen before, but something else—a raw hunger that she felt her whole body respond to. In that moment, she realized it could go either way. If he pulled her with him out of the water, she wouldn't resist. She would go back with him to the suite.

Finally, he let out the breath he'd been holding. ''Not here.''

She ran her fingers lightly along the waistband of his suit before she drew her hand away. ''I have a more private place in mind. C'mon.''

She pushed away from the edge, slicing the water with smooth, clean strokes. The waterfall she'd spotted from their balcony was on the other side of the hotel from where they were. The length of the swim would give her time to plan.

There wasn't a doubt in her mind that once they reached the cave, Lucas would make good on the promise she'd seen in his eyes and felt in his body's response to her. She'd been playing with fire for about as long as he was going to allow it. And if the truth be told, she wanted to be burned.

So what was causing the tight ball of fear to form in her stomach? Hadn't she proven to herself that if she could focus on the fantasy, she could do all the things she'd discovered in her research?

In the bar when she'd been pretending to be Sally, she hadn't even had to plan anything out step by step. Everything she'd done to him had felt so natural because…she was Sally?

Or was it because he was Lucas?

She knew exactly when he drew beside her, even before she felt the brush of his hand along her shoulder and down her back. His touch was familiar, exciting, and with each lift of her right arm as she swam, she could see him. The lean muscled arms, the broad shoulders, the narrow waist and the…

She hadn't had a chance to appreciate before how he filled out that tiny bathing suit. Every time her face went into the water, her eyes homed in on the same target. Not that she hadn't vividly pictured him in her mind when she'd chosen the suit in the gift shop. But the reality of Lucas, nearly naked and well within reach, had the fear in her stomach turning into something else.

She really wanted him. As a biologist, she could dismiss what she felt as lust. But as a woman, she was very much afraid that it was personal.

As successful as she'd been in becoming Sally the hooker, Lucas had always been Lucas. There was that kindness, that sweetness that embarrassed him. More than that, there was the feeling she got when he looked at her—that he saw her as no one else ever had. He already knew her secrets, and they didn't frighten him away.

But it was dangerous to dwell on that, dangerous to want…

No, it was much safer to concentrate on the fantasy she was about to create and slip into the persona of Fiona.

Dragging her gaze away from Lucas, she checked her surroundings, then increased the speed of her stroke. The moment she rounded the curve, she spotted the churning in the water that told her the waterfall and the little rock cave were just ahead.

She summoned the image of a ladder into her mind. All

she had to do was take it one step at a time. The first step was to create the mermaid fantasy. Concentrating, she focused on the water beyond Lucas. Though the lagoon was man-made, every effort had been made to create a facsimile of the real thing. Concrete in the shape of rocks lined the walls, and in the shade created by the palm trees on either side, the water was a deep, exotic blue-green. Shafts of sunlight lightened the color at intervals.

Slowly, inevitably, her gaze fastened on Lucas again. It was almost too easy to imagine that this was a man she'd rescued from the sea. She watched the steady ebb and flow of muscle beneath his copper-colored skin. He was so different from anyone she'd known before—so fascinating.

How often had she swum to the surface to watch him? Then the watching had turned to wanting. How she'd longed to touch him, to run her hands over that sleek, smooth skin. And now that she'd finally lured him to their destination she could reach out and...

Desire struck her then, so sharp and so piercing, she nearly doubled up from the ache. Oh, it was altogether too easy to fantasize that she was a mermaid, and Lucas was the human being she was prepared to give up everything for.

Touching him once on the shoulder, she angled to her left and swam ahead of him through the tumble of water and into the small cave.

FOR A FEW SECONDS after he'd made it through the waterfall, Lucas thought he'd entered another world. The inside of the cave was small, the light dimmed and filtered by the curtain of water falling from the rocks overhead. Mac was sitting on one of the ledges that lined the walls, the lower half of her body submerged, her hair and face drenched with water. She looked like a creature of the sea—some primeval goddess that men would have followed anywhere.

And she was beautiful. Why hadn't he noticed that before? The ache that had built the whole time he'd been swimming beside her twisted low in his body and began to spread. For a moment he couldn't move, couldn't breathe. He could only want, and the torture was exquisite.

He watched, still mesmerized as she lifted one hand out of the water and beckoned.

"I want you."

He wasn't sure who'd spoken the words. But he knew they were real—the one real thing. She wasn't a mermaid. He wasn't some hapless sailor lured off course by her song. Fantasies were never real.

It was time he put an end to the game.

Even as he moved toward her, he glanced quickly over his shoulder. The thick curtain of water provided some privacy, and the cave faced the ocean, not the hotel. Still, all that separated them from anyone who happened by was water. When he turned back, they were facing each other eye to eye. Her lips were parted and wet. Real. It took all his control to touch only her hand. "Come with me," he said.

"Stay with me."

He brushed his lips over hers.

"We don't have to be who we really are as long as we're here. We have no past. No future," she said.

He traced her bottom lip with his tongue, then tasted each corner of her mouth in turn. And all the while her words burned through him, eating at his control like the hot, hungry flames of a bonfire.

"No regrets. No repercussions."

In some small part of his mind that hadn't completely shut down, he knew that her words were the worst kind of fantasy. Every action produced an effect as surely as a pebble made ripples when tossed in a pool. There would be a price to pay. There always was.

Unable to resist any longer, he crushed her lips with his. If he could just stop the words…but he couldn't seem to prevent her from making those small hungry sounds deep in her throat. They shot through him like electric shocks.

He grabbed her hands, bracketing them in one of his behind her back. Then with a quick groan of pleasure, he slipped his hand beneath the tank top, ran it up that smooth skin and cupped her breast. Helplessly, she arched toward him and moaned. It seemed he'd waited forever to touch her like this again.

He'd known hunger before, but it had never been this deep, this desperate. Suddenly impatient, he stripped her out of the tank top, and then arching her back over his arm, he lowered his mouth and feasted. The skin at her waist was taut, smooth and cool. He'd wanted to taste her there since he'd stepped out of the cabana. He lingered, using his teeth and his tongue until she was shuddering. Then he moved on, sampling her navel, then that slender, strong torso, until he reached her breasts. They were as soft as satin, as sweet as the most forbidden fruit. He wanted to go slowly, to torture her as she'd tortured him. But as he moved his lips and his tongue first over one silky curve and then the other, the soft, urgent sounds she made vibrated against his mouth and pounded into his brain.

Twin desires warred within him. He had to have her. Soon.

He had to draw out the pleasure for them both, for as long as he could.

Taking one cool, puckered nipple into his mouth, he moved his tongue over it, then closed his teeth around it. She arched back, her hair dipping into the water, and offered him more.

He slid the palm of his hand down the slick skin of her torso and dragged the bottom of her suit down her legs. Then he pressed his hand against her soft, hot center. When his finger penetrated her, she cried out, and he covered her mouth with his. Pushing in deeper, he felt tight, slick satin pulse and pull, begging, demanding.

Need slammed into him, not an ache this time but a chain saw with a rusted blade, shredding his restraint. Control streamed away as quickly and surely as the water crashing down overhead. He couldn't think. He had to be inside her, completely naked. He had to feel hot slickness pulling him in farther and farther.

"I...want...you." The hoarse sound of her voice had the need slicing deeper. "Now."

"You've got me." Slowly, he withdrew his finger. Then releasing her hands, he gripped her waist and settled her back on the submerged rock ledge. He ran his hands up the inner side of her thighs, pushing them apart.

Her fingers were already dragging his swimsuit down. The moment he was free, he grabbed her wrists. If she touched him now...

Drawing in a deep breath, he fought against the climax he knew was close.

Then, when he was sure he could, he took her hands and placed them on his shoulders. "Wrap your legs around me." He helped her, drawing her closer until his erection was pressed just inside her core. The searing heat of it— the promise of even more heat to come—nearly undid him. In spite of the coolness of the water swirling around them, he felt sweat pearl his forehead and slide down his spine. He'd never been this close to the edge before without letting go. His entire body was clenched tight, but the desire to take her warred with a greater need.

"Open your eyes." His words were only a whisper, but her lids opened.

"Say your name," he said.

She tightened her grip on his shoulders and met his eyes. "Fiona." Then she tightened her legs around him and began to draw him in.

It took all his control to resist. "No. Your real name."

"Mac."

"And mine."

"Lucas."

He thrust into her then, hot and deep and hard. For a moment he was sure his heart stopped. He thought he'd known what it would be like, but she was tighter, hotter, much better then he'd imagined. He knew he should wait, give her time to adjust, but he couldn't stop himself from withdrawing and thrusting again. And again. And again.

He watched her eyes grow darker even as the sheath she'd wrapped him in pulsed around him.

He wanted more than anything to stop—to draw out the moment—to prolong the feeling of oneness he'd never experienced before now. But he felt her convulsions start, felt them radiate through her, and he was lost. He had to thrust even more deeply into her until his own release began to rip through him. The pleasure built in wave after wave after wave—pulling him higher and higher—until it finally thrust him free. Holding her tight, he took her with him into a breathless, airless void.

9

WHEN SHE COULD BREATHE again, think again, Mac found herself sitting on Lucas's lap on the rock ledge that surrounded the little cave. His arms were around her and her head was cradled against his chest. Against her ear, she could hear the sure beat of his heart. Contentment spread through her, and she didn't want to move, to think.

That was not good. If she were in the lab, she would be feeling that sudden rush of elation that always came when an experiment went well. She would be running the whole thing through in her mind, evaluating what had worked, what needed to be improved.

But she didn't want to analyze. All she wanted to do was to hang on to the moment—to spin it out and to pretend just for now that Lucas had really wanted her, not Fiona.

That was not only wrong, it was dangerous. An impossible fantasy. Even as fear knotted in her stomach, she pushed it away. She couldn't afford to repeat the mistake she'd made all her life of wanting what she could never have. She had to settle for what was real—her research.

"Penny for your thoughts."

She jumped when the rumbling sound of his voice startled her.

"That bad, huh?"

She lifted her head and met his eyes. They were intent, guarded.

She struggled to reach the same level of control. "That went very well, I thought. But I'd like to try it again."

His eyes narrowed. "Something was wrong? Did I hurt you?"

"No, not at all. Except…" Slowly, she smiled—the way she imagined Fiona might. "I'd like to try it again, and this time you have to leave my hands free."

His hands tightened on her. And something flashed into his eyes—the wild recklessness she'd seen before. It ignited an answering response within her—a fierce, almost overwhelming need.

"That can be arranged. But not here. We've been lucky so far…"

The rest of his sentence trailed off when a head suddenly appeared beneath the curtain of the waterfall. In one quick, smooth movement, Lucas eased them both off the rock ledge so that the water came up to his chest and her neck. Mac was suddenly aware of two things. Lucas was easing himself back into his swimsuit. And she had no idea where hers was!

"Oh. Hi," said a plump woman in her mid-fifties. "We didn't mean to interrupt. Harold here just thought it would be fun to—"

While Harold surfaced and made a show of shaking out the water from the few strands of hair left on his head, Lucas moved in front of Mac, shielding her with his body. Running her hand along the rock ledge, Mac prayed that her suit was there.

"See, Nelly, these folks had the same idea I had, I bet."

"Nonsense." Winking at them, Nelly gave Harold a playful push. "Harold's a dirty old man."

"That's the best kind, isn't it?" Mac asked as her fingers closed around her tank top. As unobtrusively as she could, she drew it in front of her beneath the water.

Harold's guffaw filled the cave. "That's what I keep telling her, young lady. That's what I keep telling her."

"C'mon, Harold. We've interrupted this young couple."

Reaching behind him, Lucas gripped Mac's arm. "Not at all. We were just about to leave, weren't we, dear?"

Before she could reply, he was edging her toward the waterfall, shielding her as much as he could. As they moved past Harold, Lucas leaned toward him.

"My wife here thought that this might be just the kind of place a mermaid would lure some hapless sea captain, if you know what I mean."

"I think I catch your drift, son," Harold said and winked.

Without waiting to hear another word, Mac clutched the top of her bathing suit close and dived under the waterfall. When she surfaced she found Lucas at her side.

"What did you do that for?" she asked. "You practically told them what we were doing."

"I thought it might add to your research. Obviously, Harold fits into the forty to fifty percent of men who like the mermaid fantasy."

"Let's hope Nelly likes it too," Mac said.

Lucas threw back his head and laughed. The warm, rich sound of it was so infectious that she had to join him. Before they were finished, they were clinging to each other trying not to submerge.

"It's not funny," Mac said, trying to stave off another wave of laughter. "I only have half my bathing suit. I lost the thong."

"A real mermaid wouldn't need one," Lucas pointed out.

"A real mermaid wouldn't have to walk into the Wainright Casa Marina Hotel."

"Let this be a lesson to you, Doc. Fantasies can be dangerous."

And they could, Mac thought. But they were also fun. And she was enjoying this playful side of Lucas almost as much as she'd enjoyed the fiercely possessive lover that she'd encountered in the rock cave. Lifting her chin, she said, "I'm going to put the top half of my suit on, and while I'm doing that you can figure out how we're going to get to the room without getting thrown in jail."

But getting into the bathing suit wasn't as easy as it looked. The tank top wasn't in the mood to cooperate. The material didn't stretch as easily when it was wet. And to make matters worse, they kept laughing and sinking under the water. And it didn't help at all that Lucas's hands were on her more than they were on the suit. Each time they touched her, she couldn't seem to remember about the suit at all. By the time they got her arms through the holes and tugged the top down over her breasts, they'd both sunk to the bottom of the lagoon.

She would have pushed up to the surface, but his hands gripped her waist, anchoring her. In the wavering shafts of light piercing the turquoise water, he looked different, more like an undersea god than a mere mortal. Suddenly, she wanted him just as fiercely as she had in the rock cave. She only had time for that one thought before he pushed them both to the surface and shoved her against the side of the lagoon.

One of his hands gripped the back of her neck, his body pressed fully against hers. Then his mouth closed over hers.

Sensations streamed through her and around her, trapping her in a world of razor-edged contrasts. The chill of the water; the heat shooting through her in bright lightning bursts wherever his body touched hers. The hard pressure of his hands at her waist and her neck; the incredible softness of his lips and the gentle insistence of his tongue as it patiently explored her mouth—as if he had all the time in the world to savor each flavor. Pleasure shot through her in wave after wave. Seductive. Overpowering.

She was drowning. It was only as they once more broke the surface of the water that she realized they'd sunk below it again. Coughing and dragging in air, she stared at him. His breathing was just as ragged as hers.

"I want you."

LUCAS WASN'T SURE who'd spoken the words aloud or if they were merely a chant in his brain. All he knew was that he'd never felt this way before. *Desire* seemed too tame a word for it. What had gripped him at the bottom of the lagoon had been so intense, so overpowering that he wasn't sure how he'd managed to get them above the water.

He'd been laughing one minute, struggling with her suit, then the need had snuck up on him and slammed into him with a force that had driven everything else away.

She'd looked like a sea goddess, her hair a red-gold crown. All he knew was that he had to have her. And he'd very nearly taken her right there on the bottom of the lagoon.

But it wasn't a mermaid who was facing him now, with a mixture of desire and anticipation in her eyes. They were no longer in danger of drowning. And the wanting had only increased.

"I want you." This time he'd definitely said it aloud, and the raspy sound of the words only seemed to intensify the need pounding in his head and burning through his blood. Using his body, he pushed her back against the side of the lagoon, then slid a hand behind her and gripped one of the rocks.

He tried to focus on looking around, checking to make sure they were alone. But any clear thoughts of decency and privacy were erased by the image of what he saw in her eyes, the perfect mirror of the desire that was coursing through his veins.

"Your hands are free this time," he said. "Use them."

As she grasped his shoulders, he wrapped her legs around him and, gripping the rock ledge behind her, he pushed into her slowly. The heat ate at his control.

"Tell me you want me." Slowly he withdrew nearly all the way. "Or do you want me to stop?"

"No," she whispered.

"No, you don't want me or no you don't want me to stop?"

"No...yes...please..."

He pushed into her again. Not fast enough, not far enough. "Hold on."

But she was already tightening her legs around him. Holding the rock ledge with both hands for all he was worth, he pushed as far as he could into her sleek, satiny heat.

She made a sound as she moved against him and drew him in even farther.

"Shh," he whispered against her lips. "You can't make any noise. Someone could come along at any moment. We can't let them know what we're doing."

He withdrew slowly, then entered her again, spinning the piercing pleasure into torture. "The water is working against us. It's going to take a long, long time."

"Lucas, please…"

"Shh," he managed to murmur. But the sound of his name had already shredded what was left of his control. Suddenly, he wasn't thinking. Couldn't think. All he knew was the dark, slippery grip of her as he withdrew as far as he could and pushed into her again. He wanted to go faster, had to go faster—but he'd spoken the truth. The depth of the water and their position against the side of the lagoon worked against him. Each time he withdrew, he felt as if he was leaving some vital part of himself behind. Then she stiffened, using all her strength to arch against him, and he felt himself shatter. Helpless, he pushed in as far as he could and poured himself into her.

For a long time, neither of them moved. Lucas wasn't sure he could. He knew he didn't want to. Palm leaves rustled overhead. The water around them gradually stilled. Then he heard the steady *slap, slap* of approaching sandals.

Tightening his grip on her waist, he drew back and eased himself out of her, then quickly adjusted his bathing suit and glanced around. Much to his relief, the area was deserted. Whoever was approaching was still hidden by the rock cave to his left.

Turning his attention back to Mac, he said, "Are you all right?"

Her eyes when they met his were focused and filled with delight. "Much better than all right." Then she leaned closer to plant a quick kiss on his lips. "It was even better than in the cave. And I like it when my hands are free. Next time I'll have to remember to use them."

He wasn't sure which surprised and delighted him more—her reply or the kiss. It had been so spontaneous, it had to have come from Mac, not her mermaid persona.

"Mr. Wainright! Mr. Wainright, sir…"

Glancing up, he saw Yancey, the young pool man, hurrying toward them and waving Mac's duffel bag. Lucas could cheerfully have murdered him. He released Mac, but used his arms to keep her caged against the side of the lagoon.

"Your cell phone has been ringing and ringing. I finally figured I should answer. Good thing too. A Mr. Tracker is trying to reach you. He ordered me to bring you the phone, so he can call back." Dropping the duffel at the edge of the lagoon, Yancey squatted to hand Lucas the phone. "Was your Mr. Tracker by any chance in the military? There's such a note of command in his voice," he asked, eyes bright with interest.

The cell phone rang.

"And he's so prompt too."

"Yes?" Lucas said into the phone.

"Are you okay?" Tracker asked.

"Of course."

"It's the first time someone else has ever answered your cell phone."

The amazement and concern in Tracker's voice had him frowning. For the first time since he'd followed Mac into the lagoon, reality was setting in. The truth was, he'd left the damn phone in the cabana along with his wallet and clothes. He hadn't given them a thought once he'd seen Mac in that swimsuit. And he hadn't been thinking of anything but her a moment ago when he'd taken her against the side of the lagoon.

He might have taken her there again if Yancey hadn't interrupted them. What was she doing to him?

"I'm inside," Tracker said.

"Inside?"

"The Serenity Spa. Look, am I interrupting something? If you and the doc—"

Lucas dragged his attention back to the phone call. "The doc and I are swimming. That's all. You can report."

"It's going to take me a while to verify that Sophie's here. I don't want to sneak into her cabin until she's asleep."

"You know which one it is?"

"Not yet. As soon as the coast is clear, I figure I'll be able to find her cabin number in the main office. Then I'll wait until everyone is asleep. I also have an updated report on the Falcones."

As he listened to Tracker give him a rundown on the two men's movements for the past twenty-four hours, Lucas found his attention refocusing on Mac as she retrieved her wallet from the duffel and gave Yancey a bill.

"I brought a couple of towels for you," Yancey was saying, "just in case you want to go into the hotel by the ocean-side entrance."

"You're a lifesaver. I'm going to tell the management to give you a raise," Mac said.

For someone who said she'd never gone on vacation with her family or stayed in a big resort before, she certainly had a knack for winding his staff right around her finger. First Waldman and the three bellhops in the main lobby and now the pool man. And, of course, the owner of the hotel. She had *him* forgetting his money, his cell phone and even the clothes off his back!

Pocketing the bill, Yancey gave them another three-fingered wave before he turned and strode away.

"You still there, boss?"

Dragging his attention back to Tracker, Lucas said, "Let me know the minute you verify..." He paused to watch Mac pull one of the towels into the water and fasten it around her waist. He thought of how easy it would be to pull it off of her once they got to the room. And there was that Jacuzzi. It would provide a much more private environment for a mermaid fantasy. They wouldn't be interrupted.

"The good doctor is very distracting, I take it," Tracker said.

"No. Yes." He had to get a grip. And the best way he knew how to do that was to put a stop to the fantasies she seemed bound and determined to ensnare him in. "Call me as soon as you can confirm anything."

10

THE SUN HAD MOVED nearly an hour closer to the horizon by the time Lucas let himself out onto the balcony of his suite. He'd urged Mac to use the larger of the two bathrooms, then taken his own shower in the smaller one. It had been a test—to see if he could stay away from her.

He wasn't sure he could pass it.

And that worried him.

The time he'd spent with Mac in the lagoon should have sated him. Making love to her in the cave had been risky enough, but what had happened afterward in the lagoon... He couldn't prevent his gaze from drifting down to the blue ribbon of water that snaked its way around the hotel. Even now he couldn't believe what they'd done, what might have happened if Yancey had come upon them a few minutes earlier. Never had he been that desperate, that reckless, not even when he was a teenager.

No other woman had ever driven him to do something that...crazy. For the life of him, he couldn't think of another word to describe it.

And there'd certainly been other women. He'd been quite young—only midway through his teens—when he'd discovered women were attracted to him. The realization that this had a lot to do with the Wainright name and wealth came later. By that time, his father had gone through three of his five marriages.

Lucas had no intention of ever following in his father's footsteps. He'd always made sure that he was in control of any relationship he had with a woman.

Until MacKenzie Lloyd. And it wasn't just his control that she was sapping. Each time he made love with her, he was losing parts of himself. Maybe forever.

A ripple of fear moved through him. Then, dragging his gaze away from the lagoon, he paced down the length of the balcony. No woman had ever frightened him before either.

How could she have that kind of power over him? She might believe that he was buying into the fantasies, but he knew better. It was always MacKenzie Lloyd he was making love to, whoever she was.

A kaleidoscope of images poured into his mind. The shy, young girl he'd met at Sophie's party was only one facet of MacKenzie Lloyd. There'd been nothing of that woman in the way she'd looked on the tarmac when he'd demanded to know where Sophie was. That MacKenzie Lloyd had met his eyes with her chin lifted, determined to shield Jill Roberts from his anger. And she'd been yet another woman on his boat. He could still recall the excitement in her eyes and the recklessness of her laughter as the wind snatched it away.

And there was the doc, so intent and focused, aiming one of her killer serves across the net, or giving him that slow appraising look as if she were going to smear him on a slide and figure him out no matter how long it took.

Stopping suddenly, he stared back down at the lagoon. Then there were the fantasy women she'd created for him— the shy Lania, the exuberant and fun-loving Sally, and the brave and determined Fiona. They were all facets of MacKenzie Lloyd.

How many more women did she have inside her? He wanted to know—and he wanted to learn how to handle each one of them. To do that, he needed to get to know them better.

Turning, he looked back at the sliding glass doors he'd just stepped through. Not here. He knew exactly what would happen if they stayed in the suite. Incredibly, he felt fresh desire ripple through him. All he had to do was open the doors and go to her.

She was probably stepping out of the shower, pulling a towel around her and tucking the ends in at her breasts. He could slip his hands beneath the towel. There'd be no chance for her to think. He would make sure of that. Then he could lift her onto the vanity and gently separate her legs to make a place for himself between them. There would be no time for her to slip into one of those fantasies. No time for her to pretend that they were anyone else but who they really were—not with their images reflected on two walls.

And there wouldn't be the pressure to rush. No one would interrupt them. This time he would take her very slowly, drawing out the pleasure for them both. His hand had closed around the door handle before he stopped himself.

Turning, he paced down the length of the balcony again. He'd come out here to distance himself, and the desire he felt now was just as fierce as it had been in that damn rock cave. He was caught up in it as surely as if he were caught in one of the dangerous riptides that lurked beneath the surface of those seemingly gentle waves pushing onto the shore.

It was just as he focused his gaze on the sea that the idea came to him. Of course. He would take the doc out on a date. That would be very familiar territory for him. Thoughtfully, he considered his options. It would have to be someplace she'd like, someplace that would keep that very agile mind of hers occupied so that she wouldn't come up with a new fantasy.

Keeping his eyes on the water, Lucas began to sift through the possibilities.

USING A TOWEL to wipe steam off the bathroom mirror, Mac finally faced her reflection. As far as she could see, she looked exactly like the old MacKenzie Lloyd. But she certainly didn't feel like her. She felt wonderful, wild and frightened, all at the same time. Pressing a hand against her stomach, she drew in a deep breath.

Wonderful and wild, she understood. She'd done it! She'd brought three fantasies alive for Lucas. And his response had been more than she'd hoped for, more than she had ever imagined.

So why wasn't she feeling satisfied, the way she did in the lab when an experiment went even better than she'd hoped it could?

Why was there a bubble of fear in her stomach instead?

Foolish question. She knew exactly why it was there. It had to do with what had happened when they'd come out of the rock cave. She couldn't rid her mind of the way it had felt when he'd kissed her underwater—as if he was determined to know every secret she had. And she was sure she'd given them all away. Any kind of defenses she'd managed to build up had streamed away in the water. She'd felt parts of herself slipping away too.

Wrapping her arms around herself, she met her gaze steadily in the mirror. Years from now she'd remember what it had felt like to be wanted so much that he'd taken her right there at the side of the lagoon.

Correction, she reminded herself. He'd taken Fiona. It had been part of the fantasy. She'd had the whole time she'd spent in the shower to analyze it. When they'd been under the water, he'd looked like some kind of sea god to her. She must have looked the same to him. He'd been thinking about Fiona the whole time. She couldn't afford to let herself forget that.

She couldn't let herself want—

No. She blocked the rest of the thought from her mind, but she couldn't prevent the fear in her stomach from expanding. Why did she always have to want the one thing she couldn't have? Lucas had been right about one thing. Fantasies were dangerous.

At the sound of the phone ringing in the other room, she

tucked the towel around herself and opened the bathroom door.

Another ring had her moving toward the phone on the desk.

Lucas wasn't in the bedroom. She told herself the sinking sensation in her stomach wasn't disappointment. Just as it hadn't been disappointment when he'd told her to go ahead and use the larger bathroom for her shower and he'd use a different one.

That one small suggestion had told her quite clearly that she wasn't Fiona to him any longer. She was just Mac. And that was fine—just as it should be.

As she picked up the extension of the hotel phone, she met her own gaze in the mirror. *Who was she kidding?*

Another insistent ring told her it wasn't the hotel phone that was making the racket. She raced to her purse and fished out Sophie's cell phone. "Hello?"

"I hope I'm interrupting a very erotic fantasy."

"Sophie." Smiling, Mac sank onto the foot of the bed.

There was a muffled groan. "I sincerely hope Lucas is not there. I would prefer not to have to talk to him."

"No, he's not here."

"What's wrong? And for that matter, why *isn't* he there? You did take my advice, didn't you? You've tested a few of those fantasies?"

"Yes."

"They didn't work?"

The astonishment in Sophie's voice nearly had Mac smiling again. She tried to force some enthusiasm into her voice. "Everything worked perfectly." *Too perfectly.* "I've turned a man who didn't like fantasies into a fantasy-aholic."

"You don't sound very enthused. Or triumphant. That *was* the purpose of your little experiment, wasn't it?"

"Of course." It was exactly what she'd wanted. Mac glanced down at her red-painted toenails. They were Sally's toes, and Lucas was totally fascinated by "Sally." She shifted her glance to her reflection in the mirror. Her hair, still mussed from the quick toweling she'd given it, was a tumble of locks around her head—the perfect mermaid do.

"You may be a brilliant scientist, but you're a lousy liar. Why don't you tell me what's really going on?"

"Things can't be that boring at the spa."

This time Sophie's reply was a sigh.

"That bad, huh? I thought you liked it. What happened to riding in a hot-air balloon?"

"This place…let's just say it isn't all it's cracked up to be. Maybe I ought to borrow one of your fantasies."

Mac blinked and thought. "I'm not sure I have anything appropriate for an all-women spa."

Sophie laughed. "You have such a wonderfully literal mind. But you can relax. If I were going to actually field-test one of your fantasies, I'd definitely go AWOL."

"Sophie—"

"Just kidding. After all this effort and subterfuge, I'm at least going to stay the week out. But if you want to make sure I don't do something desperate, you're going to have to keep me entertained by telling me what's really going on."

Leaning back against the bed, Mac tried to find words for the thoughts that had been tumbling around in her head while she'd showered.

"Or maybe I should just take a wild guess. Lucas likes the research, but you'd rather he liked you."

Sophie's succinct summary of the situation had Mac bolting upright. "No."

"Denying the truth is never an effective way of dealing with reality."

The bubble of fear she'd felt before was sharpening, tightening in her stomach. "But I don't…he doesn't…I can't…"

Sophie laughed. "I love to hear the preciseness of a scientific mind at work."

Mac sank onto the bed again. "Lucas is not interested in me as me."

"What makes you so sure of that?"

"Island girls, mermaids and hookers are much more exciting. He's making love to them not me."

"Hookers I can figure out. Maybe even the island girls. But mermaids? When we have more time, you are definitely going to have to tell me about that one. In the meantime, there's one way to find out if Lucas wants you as you. Take a night off from the fantasies and be yourself. Seduce him all by yourself."

Mac glanced quickly at the closed door to the bedroom. "But I'm sure Lucas is expecting—"

"Don't give him what he expects. Surprise him. Surely your Madame Gervais included that piece of advice in her instructions."

"Well, yes, but—"

"The problem is you have no confidence in yourself. And the only way to build confidence is to practice. What have you got to lose, Mac?"

Everything.

"Just do it," Sophie said.

Once again, Mac stared at her reflection in the mirror. Did she have the courage to take that kind of risk?

"And for once in your life, don't plan it all out. Not that there would be much to plan on that island of my grandfather's."

"We're not on the island," Mac explained. "We're at the Wainright Casa Marina."

"You're what?"

"It was Lucas's idea to come here."

"Don't say anything else for a minute. I'm trying to picture in my mind hookers and mermaids in a public setting where Lucas could be seen and recognized." Sophie began to laugh. "This is just too delicious."

Mac found herself smiling in response. "I don't think

Yancey, the pool man, recognized him at first, but Lucas told the manager in the lounge that we were married.''

There were two beats of silence before Sophie said, ''I don't think you need my advice, Mac. You seem to be doing fine on your own. Plus, I think I see the room service golf cart wending its way toward my door. Just tell Lucas I called and that I'm having the time of my life.''

For a full minute after Sophie cut the connection, Mac stared at her cell phone. She could have sworn that Sophie was not having the time of her life. She was about to call her back when a knock at the door had her shooting to her feet. ''Yes?''

''Are you decent?'' Lucas asked.

Decent? This from the man she was becoming addicted to being indecent with?

''Yes.''

Later she would wonder if Lania, Sally and Fiona had become permanent facets of her personality—or perhaps it was just one of those moments of perfect timing. But the moment that Lucas stepped into the room, the towel she'd wrapped herself in slipped silently to the floor.

TRACKER SWORE SILENTLY as he shifted in the tree he'd selected for his long vigil. It had taken him three hours and a lot of sweet-talking to get himself smuggled into the Serenity Spa. But he was beginning to believe he'd wasted five hours of his life dressed as a woman for nothing.

The Princess was going to pay for this.

He glanced down at the outfit he'd carefully selected at the general store in town—pale, stone-washed jeans, a pink shirt and a jean jacket. He didn't regret buying them. His pretty little informant, Millie Jean, had been right on the money. She'd sworn she couldn't smuggle him in on the floor of her van, and she'd been correct. The two amazons at the gate had searched it. But the wig and the makeup he'd worn had earned him only a cursory glance from the two guards before they'd waved them through. According to Millie Jean, they never bothered to check the van on the way out.

He shifted his attention to the main building that housed the kitchen, dining rooms and administration offices. Women were still drifting toward it in twos and threes, heading for dinner. So far, none of them walked with that confident, ground-covering stride that seemed to be so much a part of Princess Sophie.

But that didn't mean a thing. In the past hour, he'd seen the golf carts ferrying trays of food back and forth to various cabins. If Lucas's sister *was* here, he figured one of those golf carts had gone to her cabin.

Frowning, Tracker shifted again on his tree limb. What reason did he have to believe that she wasn't here—aside from instinct? The problem was, his gut instincts hadn't been working where Sophie was concerned since that day in Lucas's office when she'd begun to sob in his arms. He'd always thought himself immune to a woman's tears, but Sophie's had gotten to him. Perhaps because there hadn't been any weakness in the tears. She cried with as much energy as she fought.

And it hadn't been to get attention or to get her way. One minute she'd been fighting mad, and the next she was crying her heart out. All he could do was hold her until she stopped.

She'd really had feelings for that Davis jerk.

Well, he knew what it was like to be betrayed by someone you loved. That was why he'd taken it upon himself to look out for her. And she'd spotted him.

A good security professional didn't ever let his job get personal. He had, and now he was paying the price.

Muttering under his breath, Tracker shifted again. The damn tree limb was going to leave permanent markings on his backside. And to top it all off, he was beginning to suspect that he would find Sophie Wainright sound asleep and very safe in her bed.

A glance at his watch informed him that only three

minutes had gone by since the last time he'd checked. The rain had stopped, but in the gray mist that clung to the mountains like a favorite cloak, it was impossible to guess exactly how long until sundown.

Tracker was literally counting the seconds. Sundown was nighty-night time at the Serenity Spa, and that meant that he could get into the offices and find Sophie's room number. He was allowing himself an hour to locate her, verify that she was here and then...

Well, then he figured he'd even have time for a nap before Millie Jean made her morning delivery.

And this time he was going to make sure the Princess never knew she'd been checked on.

As LUCAS WATCHED THE towel drop to the floor, he was quite sure he'd never felt the blood drain so quickly from his head before.

In the soft glow of the bedside lamp, her skin had the pale, creamy hue of porcelain. He knew exactly what it would feel like beneath his hands—still cool and slightly damp from her shower. He could smell the soap even from a distance.

He hadn't moved. He didn't know if he could. In the back of his mind he knew that he'd had a purpose for coming into the room. But all he could do now was look at her. Knowing that she was here, naked in his bedroom, understanding that she could be his in the time it took him to take three quick strides across the room—all of that had the need to touch her boiling in his blood.

"Lucas..."

He wanted her beneath him on that bed. Now. That thought, along with a sharp stab of desire, freed him from the paralysis that had gripped him since her towel had dropped. He'd taken those three steps toward her before he stopped himself.

This wasn't what he'd planned. Ruthlessly, he tried to dredge up the details he'd carefully mapped out. He was going to take her out…on a date. For the life of him, he couldn't remember where.

"Lucas…"

If she continued to look at him that way, there wasn't going to be any date.

She moistened her lips with her tongue as she moved toward him and laid a hand on his chest. "What I have in mind is…"

Bells began to ring in his head. There was a shyness in her voice, a tentativeness in her approach that hadn't been there with Lania or Sally or even Fiona. If this was yet another fantasy, he had to nip it in the bud.

"You dropped something," he said. He saw the quick leap of surprise in her eyes and something else before she lowered her gaze. Embarrassment? Hurt? He stooped over to retrieve the towel, then handed it to her. As she wrapped it around herself and tucked it securely into place, he became certain of one thing. This was Mac standing in front of him. Lania, Sally and Fiona weren't shy at all. But Mac was. She was also very neat and thorough about the way she tied a towel around herself.

And he'd just hurt her. He knew he had to make it right. Wanted to with all he had. More than anything, he wanted to pull her into his arms and hold her. But he didn't trust himself to touch her. Still, he needed to erase the pain he'd seen in her eyes.

"Look at me, Mac."

When her eyes met his, he said, "For the record, I want to make love to you more than anything right now."

"Then why did you pick up my towel?"

"Because I was rough on you down in the lagoon, and I think we should both take a little break from…your research. And since it is finally my turn to call the shots—"

"It's not your turn."

Lucas frowned. "Time out. In the lobby earlier, you said it was your turn until we made love. We did. That means it's my turn."

"We made love two times. The second time was your turn. Now it's mine."

She had a point. More importantly, the hurt look had vanished from her eyes. "Look, we can argue about this, or we can compromise. What I was going to suggest is that we go out—on a date."

Mac blinked. "A date?"

She sounded as if she'd never heard the word before, and quite suddenly Lucas began to enjoy himself. For the first time since Mac had stepped off his plane, he was beginning to feel as if he had a slight advantage. He intended to keep it. "That didn't pop up in your research? I'm thinking of the kind of thing where a guy asks a girl out to dinner, maybe dancing. It's an old-fashioned way of getting to know one another—"

"I've heard of a date before."

The dry tone had him grinning. "I think we're overdue for one, don't you?"

"But we know each other."

"Most definitely in the biblical sense. However, there are lots of things we don't know yet. What's your favorite flavor of ice cream?"

"Rum raisin."

"What do you have nightmares about?"

"Falling."

"Ah. That fits with the fear of heights. But the rum raisin is a surprise. I would have picked you for a strawberry girl."

She frowned, studying him as she turned over his proposal in her mind. Finally, she said, "This date wouldn't count as anyone's turn?"

"Scout's honor."

Still, she hesitated.

"Doc, it's just a date. I'm not asking for your hand in marriage. I want to go out with you for one evening in Key West. Just you and me. Mac and Lucas. We leave Lania,

Sally and Fiona here in the room with John and the ship-wrecked sailors.''

She said nothing, and in the silence he could almost hear the wheels turning in her mind. He couldn't recall ever having a woman hesitate about accepting a date with him. Instead of being annoyed he had to clamp down on the urge to hug her.

"You're a tough sell, Doc. Let me sweeten the deal. If you'll come along quietly, I'll let you sneak in some of those questions on your questionnaire."

She studied him for one more minute before she held out her hand. "It's my turn when the date's over and we come back here to the room."

"You have my word on it."

While they were shaking on it, he said, "One other thing. I get final approval on what you're wearing this time."

"Don't push your luck."

11

THE MOMENT THEY WALKED through the door, Mac felt her senses being bombarded from every direction at once. What she saw was a crowded, dimly lit room that might have been the set of a forties movie. If the lights had been brighter, she thought she might have even glimpsed Humphrey Bogart straddling one of the stools at the bar. She smelled perfume, liquor and cigarette smoke, mixing with the spicy scent of a pizza on the tray of a passing waiter. And through it all, she heard and felt the haunting, bluesy sound of a sax.

Nerves knotted in her stomach. How was she supposed to seduce a man in a crowded, noisy bar? Sally wouldn't have had a problem, but she'd promised to be Mac. And Mac didn't even have step one figured out in her mind.

"Lucas." A large man in tan slacks, a crisp white shirt and wide red suspenders slid from a bar stool and hurried toward them. Mac guessed his age to be in the seventies. "Welcome. It's been a long time." He grasped Lucas's hand and thumped him on the back. "I've got your grandfather's favorite table ready for you."

While Lucas introduced her to Joe Johnson, the current owner of the place, the large man ushered them past the band to a booth in a back corner. It was U-shaped with wooden partitions rising high on three sides and offering an illusion of privacy.

"You enjoy yourselves, hear?" Joe said as he left them.

"I've never been in a place like this," Mac said as she slid into the seat.

"Good."

But she wasn't so sure of that.

"I'd like to be able to tell you that Ernest Hemingway wrote *To Have and Have Not* while he was sitting at this very table."

She glanced down at the scarred wood of the table, then back at him. "But you're not telling me that."

"Not with absolute certainty. The place has been renovated since the days when he used to hang out here." He paused to glance around the room. "Some of the furniture goes back that far, I'm sure. What I can tell you is that this is the place where he wrote a lot of that novel—and others."

Mac stared at him. "But this isn't Sloppy Joe's. It says in the guidebooks that's where he wrote."

"This is the building that housed the original Sloppy Joe's. My grandfather used to bring me here, and then he'd tell me stories about the days when he and Papa Hemingway used to drink and fish. There's a back room they used to play pool in." He gestured toward a doorway next to the bar. "Each time he brought me here he'd swear that the table we were sitting at was the exact place where Hemingway had penned this or that story or scene."

Mac glanced quickly around the room. "Which one were you sitting at?"

Lucas grinned at her. "We were at a different table each time we came here."

She ran her hand reverently over the scarred wood in front of her. "But this was your grandfather's favorite. So it really could be the one?"

"Could be." He reached over and tucked a strand of hair behind her ear. "I heard you talking to the bellhops in the lobby of the hotel. I thought you might like this even better than the museum."

"I do." She met his eyes then. "Thank you. You're a very kind man."

"No." His grin faded as quickly as it had appeared.

"Don't make the mistake of thinking that. Hasn't Sophie disabused you of that notion?"

Mac reached for his hand then. "Sophie appreciates that you care for her. Or she will as soon as she gets over that Bradley creep."

Lucas studied her for a moment. "When did you decide that Bradley was a creep?"

"The first time I met him."

"And Sophie knew your opinion?"

She shook her head. "Of course not, although sometimes I had to bite my tongue. She suspected that I didn't like him, but I would never have told her not to date him. Haven't you noticed that she immediately does the thing that she's been told not to do?"

Lucas laughed. "Yeah. I've noticed that pattern in her behavior."

"If you ever really want Sophie to do something, tell her the opposite," Mac said. "It's the forbidden-fruit syndrome. It works every time."

He could testify to that. His determination not to touch Mac was fueling his desire to do just that. And it had been growing steadily since he'd slid into the booth beside her—no, even before that, when she'd bent to get in the taxi and he'd caught a glimpse of that soft smooth skin at her navel, just below the spot where she'd knotted her shirt. He could reach out to brush his fingers along it right now.

It didn't help one bit that her hand was still in his. It would be so easy to raise her fingers to his lips, scrape his teeth over her knuckles and watch her eyes cloud. She was so responsive…so tempting. But he'd promised her a date, and he was going to give it to her.

When he caught himself staring at her mouth, he cleared his throat and said, "I'll have to remember that. About Sophie, I mean. The forbidden-fruit syndrome—the next time I want to handle her." Good grief, he was babbling. He had to focus. Ask a question. "Why are you so afraid of heights?"

Mac blinked and stared at him. "Why would you ask that?"

He settled himself against the back of the booth. "Because I want to know. You must have given it some thought—tried to analyze it."

She had, but it had been a long time since she'd dredged it up. She wasn't sure she wanted to now.

"C'mon. We're on our first date, remember. We get to ask questions so that we can learn more about each other. You can trust me, Mac."

The look in his eyes was so calm and patient, she found herself saying, "When I was five, my father built me a swing set in the backyard. There was a trapeze on it, and he'd been disappointed in me because I couldn't sit on it. I've never been very athletic."

"So?"

"My father had wanted a son. That's what my mother told me after he left us. Anyway, this one night I wanted to please him when he came home from work, and so I climbed up on the trapeze and tried to do this trick. I wanted to swing all the way around the trapeze bar like they do in the circus. I kept swinging higher and higher, but the trick wasn't as easy as it looked and I fell and broke my arm. My mother blamed my father for building the swing set, and my father was furious. The next day he packed up and left. Ever since then, I've been afraid of heights."

Lucas's fingers tightened on hers. "And you blamed yourself because your father left."

"At the time, I did. It was a long time before I understood that he'd found another woman he loved better than he loved my mother and me. She gave him the son he wanted. And eventually my mother found someone too. They're both very happy with their new families."

"And you're still afraid of heights."

She shrugged. "Fears aren't rational."

"No. It takes a brave person to battle them."

When he raised her hand to his lips and kissed it, Mac felt something inside her dissolve and stream away. No one had ever had this effect on her. She'd never allowed it. But when he looked at her the way he was now, she couldn't seem to prevent it. And she wanted, more than anything, she wanted to know that she truly was the person he'd made love to in the lagoon. Sophie's advice streamed into her mind—that she should seduce him as herself.

Wasn't it her plan to do just that?

"What can I get for you folks?" The waitress, a thin woman with a blond ponytail, beamed a smile at them.

"What kind of beer do you have on tap?" Lucas asked.

What if she wasn't the woman he'd made love to in the lagoon? What if she found out that Lucas was just being kind to his sister's friend? She'd forced herself to face other fears, but this—

She watched Lucas's eyes light with laughter at something the waitress said.

If she didn't at least try, she was the worst kind of coward. But she couldn't attack him the way Sally had. No, he would have to know it was Mac. She'd have to start with the questionnaire. When she pulled it out of her bag, her fingers were trembling.

The moment the woman hurried off, Mac smoothed it out on the table, "Before I drink any beer, I'm going to get you started on these questions."

"You know, I wish I had my camera with me. I'd like to capture that on film."

"What?" She glanced quickly around.

"The way you turn yourself from Mac, the woman who is enchanted because she might be sitting at a table where Hemingway wrote, into the focused, very serious-minded Dr. Lloyd."

"I didn't. I—"

"Oh yes, you did, the moment you pulled out that questionnaire. It wasn't quite as dramatic as Mr. Hyde turning into Dr. Jekyll. But I think I could definitely capture it on film. Your smile fades, then your eyes become darker, very intent, and I can almost hear the wheels start to turn in that pretty little head of yours.''

As he talked, she studied him as closely as he was studying her. He was teasing her. She was almost sure of it. But there was something else in his eyes that she was equally sure was dead serious. ''You're starting to make me feel like I have a split personality.''

''Maybe you do, in a way. My theory is that you turn into the doc when you want to escape.''

Mac stared at him. He was right. Why should it surprise her that he knew that about her?

''My question is, why? You're certainly not a coward.''

''It's easier to be Dr. Lloyd.'' The words tumbled out before they'd been fully formed in her mind. ''She can be clinically detached. She doesn't get hurt as easily.''

For a moment she thought she saw a flash of understanding in his eyes.

Then the waitress appeared. ''Two beers,'' she said as she slapped them on the table.

The moment the woman moved away again, Lucas said, ''Okay, you can be the doc—for a few questions. Then I want Mac back.''

Then I want Mac back. His words moved through her, weakening her and strengthening her at the same time. Blinking twice, she glanced down at the questionnaire and asked the first question she focused on. ''Have you ever had anyone make love to you while you were blindfolded?''

''Blindfolded?''

''So that you can't see, and you can't tell what your lover is doing exactly. The sensual pleasure is incredibly heightened.''

''Really.''

She waited for a beat, then said, ''You haven't answered the question. Have you ever let anyone make love to you while you were blindfolded?''

"No."

She nodded. "Because you want to stay in control."

"Perhaps. What's the next question?"

She glanced down. "What is your favorite position for sex?"

"My favorite position?"

She looked at him. "You know—on top, on the bottom, behind?"

"I know what you're asking. Let me see that." He pulled the papers closer and skimmed the page quickly. "Where did you get these questions?"

"I compiled them myself."

"And who else have you done this questionnaire with?"

"No one. I developed it especially for the man who would be my research partner."

"And that's me?"

She nodded and saw some of his tension ease. Was he jealous? Was that why he sounded so tense and annoyed? The possibility sent a little wave of pleasure through her. "You haven't answered the question yet." And she was suddenly curious. They certainly hadn't used any of the normal positions yet. "What *is* your favorite sexual position?"

Lifting his beer, he took a drink. "I pretty much like them all."

"That's not a very explicit answer."

He narrowed his eyes at her over the rim of his glass. "Give me another one. I'll try to do better."

She skimmed the page, then flipped to the next one. "Why don't I make it easier for you? There's a section here about sex toys. I'll just name them, and you can rate them on a scale of one to five—one meaning you've never used them and five meaning *wow*. All set?"

When she glanced up, she saw that his eyes had become very intent, and the dark, reckless gleam was back. Her throat went suddenly dry.

"I'll make it easy for you. Give them all a one. I've already told you I'm partial to reality."

Mac moistened her lips. Staring into Lucas's eyes for any length of time was paralyzing and, at the same time, exciting. She imagined a predator must look at his prey this way, just as he was about to spring. She forced her gaze back to the page and tried to focus. "No sex toys. Let me see…does it turn you on to watch your sex partner masturbate?"

When he didn't answer, she didn't meet his eyes. Already, she regretted the question. She didn't want to know, didn't want to picture him watching another woman pleasure herself.

When she finally did glance up, she found that he was close.

"I know that I would enjoy watching you touch yourself intimately." His hand moved to rest on her knee. "You could show me what you like, tell me what you'd like me to do. Explicitly."

His fingers began to trace a pattern on the inside of her knee. "Do you like this?"

Mac felt the heat rush through her. He was barely touching her, but her legs had already spread to give him more access.

"Ah, you do like this. Or do you want me to stop?" His hand stilled on the question.

"No." She didn't want him to stop. He hadn't touched her this way before. When he'd made love to her, his hands had been hard, demanding. Now she could barely feel the movement of his fingers. "But someone will see…"

Leaning closer, he feathered a kiss over her lips. "Tell me about your research. That way, no one passing by will know what we're doing."

"My research…?" His eyes and mouth were so close. His hand wasn't nearly close enough.

"Sophie says you had a breakthrough."

Mac tried to ignore the melting sensation in her lower

body as his fingers moved a little higher. "I'm working on something—you…really shouldn't…"

"I can't seem to help myself. You started it with that question. Now I can't seem to stop picturing you touching yourself. Like this."

In his eyes, she could see the same mixture of emotions she'd seen when he'd backed her into the wall of the lagoon. Desire and something else too. Was it possible that he felt as vulnerable and as out of control as she did? Something softened within her.

"Have you made any progress?"

"Hmm?"

"On your research? Have you made any progress?"

He had made progress. The tiny circles that his fingers were making inched higher. What he was doing to her seemed even more erotic contrasted with what she was trying to think about, talk about. She drew in a shaky breath. "I've had some success with…" One of his fingers was stroking down the silk of her panty and was close to…

"Success with…?"

She dragged her thoughts back. "Animals," she managed to say. "They're not aging as quickly. Wilbur, one of my lab rats, has been with me from the beginning. He's lived to be…"

His finger slipped beneath her panties and entered her.

"Lucas…"

He leaned very close so that his lips were nearly brushing hers. "I can't do here what I could have done back at the hotel. If we were there, I would take you into the bathroom and sit you on the vanity. That's what I wanted to do when you dropped your towel. We could watch in the mirrors while I entered you. I want you to see both of us when I'm inside you. I want you to know it's just you and me. No fantasies."

But it was. It was the most seductive fantasy he could have conjured up. And she wanted it more than anything.

She wanted Lucas to want her just the way she wanted him. Once more, Sophie's advice filled her mind.

"Come back to the suite with me, Mac."

No. Shaking her head to clear it, she met his eyes steadily. If she went back there, it wouldn't matter whose turn it was, she would fall under his spell just the way she always did. Just the way she was right now. She had to know that she could seduce him. "One question first."

She watched his eyes narrow and darken. Here was the recklessness and the danger that had drawn her from the first. "Not from that damn questionnaire?"

"No, it's a simple date question. Would you play a game of pool with me?"

His hand finally stilled as he stared at her. "Are you always going to be able to surprise me?"

"I asked my question first."

"The answer is yes, just as long as I'm playing with Mac."

"You've got a deal." And, as Mac, she finally had a plan.

12

"MY GRANDFATHER TAUGHT ME to play pool in this room," Lucas said as he led the way through the door at the end of the bar. "I loved it." Past tense. Pool was the last thing on his mind right now. What he wanted to do more than anything was throw Mac over his shoulder and carry her back to the hotel. If they made it that far. The way he was acting, they might not make it farther than the first shadowy doorway along the street.

Ruthlessly, he pushed the image out of his mind. He'd asked her here on a date because he'd thought it would be safe.

Was there anyplace in the world where she would be safe from him? Or anyplace where he might be safe from wanting her?

He watched her walk over to the rack of cue sticks and run her hand down one. He couldn't blame his reaction on a fantasy this time. Mac was the one who'd set out to tease him with that questionnaire.

"Ready?" she asked as she turned back to him.

He glanced at the pool table. He was ready all right. And he could make sure that she was in seconds. All he would have to do...

A loud burst of laughter had him shifting his gaze to the open doorway. The crowd around the bar was growing, and the pool table was in plain sight.

Moving to the rack, he selected a stick. When he turned to her, he found her looking at him in that quiet, intent way he was becoming familiar with.

"You really loved your grandfather, didn't you?" she asked.

"Yes. He was a remarkable man. He worked very hard to build Wainright Enterprises." He chuckled. "And he always took the time to play hard too."

"You were lucky to be able to spend time with him. I've heard that grandparents are a lot less judgmental than parents."

Lucas glanced up from racking the balls. "Your parents judged you a lot?"

"My mother. I think I'm a constant reminder to her that she failed in her first marriage."

He thought of his own parents—his mother who had left when he was barely five and his father who'd remarried within a year. "Mine pretty much left me to nannies, and whenever that didn't work out, my granddad took over."

Her eyebrows lifted. "The nannies didn't work out?"

"Bad things always seemed to happen to them—frogs in their beds, cockroaches in their tea cakes. It was almost as if the house were haunted."

"Shades of *Turn of the Screw?*"

Grinning, he propped a hip against the pool table. "Not quite that bad. Just enough to get my grandfather's attention. What about you? What's the worst thing you ever did to your nannies?"

A smile hovered at the corners of her mouth. "The worst I ever did was to give them the slip and disappear for the day."

"I can't picture Dr. Lloyd playing hooky, so it must have been Mac." He tucked the new insight away. "What did you do when you gave them the slip?"

Her chin lifted. "Maybe I learned to shoot pool."

"Did you?"

"You're about to find out." Turning, she walked toward the table.

"It's a good idea to chalk the sticks first."

After he demonstrated, he watched her imitate his actions perfectly. "You're a very quick study, Doc."

She shot him a very level look. "I'm Mac. Or did you forget?"

His grin widened. "Touché. When Grandfather and I played, we always used to have a friendly wager, just to keep the game more interesting."

"Sure. Have you ever played strip pool?"

Lucas stared at her.

"It's basically like strip poker. When you win the first game, you tell me to take something off, and—"

"I know what the wager in strip poker is." She'd tossed it out as if she'd been playing pool for years, and that was her usual bet. And she was suddenly close enough to run a finger down the buttons of his shirt.

"Of course, we probably couldn't really strip—not here. Not if I have to be Mac and you have to be Lucas. But we *could* pretend. I could tell you exactly what I'm taking off, and you could imagine." She leaned closer until her body just brushed against his. "You do have a pretty good imagination, don't you?"

"Yeah." His imagination was both excellent *and* fertile. The picture of what she'd looked like standing in his bedroom earlier had beamed itself right into his mind. Now he was projecting what she would look like lying on that pool table, wearing absolutely nothing.

"I'll go first."

His gaze tracked her as she moved to where he'd racked the balls, and he managed to follow her just in time to see the skirt she was wearing hike up a full two inches when she leaned over the table.

Glancing over her shoulder, she said, "Any suggestions on what I should do next?"

Later he would wonder if it was the heat in her look, the sultry invitation of her tone or the images she'd managed to conjure up in his mind. Perhaps it was the whole package. The only thing he was really aware of was that he couldn't resist her. And if he moved toward her how, touched her now, he was afraid...

He'd taken one step when she straightened and grinned at him. "I can't believe it."

"What?" He was amazed that he'd managed to get the word out.

"I was just being myself. Mac. I swear I was. I didn't know I could do that. And it was *working!* I could see it in your face, in your eyes."

Lucas narrowed his eyes. She was baiting him. She'd known exactly what her suggestion had done to him and precisely how her skirt would hike up when she'd leaned over that table.

"You amaze me," he said. And he realized that nothing he said could have been truer. He wondered if he would ever figure her out. But he did know that two could play at the little game she'd begun. He tapped his cue stick against hers. "Why don't you turn around and I'll show you how to break the balls?"

She grinned at him. "I don't think so." She shot a quick look at the open door they'd walked through.

When he followed her gaze, he saw the crowd in the bar had grown even more, so that there were groups standing, drinks in hand, just outside the room.

"Even as Lucas, I don't think you'd want to get arrested for..." She glanced back at him, the laughter clear in her eyes. "What exactly was it you had in mind a few seconds ago?"

"You're playing with fire, Mac."

When she laughed, he couldn't help but smile.

"You stand over there like a good boy," she said.

Lucas very nearly laughed, himself, when he did exactly what he was told. Meekness had never been one of his strongest virtues, probably because he didn't believe that the meek would one day inherit the earth. But then, thanks to the doc, he'd done a lot of things out of character in the past day and a half. Of course, it wasn't the doc ordering him around now. It was Mac.

Leaning against the wall, he watched her take the rack off the balls and bend over the table. As she ran the stick through her fingers in short little strokes, he watched her hands. Her fingers were long, delicate-looking. But he recalled how strong they'd felt on his skin, pressing, demanding. Taking.

Straightening, Mac lifted, then relaxed her shoulders in a circular motion. This time, she planted her feet farther apart before she bent back over the table.

If they were alone, he could walk right up to her and... Out of the corner of his eye, he saw someone glance into the room, then walk away. He could easily shut the door and prop a chair against it. Then he could go to her, lean over the table with her... She would gasp in surprise as he pressed against her, pinning her against the table. Then he would whisper in her ear, "You don't know me. I'm not even going to tell you my name." He would tell her exactly what he was going to do, describe every action, even as he did it. He'd make quick work of pushing the skirt up to her waist. Then he'd release his zipper and free himself so that she could feel him pressing against her with nothing but her panties separating them. All he would have to do then was push her down against the table and tear away that last, thin, silky barrier. Then he could bury himself in her. Lose himself—

The sharp crack of the cue ball smacking against the others sent Lucas's fantasy splintering off in as many directions as the balls. Drawing in a deep breath, he let it out slowly and dragged his attention back to the pool table. He thought he saw three balls sink into pockets.

"Aren't you going to congratulate me?" Mac beamed a smile at him as she moved to the other side of the table.

"Congratulations." He struggled to free his mind of the remnants of the fantasy he'd woven.

"That doesn't sound very sincere. I don't think you were paying attention."

Could she see into his mind?

"Watch," she said as if she were talking to a recalcitrant child. "I'll show you again."

To Lucas's astonishment, she did.

"Well?"

"Do it again," he challenged. This time he watched more carefully as she set up a complicated bank shot. It wasn't the one he would have chosen, but the moment she set it into motion, the cue ball careened off the side of the table into three others and sent them spinning into three different pockets.

"You hustled me," he said.

"I did no such thing," she said, moving toward him. "You assumed I didn't know how to play, and you're the one who wanted to make a little wager, just to keep the game more interesting."

"Were you telling the truth? Did you really learn to shoot pool when you were playing hooky from your nannies?"

"I learned in college. I was too young to date, but there were a lot of guys who didn't mind a kid sister–type tagging along. Especially if she could tutor them in physics or biology or calculus."

"That's all they wanted you to do? Tutor them?"

"I started college at fourteen. The deans and the resident directors had read all the guys the riot act. Not that they were tempted. I was a total geek, a one-hundred-percent nerd."

Mac at fourteen. Lucas tried to form a picture of it in his mind. It reminded him of the person he'd glimpsed at Sophie's party—a timid little bird, eager to help but determined to remain on the sidelines. Probably because she was so sure she wouldn't fit in.

"Did you beat them all at pool?"

She shrugged. "It wasn't hard. Getting them to see the utter simplicity of calculus was hard."

"I'll bet." He could barely keep a straight face at the seriousness of her expression. He wanted to grab her and hug her, twirl her around the room. But he didn't trust himself to touch her at all. And if he was patient now, he might learn more about the woman who hid behind the facade of Dr. Lloyd. Look how much he'd learned already. It was a good enough excuse to wait—almost.

He watched her lean across the table for a very long shot. She could have taken it more comfortably from the other side of the table. Was she doing it because she didn't see that, or was she doing it so that he could see the lacy edge of her panties when her skirt moved up? He took another drink of his beer to ease the dryness in his throat and watched the ball sink.

By the time she'd cleared the table, he'd had several more views of the edge of her panties. He was just about through waiting.

She collected and racked the balls before she approached him. Then she put a hand on his arm and said in a voice only he could hear, "Time to pay up. Picture this—I'm taking your pants off right now. Of course, I can't really take them off." She glanced toward the doorway. "Someone might come in, so we'll just have to imagine that you have to take your shots wearing only your boxer shorts."

He leaned down and whispered into her ear. "I'm not wearing boxers *or* briefs. Picture that."

The quick hitch of her breath had him grinning as he moved to the door, shut it and jammed a chair beneath the knob.

When he turned back to her, she was taking off the string of pearls she'd worn around her neck. "Now you can really take off your pants."

He walked toward her. "Now I can do a lot of things I've been planning."

She let the pearls swing from two fingers. "I've been thinking of something too."

He lifted her onto the pool table and began to ease off her panties.

"You were supposed to take off yours first."

There was laughter mixed with the excitement in her eyes. He couldn't have wanted her more. "No problem." Pulling the belt loose, he let his pants slip to the floor.

"I suppose you're going to insist on going ahead with your plan first."

"Absolutely," he said as he gripped her hips and pulled her to the edge of the table. "But I promise to let you have your turn next."

VERY SLOWLY, Sophie twisted around on the bar stool and let her gaze move over the crowd. The room was dim, the music live and pulsing with bass. Laced through it was the din of conversation and laughter.

She was in her element. She should be having a good time.

And the prickling sensation at the back of her neck was just due to the fact that she was in a place where people came to meet other people. Of course, they would be looking at her—perhaps even staring. She glanced down at the dress. Hadn't she chosen it just to get some attention?

She'd bought it Monday on that shopping trip with Mac. The green color went particularly well with the red wig she was wearing tonight. When she'd walked through the lobby of the hotel and caught a glimpse of herself in the mirror, she'd been amazed at her resemblance to Mac.

Lifting her glass, she took a sip. Tonight she was MacKenzie Lloyd and not Sophie Wainright, and she *was* going to have a good time.

The concierge at her hotel had been right on the money with his recommendation. The Side Street Grill was crowded with people, mostly singles, or at least pretending to be. The last man she'd danced with had forgotten to take off his wedding ring. Tables circled a dance floor, and on the second level, pressed against a balcony railing. On one wall, tall glass windows looked out on a patio lit with Chinese lanterns.

She caught herself rubbing the back of her neck again and immediately dropped her hand to her lap. She was being ridiculous, paranoid. Gripping her wineglass between her fingers, she began to turn it in slow circles on the bar.

Why not admit the truth? She was bored. Lifting her wineglass, she licked a drop off the rim, then set it back down.

Perhaps she should go back to D.C. If only Mac were here to talk to, or even— She set the glass down so fast she nearly overturned it. She couldn't be wishing that the *Shadow* were here, could she?

Definitely not! She wanted to torture the man, slowly, not…what? She certainly wasn't thinking of using some of Mac's research on him! She didn't know anything about him, other than that he was big, bigger than Lucas even. And strong. Smart too. When she'd cooled down enough to read the file he'd compiled on Bradley, she'd found his report thorough, well written and concise.

And he'd held her when she'd cried. A lot of men couldn't stand a woman's tears, but the Shadow hadn't been fazed.

She ran her finger around the rim of her wineglass. Well, she certainly wasn't going to soften toward him because of that.

And if she was wishing him here, it was just because it would give her great satisfaction to give him the slip again. Although if she were to consider using Mac's research on him… She ran her finger around the top of her wineglass again. There was more than one way to torture a man. She dipped her finger into the wine, then licked the drops off.

"I've never seen anyone do quite so many things to a wineglass without actually drinking the wine."

Sophie froze in her chair. Damn! She knew that voice—

Sonny Falcone. Had he recognized her in spite of the wig? How would she explain that she'd told him she'd had to work on her presentation?

"Why don't you let me buy you a fresh glass? I can recommend one from a local vineyard."

He hadn't recognized her. But he still might.

Pushing down the nerves in her stomach, Sophie turned. "No thank you. One is my limit, and I made the mistake of ordering a second one."

"You know, I have the funniest feeling we've met before. And that's not a pickup line. You remind me of someone…"

"I do that to a lot of people. But we haven't met. I just arrived in California today."

"It's probably the lighting in this place. But I can see I was mistaken. If I'd seen you before, I wouldn't have forgotten your face."

Oh, please! What had she ever seen in this man? Had her breakup from Bradley made her this blind? This desperate?

"If I can't buy you a glass a wine, perhaps I could persuade you to dance?"

"I'd love to dance." She risked a quick meeting of eyes and felt the nerves settle. He still didn't recognize her. And she would make sure that he didn't. "But first I need to freshen up."

"I'll be waiting right here."

For longer than you'd probably like. Sliding from the stool, Sophie threaded her way through the crowd in the direction of the ladies' room. But she didn't go inside when she reached it. Instead, she pulled open the door next to it marked Exit. The cool night air was refreshing after the smoky closeness of the bar. Drawing it in, she hurried down the path to the parking lot.

A glance at her watch told her she could still catch the red-eye. Her decision made, she suddenly felt free. Happy. There was only one thing she regretted. She was going to head back to D.C. without ever going up in that hot-air balloon.

But there had to be places to take a balloon ride in Maryland or Virginia. It would be a nice wild-goose chase to take the Shadow on. She was still thinking of that, laughing almost, when she reached her car.

It all happened very quickly. Arms grabbing her, holding her tight. A prick in her arm, and darkness swallowing her up.

13
___

MOONLIGHT POOLED on the bed, spilling over Mac as she slept.

Mac. Propping himself up on an elbow, Lucas shifted slightly so that he could see her better. She'd fallen sound asleep in the taxi on the way home from the bar. The last thing she'd said to him before she snuggled her head against his shoulder was that since he'd enjoyed the pearls, she knew he would love being wrapped in plastic wrap.

"Plastic wrap?" he'd asked.

"Mummification," she mumbled against his shirt. "It turns some men on. You can't move. I can. I can do anything I want. I bet you'll like it."

"I don't think I'll enjoy smothering to death."

"You won't." She'd giggled then and yawned. "I'll leave your mouth and nose free and, I think, one other part of you. Maybe I'll use the pearls again." He felt her mouth curve against his chest as she moved her hand from where it rested against his chest to the waistband of his slacks. He gripped it there.

"The picture is becoming clearer."

"The moment you told me you weren't wearing any boxers or briefs, I knew I had to try the pearls. And they worked."

They worked all right. Just thinking of the way she'd looped them around his erection and drawn them slowly upward...

She'd moved then, wiggling against him, exactly where he'd grown very hard. "I bet you'll enjoy the plastic wrap too. I packed a whole roll. We can do it right after we get back to the hotel.''

But they hadn't gotten to it. They hadn't gotten to anything. Yet.

MacKenzie Lloyd slept like a rock. He'd had to carry her into the hotel, and he hadn't had the heart to wake her when they reached the suite. As he'd undressed her and tucked her in, he'd noticed the dark smudges under her eyes. She was exhausted.

And no wonder. When he thought of what they'd done on that pool table. They'd taken turns, and when she'd suggested a position he'd never heard of before, they'd even compromised. He was going to have to get a hold of her research. He certainly was never going to be able to concentrate on his pool game again.

Because he couldn't help himself, he brushed one finger lightly over the fullness of her bottom lip.

At last he'd met the real MacKenzie Lloyd. And if the glimpses that he'd caught of her before had intrigued him and surprised him, the real deal fascinated him. She played pool as if she'd been raised in a pool hall. Yet he'd seen traces of the scientist too, in the way she set up her shots and measured the angles, almost as if she was solving some kind of problem.

He reached out to brush a curl back from her forehead. But it wasn't just the logical side of her brain that he admired. It was the imaginative side that quite literally had knocked his socks off.

And when she set out to seduce him, she drove him...crazy.

Tracing a finger down the soft curve of her cheek, he smiled. Who would have thought that the prim and proper Dr. Lloyd had an alter ego who was wicked and wild?

But then he'd never thought of himself as a man who could get caught up in wild fantasies or risky sexual games. What they'd done tonight had been plenty risky—but fun.

Anything might be fun with Mac.

Except for the plastic-wrap thing. He was going to have to draw the line at being rolled up in that. Then suddenly he grinned. Perhaps he'd have to turn the tables on her and see just how much she liked "mummification." He traced a finger lightly down her throat and over the rise of one breast until he let it rest on the peak. Of course, he'd have to leave some parts free.

As the images began to fill his mind, he shook his head to clear it. If he allowed himself to pursue that fantasy, he wouldn't let her sleep. He wouldn't get any sleep himself. And they would have plenty of time.

Time. Just that one word sent the first little ripple of unease through him.

He wanted to go on seeing Mac. And he could. There was nothing to prevent their spending more time together when they returned to D.C. He could picture her there even now. In his apartment, in his office…in his life?

The direction his thoughts were taking had the ripple of unease growing into a full-blown wave.

As quietly as he could, Lucas slipped from beneath the sheet and eased himself up from the bed. After glancing back once to make sure that she hadn't stirred, Lucas pulled on his slacks and let himself out of the bedroom.

Moonlight streamed into the large sitting area, bright enough to have him squinting a little as he crossed to the bar and poured himself a snifter of brandy. He had to think, to plan. Somehow, lying there beside Mac, he'd stopped doing that. He'd felt so—he struggled to find the right word—content.

Lifting the glass to his lips, he took a long swallow and welcomed the burn as it slid down his throat. He didn't want to feel that way. It didn't last. There was no one that you could allow yourself to depend on that much. Those were the rules he'd lived by. Survived by.

Moving to the balcony door, he opened it and slipped through. The moon was full and bright. Beneath it, the ocean was black, laced with flashes of silver. His granddad had told him once that the sea was a lot like life—always dangerous, often surprising and, every so often, magical. For a while he stood there, just concentrating on the flashes of silver.

What would Mac think if he told her he wanted her in his life once they got back to D.C.? Somehow, he didn't think she'd be any more pleased with the idea then he was. He took another taste of his brandy, just a sip this time. She might run.

He would catch her.

Or she might come on this very balcony to get her courage revved up. He'd recognized, though, that she had no understanding at all of how really brave she was.

Surely brave enough to take the same risk he was taking. And if she wasn't, he'd just have to convince her. He smiled slowly. With plastic wrap, if nothing else worked.

Tossing off the rest of his brandy, Lucas glanced at his watch—3:00 a.m. He could wake her and begin his campaign right now.

Or he could catch what little sleep he could and wake her when the sun came up. The wide yawn that suddenly overtook him had him choosing the latter. His resolution strong in his mind, he turned and walked back toward the bedroom.

AT 3:00 A.M. TRACKER glanced at his watch, then aimed a murderous glance through the crack in the closet door. His back was killing him and he wasn't sure if his legs would ever unbend again. If looks could have maimed or killed, the woman sitting at the desk would have died a very painful death several hours ago.

He'd waited until after eleven to break in. By that time, all the lights had been turned out except the ones illuminating the walkways between the cabins. He'd no sooner let himself into the office than he'd heard the key turn in the outer door.

The closet had been his home ever since.

The sudden whir of the computer told him that the blond amazon might have finally finished her nocturnal book-keeping. He would have put her out of commission earlier, but Lucas's orders had been very clear. He didn't want any kind of disturbance at the spa that might alert Sophie to the fact that her big brother was keeping tabs on her.

The moment the computer stopped whirring, the blond amazon closed the ledger and put it in the top drawer. Tracker pinched himself just to make sure that he wasn't dreaming when she rose and moved toward the door of the office.

He waited two minutes before he crawled out of the closet. When it only took him another five to find what he was looking for, he swore softly beneath his breath. If he'd climbed out of that tree ten minutes earlier, he would have had the number of Sophie's cabin before that blond amazon had ever settled in for her nighttime rendezvous with the books, and wouldn't have wasted so much time.

Quickly he checked the number against the map on the wall and discovered that the cabin Sophie had been assigned to, number 58, was nearby. Perhaps his luck was about to change.

Once he let himself out of the building, he slid into the shadows offered by the trees and made his way to number 58. The kinks had just about worked themselves out of his legs when he reached it.

A light poured through one of the windows and pooled on the flower beds below.

Did anyone sleep normal hours around here?

Ducking low, Tracker moved quietly to the cabin. Then pressing his back against the logs, he rose slowly, inched his face closer to the window and risked a quick peek.

It was the bedroom window all right. A woman had propped herself up against a pillow to read. The good news was she hadn't seen him.

The bad news was that the woman wasn't Sophie.

Tracker ran through the evidence in his mind as he

moved quietly to the front door of the cabin. It always paid to be thorough. The porch light confirmed that this was indeed Sophie's cabin. So he hadn't made a mistake. And the blond wig he'd spotted sitting on the dresser had been styled to resemble Sophie's hairdo.

There were times he hated it when his instincts were right. He let himself quietly into the cabin. The time for careful subterfuge was over. He intended to get some answers.

WHEN SHE DRIFTED UP through the layers of sleep in the early hours of the morning, Mac discovered she and Lucas were nestled in bed together like spoons. She felt his breath warm on her ear, his body even warmer along her backside. One of her feet was trapped between his legs, and he had one arm wrapped around her waist, the other hand planted firmly on her thigh. Just as if he wasn't planning on letting her go.

She didn't want to go anywhere.

She opened her eyes only a crack, only long enough to see that thin gray light was creeping into the room.

Closing them tightly again, she tried to recapture the dream she'd had—of Lucas slipping in beside her during the night and pulling her to him. He'd touched her so gently, loved her so softly, she'd known she was dreaming. His lovemaking had been nothing like the other times. There had been none of the desperation, none of the demand. She had never felt so cared for, so cherished. Each time she'd drifted close to the surface, he'd whispered to her to go back to sleep, to dream, to just feel how much he wanted her.

In the dream, Lucas had wanted *her,* not just the fantasies she'd conjured up for him. He'd wanted Mac. When he'd whispered that in her ear, the pleasure had streamed through her so sweetly, so deeply, that she'd shattered into a million pieces.

It had been the most wonderful dream she'd ever had.

And as impossible as it was, she wanted it to go on and on. She wanted it to be true.

In the half light of dawn, still wrapped in his arms, she could admit that she'd fallen in love with Lucas Wainright. She'd known it with the same certainty she felt at times in the lab, just when an experiment was about to go right. If she wanted to be Dr. Lloyd and analyze it, all she had to do was remember her research. When admiration was mixed with physical attraction, the chances for combustion were greatly enhanced. Mix in liking and trust, and you might have the perfect formula for love.

Mac didn't need the analysis. She just knew it was true. She never could have attempted what she had in that poolroom if she hadn't been doing it to Lucas.

She loved him.

Keeping her eyes tightly closed, she hugged the dream and the knowledge closer. As long as she did, she wouldn't have to allow the part of her that was Dr. Lloyd to spoil this moment by coming up with a tidy list of reasons why a future with Lucas Wainright was impossible. That would come soon enough. For now she'd let the Mac she was discovering inside of herself rule. Because Mac knew how to dream.

The first ring of the cell phone had her frowning and opening one eye. Sophie surely couldn't be calling her at this hour, not if she was bound and determined to avoid speaking to Lucas. In fact, Sophie didn't even get out of bed at this hour.

The second insistent ring had Lucas stirring behind her and another thought springing into her mind. What if Sophie was in trouble?

Mac struggled to free herself, but Lucas only tightened his grip.

"The phone," she said. "I have to answer it."

"Why?"

His voice was sleepy, but his body wasn't.

"It could be So—I mean, there could be a problem…at

the lab.'' There. If it was Sophie, she could still pretend it was someone else.

The second Lucas relaxed his arms, she slid from the bed and raced to the dresser for her purse. Dumping the contents, she grabbed the cell phone.

''Just how often do you have trouble at your lab?'' he asked, sounding more awake.

''There was only that once.'' She flipped open her phone. ''Last weekend someone broke in. Hello.''

The third ring sounded.

''It's mine,'' Lucas said.

It wasn't until she turned back to him that she realized she wasn't wearing any clothes. They were lying neatly folded next to the pants Lucas was lifting off a nearby chair. Mac couldn't remember taking hers off. In fact, the last thing she recalled was falling asleep in the taxi on their way back to the hotel.

She never slept in the nude. But she'd definitely been nude when she'd dreamed that Lucas had made love to her. Or had it been a dream?

''Yeah?'' Lucas rubbed a hand over his face as he spoke into the phone. ''No...okay.'' Dropping the phone to his side, he turned to her. ''My security man has a rather lengthy report to make. I thought I saw the makings for coffee out at the bar. Do you think you could...?''

''Sure.'' She moved quickly to the chair, but before she could pick up her clothes, he handed her his shirt.

''I want to have coffee with Mac, not Dr. Lloyd.''

He wanted to have coffee with Mac. Forgetting to slip into the shirt, she hugged the thought to her all the way to the door.

A SMILE CURVED his mouth as Lucas watched her walk out of the bedroom. He had to clamp down on the urge to follow her. Making love to her during the night had only whetted his appetite. He wanted more, and this time he wanted her wide awake and alert to every sensation when he was inside her. He wanted her to know exactly who it was who was touching her, tasting her, making her come.

He started toward the door. Hell, the coffee could wait. And so could Tracker's report. Lifting the phone to his ear, he said, "I'm going to have to get back to you."

"Sophie's not at the Serenity Spa."

Lucas stopped dead in his tracks. "You're sure."

"I've spent the past two hours confirming it. Once I found an impostor in her cabin, I decided the time for disguise was over. I even persuaded the amazon in charge of this place to let me check every single client at their morning yoga exercises."

As Tracker filled him in, Lucas paced the length of the bedroom and back. Fear flooded through him along with questions. He clamped down on both of them, concentrating on the facts that Tracker was feeding him.

"They switched at the airport in Charlotte?"

"According to the actress Sophie hired to impersonate her, they both went into stalls in the ladies' room where they donned wigs and changed clothes. Then they exited at different times."

"And it was shortly after that Sophie called me to let me know where she was, and I told you Mac was with me."

"Right. The actress in Sophie's cabin swears she knows nothing about where Sophie was going. I believe her mostly because I don't think Sophie would have told her. She planned this thing out pretty carefully. She wouldn't want us to be able to trace her easily. I've got men checking the flight manifests out of Charlotte right now. So far, they haven't come up with anything."

"Falcone's got her."

"We don't know that."

"I know it. That's what the phone call was about. He told me he had something that would make me reconsider. He was talking about Sophie."

There was a pause before Tracker replied, "He won't hurt her. He wouldn't dare."

The fact that Tracker wasn't arguing with him sharpened the fear in his stomach. He had to believe Falcone wouldn't hurt Sophie. Turning, Lucas paced the length of the room again. He had to keep telling himself that. More than that, he had to think, to plan.

As he strode by the dresser, his gaze fell on the stuff Mac had dumped out of her purse. In addition to the cell phone, which matched the same pearl color of his sister's, a wallet, a small plastic makeup case and loose change littered the top of the dresser.

"My office is checking the flight manifests out of Charlotte. So far they haven't found any record of a Sophie Wainright flying out."

"Maybe she used another name," Lucas said.

"Easier said than done. With the new security, she'd need a pretty accurate picture ID. And I already checked. She flew into Charlotte on a round-trip ticket under her own name."

"Maybe the actress used that ticket." Turning suddenly, Lucas walked back to the dresser and stared down at the cell phone. The evidence was right there.

Dr. Lloyd wouldn't have loose change lying in the bottom of her purse. Nor could he imagine her having a pearl-colored phone. Hers would be black, practical. He pictured Mac as she'd stepped of the plane. She'd taken off the blond wig, but if she'd been wearing it, she would have looked a lot like Sophie.

The sharp, jagged fear that had been slicing through him suddenly turned cold and hard. He knew even before he opened the wallet what he would find.

Sophie's picture on the driver's license stared up at him.

"Sophie used Dr. Lloyd's ID," Lucas said. He could feel the fury beginning to bubble up, but he clamped down on it tightly.

"Dammit," Tracker said. "I should have thought of that.

The two of them must have switched everything before they left Sophie's shop.''

''Yeah,'' he murmured. ''I should have figured it too.''

With one part of his mind, he listened to Tracker outline what he was going to do. But another part of his mind was sifting through everything that the doc had done in the past twenty hours. Images and sensations swirled through him.

Nothing could have been calculated to keep him more distracted. Hell, he hadn't been thinking straight since he'd seen her step off that plane.

Had it been all her idea—or was she merely following a scenario that his sister had mapped out? Pain sliced through him, deep and sharp. Suddenly he recalled Mac's initial reaction when the ringing of the cell phone had wakened him.

It could be So—

She'd expected it to be Sophie.

''Does the doc know where your sister is?'' Tracker asked.

''I'm going to find that out right now.''

14

LUCAS FOUND HER on the balcony standing in the same spot where he'd realized that he wanted her in his life.

He shoved the thought out of his mind. But it wasn't so easy to shove the woman out, or the feelings coursing through him. It hurt to look at her. Pain shimmered inside him, fueled by the fact that he still wanted her. He took a step toward her, and when she turned, for one second he allowed himself to absorb the look on her face.

Then he reminded himself that it was a lie. She was a lie.

"Where's Sophie?" he asked.

"At the spa. In North Carolina."

"No, she's not. She never went there."

He watched each and every emotion flicker over her face—surprise, confusion and a trace of concern. She was good.

"I don't understand. She told me she was there."

He held out the wallet then in the palm of his hand. "You've got her wallet, her driver's license. Does she have yours?"

"Yes. We switched by accident in her shop."

"By accident? And was it an accident that she hired an actress to impersonate her at the spa?"

She stared a him. "An actress? What are you—"

"Let me spell it out for you, Dr. Lloyd. My sister was very angry with me, so she decided to teach me a little lesson. I'm sure she shared all this with you. She hired someone to take her place at a spa. Then she got you to fly down here in her place and distract me so that she could disappear. You tell me she's at the spa. She calls me and pretends she's there. If I call there, they tell me she's all checked in, and as far as they're concerned, she is. Still, I might have checked further, but she told me you have a problem you wanted to discuss and asked me to help you out. I've got to hand it to the two of you—it was a brilliant plan to distract me.''

Mac lifted a hand, then dropped it. ''I know what it looks like, but I—I didn't know—I—''

He studied her as she spoke, but he couldn't trust himself to read her. She'd made him lose his objectivity, his control. She'd made him lose everything. ''How many times has she gotten in touch with you since you got off my plane?''

''Two…no, three times.''

''And she never once told you where she'd really gone?''

''She told me she was at the spa. She was happy there at first. Last night I thought she sounded a little restless and bored, but she denied it.''

''And you expect me to believe that? You're not that good a liar, Dr. Lloyd.''

He watched the hurt spring to her eyes and the color drain from her face. There was some satisfaction to be gained from that. It wasn't enough. ''You played me, Doc.'' He took a step toward her then and watched her step back into the railing. The need boiled up within him to grab her and shake her hard, make her tell him the truth.

But there was fear too—that if he touched her even now, he wouldn't be able to let her go. Fisting his hands, he shoved them deep into his pockets.

''The two of you must have had a few good laughs at my expense. How long was the charade supposed to go on? And who dreamed up the little research project on sexual fantasies?''

She flinched at each of his questions as if he'd slapped her, and he felt disgust roll through him. Struggling for control, he turned away from her. He had to focus on the fact that all signs pointed against her. Drawing in a deep breath, he said, "Look, I'm begging you to just tell me where she is. I wanted her down here in the Keys with me for a reason. I've made an enemy in the last week. She could be in danger."

"I'd tell you if I knew. She told me she was at the spa."

He whirled on her then. "Then why did you agree to the switch in identities?"

"I didn't. We took each other's purses by accident when we put the wigs on in her shop."

"And the wigs were for…?"

She raised her hands and dropped them. "The fantasies."

"Of course. Well, I have to hand it to you. They were very good. Just one question, Doc. Is there anything about you that's real?"

She didn't answer. But he heard the sharp catch in her breath, saw the tears, just a flash of them, before she lowered her eyes. They only seemed to increase the hurt that threatened to consume him. Digging deep within himself, he struggled to rebuild the shield that for so many years had protected him. "One last time. If you know where my sister is, tell me."

She didn't look up but merely shook her head.

He moved to the glass doors, turning back only when he'd stepped through them. "Congratulations, Doc. You lead me right down the garden path."

Never again. He didn't say the words aloud, but they drummed in his mind as he walked away.

GRABBING HER CLOTHES out of the closet, Mac stuffed them into her suitcase, hangers and all. She had to get out of the suite, out of the hotel. Once she did, she could stop thinking about Lucas. Then she'd be fine.

In the bathroom, she swept everything on the vanity into her cosmetics bag. A plastic bottle of shampoo hit the floor and bounced. Bending over, she scooped it up, but it slipped out of her hand and bounced off the floor again, this time onto her foot. A kick sent it sailing into the wall, and this time it boomeranged back into her leg.

Taking a deep breath, she made herself stand perfectly still. This wasn't like her at all. She usually packed meticulously. And she'd never before had a fight with a shampoo bottle.

Turning, she held tightly to the edge of the vanity. She had to get a grip. She made herself look in the mirror. The dark circles under her eyes didn't surprise her, but the tears stunned her. She couldn't remember the last time she'd cried. Dr. MacKenzie Lloyd never cried. Evidently, Mac did.

Who was she?

Before she'd met Lucas, she thought she'd known the answer. She was a research scientist who had a job she liked and whose work was going well. The only thing that had been lacking in her life had been a family of her own.

She'd taken the first step toward solving that problem just the way she would have approached a problem in the lab. It had seemed so logical, so simple. Maybe Dr. Lloyd's plan would have worked, if it hadn't been for Mac.

Sinking onto the toilet seat, she buried her face in her hands. She just needed to get back to D.C. She still had her work. She could go to her lab and bury herself in it. With time she would forget Lucas Wainright. And the way he'd looked at her before he'd left the suite.

He had every right to be furious with her. She'd deceived him. And she could never forgive herself if she'd put Sophie in any kind of danger. It might have been Sophie's suggestion that she fly down to the Keys in a disguise, but she'd gone along with it easily enough. She could see now that it was Mac who'd gone along with it because she'd wanted to try out her research on Lucas. Had she loved him even then?

No, she wouldn't let herself think about it. Turning, she

walked into the bedroom. She was going to pack and get out of this room that smelled like him.

The chimes rang just as she was jamming her cosmetics bag into the suitcase. One thought filled her mind as she raced to the door. Lucas.

But it was the manager who'd gotten the chair for her in the lobby, and he was shaking his head at her. ''Mrs. Wainright, you really shouldn't open your door without ascertaining who's there.''

''I thought it might be Mr. Wainright.''

He smiled at her. ''That's why I'm here. Mr. Wainright spoke with me before he left. He told me to tell you that the staff has instructions to make your stay, for however long you wish to remain, as pleasant as possible.''

Mac blinked back the sting of new tears. Lucas was furious with her, and yet he'd taken the time to make sure the hotel would take care of her.

''Is there anything I can do for you right now?''

''Yes,'' Mac said. ''I'd like you to make a plane reservation for me back to D.C.''

''Oh. Well, of course. Although we'd much prefer that you stay, I'd be happy to take care of that. If you'll just give me your first initial, Mrs. Wainright? They'll want to know for the reservation.''

For just a moment, Mac hesitated. Then she said, ''*S.* For Sophie.'' If she had to fly in a commercial plane, she would have to present a picture ID to get on the flight. She'd just have to use Sophie's, and she'd have to wear the blond wig so she'd look like Sophie's picture.

''I'll see to it right away.''

She was closing the door to the suite when it struck her. Had Sophie used her ID in the same way?

Leaning back against the door, she forced herself to think. It had been fun buying the wigs and then putting them on in the back room of Sophie's shop. But what if it had been more than just a lark for Sophie? Was it possible that she *had* switched the purses on purpose?

Thinking back, Mac tried to recall Sophie's exact words in the tree house. *The next time I find a man I like, I'm going to make sure he doesn't know I'm Sophie Wainright.*

It had been Sophie's idea to buy the wigs and the matching purses and raincoats. She'd blamed it on the fact that Lucas was having her followed, and that she desperately needed a break. What if her plan all along had been to go somewhere and actually pretend to be someone else? *Like MacKenzie Lloyd.*

Mac strode down the hall to get her bag. The sooner she got to D.C., the sooner she would be able to figure out where Sophie had gone.

"REPORT." Vincent Falcone gestured his son into a chair on the other side of his desk. In his hand, he held a glass of Falcone Vineyards 1998 Cabernet Franc. Currently it was his favorite vintage, and it would only improve with age. Beyond the glass that walled his office on two sides, grapevines marched in neat little rows until they began to climb the hills in the distance.

"A crew will be here shortly after three on Saturday to inflate the hot-air balloons. They can take any of our guests up until sunset."

Vincent lifted his glass of wine and watched the play of light in its depths. Sonny had purchased four hot-air balloons just last week. Offering free rides would draw crowds to the vineyards and sell more wine, Sonny had said in defense of his expenditure.

"And about the other business?" Vincent asked.

"Everything's going as planned."

"You have a signed contract?"

Sonny shifted in his chair. "I will by Saturday."

"You said you'd have it last week."

"I know, but there's been a little delay."

"In business, delays can be fatal."

"I have a man on the inside who assures me that I will have the contract by Saturday."

Vincent said nothing.

Sonny shifted again in his chair. "I am perfectly capable of running Lansing Biotech. I know you don't trust me. But I've got everything under control."

His son was lying. Worse than that, he was a fool. Vincent took a sip of his wine and let the flavors linger on his tongue. There were fools in every family, almost as if the stronger genes that ran in a bloodline had to take a break before they could appear again.

In the Wainright family, the weak genes had made their appearance in Lucas's father. It was too bad that Lucas hadn't inherited more of those weaknesses and fewer of his grandfather's strengths.

But in the end, it wouldn't make any difference. Vincent was not going to allow his business connection with Wainright Enterprises to be severed. That was why he'd arranged for Lucas's sister and Sonny to meet in Georgetown.

And that was why he'd held his tongue about the balloons when he'd learned that they were part of Sonny's campaign to impress Sophie Wainright. Vincent could picture her now, riding in one of them with Sonny just as Lucas arrived at the party. A picture was often worth a thousand words.

"Why don't you bring Sophie here for dinner tonight?" he said as he lifted his glass to his lips and took another sip.

"She's busy. She has to make a presentation tomorrow."

"A presentation? I thought she flew out here specifically to see you."

Sonny frowned. "She did. But…she hasn't yet admitted to me that she's really Sophie Wainright. She's still pretending to be this Susan Walker person. I thought of telling her today that I'm aware of the masquerade."

Vincent shook his head. "Best to wait until she tells you." And the fact that she hadn't told him wasn't a good sign. Sonny had always had a way with women, so bringing the two of them together had been worth a shot.

Setting his glass down on his desk, he said, "You'd better go work on that contract."

He waited for his son to leave the office before he sighed.

It was a damn good thing he had a backup plan to handle Lucas Wainright.

HOME. It was the foremost thought in Mac's mind as she paid the taxi driver and climbed the porch steps of her duplex. She knew where Sophie was, and she was safe. Just as soon as she got inside, she would face the task of calling Lucas's office to let him know. He wouldn't take the call though. She'd convinced herself of that. He wouldn't want to speak with her ever again, so she wouldn't have to hear his voice. All she'd have to do was leave the information with his secretary.

Setting her bag down, she fished in her purse for her keys. All she'd had to do was call the 800 number on her credit card and ask for the latest posted charges. It was all there—an airline ticket to San Francisco and another charge to the Château Mirabeau in the Napa Valley. Sophie hadn't answered the phone when she'd called, but the desk clerk had promised to give her the message.

She swept her hand one last time across the bottom of her purse. Where were her keys? Then it hit her. She didn't have them because Sophie had her purse. Moving quickly to her neighbor's door, she knocked but without much hope. The stockbroker who shared the Georgetown duplex with her wasn't likely to be home from the office yet.

After a few moments, she dropped her bag on the porch and hurried around the side of the house. She was going to have to break in, and one of the basement windows was her best bet. Dropping to her knees, she picked up a good-size rock. Then, just to make sure, she leaned close and peered through the glass. The latch was secure.

"Ma'am?"

Startled, Mac whirled to face the man standing directly behind her. "Who are you?"

"Detective Ramsey, District of Columbia Police Department." He showed her the badge he'd removed from his pocket. "Now, why don't you tell me who you are?"

"I'm MacKenzie Lloyd. I live here."

"And the rock in your hand is for…?"

Mac quickly put the rock down on the ground. "I don't have my key, and my neighbor isn't home to give me the spare."

The detective studied her for a moment. "You have some I.D.?"

"Yes." She was reaching into her purse when she realized that she didn't. "No. My friend and I switched purses. Her name is Sophie Wainright and I have her I.D." She handed the detective her wallet.

After glancing through it briefly, he said, "According to the security people at the university, MacKenzie Lloyd has red hair. Yours is blond."

Mac lifted off the wig. "I had to wear it so that I could get on the plane. All I had was Sophie's I.D." Running her hands through her hair, she glanced up at him. "Isn't this where you advise me that I have the right to remain silent?"

Fishing a photo out of his pocket, he glanced at it, then at her. "I don't think that will be necessary. You look a lot like the picture I have of Dr. Lloyd. We've been trying very hard to get a hold of you, Doctor. Don't you ever answer your cell phone?"

"Yes, of course." She pulled it out of her bag and then stared at it. It just hadn't been her cell phone she'd been answering. "My friend has mine."

Detective Ramsey nodded. "Well, she's not answering it either. Where have you been, Dr. Lloyd?"

"I took a few days off and went down to the Florida Keys."

He nodded. "That fits with what the university told us. But they were worried when they couldn't get hold of you. I have some bad news for you. Sometime on Wednesday, your apartment was broken into. One of your neighbors called it in, and then tried to reach you at the university. Somebody high up at the college is very concerned about you and your research and they called us. They think the break-in here and the one at the university are related. They also said you'd planned to take a few days off, but no one at the lab, not even your colleague Dr. Stafford, knew where you were. The timing of this break-in made them worry that perhaps…you hadn't gone away voluntarily.''

Mac's eyes widened. ''They thought I was kidnapped?''

''They wanted to file a missing persons report. Officially, we can't let anyone do that for forty-eight hours. In the meantime, the commissioner assigned me to keep an eye on your place. A lot of people are going to be relieved that you're back.''

Mac stared at him. ''I just went to the Florida Keys for a little…vacation. I'm fine.''

''Well, the bad news is your apartment isn't. Whoever broke in was looking for something and they were pretty thorough. If you feel up to it, I'd like you to take a look and tell me what's missing, or what they might have been after.''

''Of course.'' She could hardly refuse. But she wanted to. During the short time it took the detective to lead her back to the front porch and open the door, she tried to prepare, to steel herself for the sight. She still remembered what it had felt like when she'd first learned about the break-in at the lab. Her head pounded, her stomach clutched at the memory. This would be easier, she told herself as Ramsey led her inside.

It wasn't. The place was in a shambles—sofas and chairs overturned, lamps shattered, pictures torn out of their frames. In the kitchen, the cupboards and even the refrigerator had been emptied. Shards of glass and china lay over everything.

Drawing in a deep breath, she tried to reach for control.

Lucas had weakened it, but it still had to be there. If she could just reach deep enough.

''Is there any way to tell if they found your research?''

Mac shook her head. ''It's not here. Why would they do this?''

''They were angry,'' Detective Ramsey said. ''Probably because they couldn't find what they were after.''

''All they did at the lab was break into the safe and search through my file drawers.''

''There are some very influential people at the university who think they might have been after more than the formulas here,'' Ramsey said as he led her back out to the porch.

''What then?''

''According to the university security people, you usually work in your lab on Sundays. The Sunday of the break-in, you didn't. Then you should have been home on Wednesday. Your voice mail on campus was letting all callers know that's where you were.''

Mac drew in another breath. ''What exactly are you saying, Detective?''

''It's possible that whoever did this to your lab and your apartment might have been looking for you. When you weren't here, they got upset and trashed the place.''

She didn't want to believe it, not for a moment.

Then she thought of Sophie who'd been using MacKenzie Lloyd's name and traveling with her ID. And it was Sophie who'd disappeared. If there was any chance that what Ramsey was saying was true, she'd just learned how easy it was to find out where MacKenzie Lloyd was staying.

''Detective, if you're right, there's someone I have to get in touch with right away.''

15

SOPHIE DRIFTED in that gray world, halfway between wakefulness and sleep. Once or twice, she'd nearly reached consciousness only to slip back under. But gradually, moment by moment, awareness was creeping in. The throbbing in her head grew more intense. As did the light, growing steadily brighter beyond her eyelids. And she was lying on a rock—a hard and lumpy one.

It was only when she tried to shift to a more comfortable position that she realized she couldn't move her arms or legs. A quick spurt of alarm shot through her.

It had to be a dream. That had to be why she felt paralyzed. Clinging hard to consciousness, she struggled to wake up.

The memories came then—in bits and pieces. California, that's where she was. And Sonny… As his face appeared in her mind, she tried to focus. She'd come to California to see him…to teach Lucas and his security chief a lesson. The flash of satisfaction was short-lived, erased by a wave of fear.

She couldn't move her hands and feet because they were bound. She couldn't see or move her lips. They were covered by something. What? How? Why?

Even as the questions poured into her mind, she turned over to one side and ran into a solid wall. A quick, panicked roll in the other direction led her smack into another wall.

Where was she?

This time she took her time, but she reached the opposite wall in three rolls. A small room. A cell? She fought against the fear even as it clawed its way to her throat. Breathe, she told herself. The air was fresh, warm. There had to be an open window nearby. Drawing in another breath, she felt the sharpness of her fear fading. And her mind was clearing.

Think, she told herself. She was in California—where?

And then she remembered—running into Sonny, slipping out of the restaurant, the sharp sting in her arm.

Someone had drugged her. Who?

"You gave her too much of that stuff, I tell you."

The voice came from close by. Acting purely on instinct, Sophie curled into her original position.

"You wanted it quick and clean. You got exactly what you asked for."

"The boss wants to talk to her."

There was a sound nearby, and Sophie could have sworn that the floor she was lying on shook as if someone had jumped on it.

"Relax. She's probably coming around right now."

The voice came from over her head, then the same noise she'd heard before, and the floor shook again. She braced herself. If they wanted her to come around, it was the last thing she was going to do.

"She's still out. She hasn't moved since the last time we checked her."

"Let's just see."

She had just enough time to steel herself before she felt the sharp slap on her cheek.

"I told you. You gave her too much."

Fingers gripped her pulse. "If you don't shut up I'll give you a dose."

"It's not me you have to worry about. He's not going to tolerate any more mistakes."

"Will you relax?" The voice sharpened even as her wrist was freed. "Her pulse is steady. She's fine. Besides, he won't be out here to see her until tomorrow."

"I don't like it."

Sophie barely let herself breathe until she was sure the two men had gone. Wherever she was, it was a place the men had entered from above. There had been no sound of a door.

Was she on some sort of truck bed?

And who wanted to see her? Sonny? Had he recognized her in the bar after all?

But that didn't make any sense. Why would Sonny Falcone kidnap her? The motive for that was money. And he didn't even know who she really was.

When the headache behind her eyes began to throb, Sophie pushed the questions aside. The answers wouldn't get her out of her present predicament. Rolling over, she drew her legs up until she could touch her ankles.

Tape. That's what was binding her legs and hands. Moving to the wall, she wiggled and pushed herself into a sitting position. The first thing she was going to do was see if she could find anything to cut herself loose.

LUCAS PACED back and forth in his office listening to Tracker's report over his cell phone. They'd been in constant contact all day.

"So you're telling me that you know where Sophie is staying but she's disappeared?"

"What I'm saying is that she's not here right now. Last Wednesday, she registered as MacKenzie Lloyd at the Château Mirabeau in the Napa Valley. I've questioned nearly everyone who works here. The clerk says that she went out last night. No one has seen her this morning and the maid claims her bed hasn't been slept in."

"Have you notified the police?"

"No. I don't think we should do that just yet. We may be overreacting."

Lucas began to pace again. "My sister has been missing all night and you think we're overreacting if we notify the police?"

"Just hear me out. The tail that I had on Sonny Falcone

says that a blond woman matching Sophie's description had lunch with him on Thursday."

"Are you suggesting that she may have flown out there on purpose just to be with Sonny, and she may be with him now?"

"I'm not liking it, but that's what I'm saying. You told me yourself that she doesn't know anything about what goes on at Wainright. She wouldn't even know the name Falcone, let alone about Vincent's other less legitimate business dealings. And Sonny has a reputation for being a real ladies' man."

Lucas stopped pacing in front of his window. The heat of the day still clung in a misty shroud around the Washington Monument. For the first time in his life he questioned his decision to keep his family isolated from all the problems at Wainright Enterprises.

Maybe Tracker was right and he was overreacting. He'd been letting fear and anger cloud his mind ever since he'd realized Sophie was missing. He had to start thinking clearly if he was going to help his sister. More than that, he had to stop thinking about Mac. He was hundreds of miles away, and he still couldn't get her out of his mind.

"Boss, you still there?"

"Yeah. I don't like what you're saying, but you may be right."

"I don't like it myself, but I want to check it out. I have someone finding out whether or not she stayed at Falcone's villa last night. It will take a little time, but I should know something soon. In the meantime, I'm going to personally check out the list of places that the concierge recommended to Sophie last night. Have you heard anything from Vincent Falcone yet?"

"No."

"For what it's worth, I don't think he had anything to do with your sister's disappearance. I know you don't trust him, but think about it. If he wants to reestablish a business connection with you, kidnapping your sister is not his best move.''

Lucas sat on the edge of his desk. ''He might be planning to use her as a pawn to blackmail me into investing with him again.''

''Thought of that. But you always said he's a shrewd businessman. After threatening your sister, he'd have to figure it wouldn't be long before you got your revenge.''

Everything Tracker was saying made sense. As much as he didn't like it, he'd much rather imagine his sister dating Sonny Falcone than being at the mercy of Sonny's father.

''If Falcone is aware that Sonny and Sophie are an item, that could be the reason he told you that his connection with Wainright Enterprises isn't finished yet. That could also be the reason he's invited you out to his vineyard. Dr. Lloyd's pretty smart, and she knows Sophie. Why don't you run my theory by her and see what she thinks?''

''She's not here. I didn't bring her back to D.C.''

Tracker didn't reply.

Restless, Lucas began to pace again, until he caught himself. He never paced. Since MacKenzie Lloyd had come into his life, he'd done a lot of things he'd never done before.

''Aren't you going to ask me why I left her there?''

''None of my business.''

''She lied to me.'' Lucas listened to the words as they hung on the air. He'd needed to say them out loud. But they didn't ease the hurt. They only made it grow.

''Women are known for that. Pretending they want one thing when they're really after something else. The best way to handle that problem is to nip the relationship in the bud.''

''Exactly.''

''No offense, but I think your sister wins the prize when it comes to lies. If I'm right about what's going on, that is.''

''Yeah.'' Lucas rubbed his free hand over his face. How

long was it going to be before he could get rid of the image of Mac standing there on the balcony as he left their suite? The whole time he'd packed his things, she'd just remained at the railing, staring out to sea. "Do you have a contact in Key West, someone who could check on her and see that she's all right?"

"Dr. Lloyd? Sure thing, boss. I'll get right on it."

Tracker had no sooner cut the connection when the intercom on his desk buzzed.

Lucas pressed a button. "Yes?"

"There's someone— Miss, you can't go in there."

The door to the office opened, and Lucas started forward the moment he saw his sister framed there.

"Sophie—" He stopped short the moment she pulled off the wig.

It was Mac. No, he corrected himself again. It wasn't Mac either. It was the doc. She was wearing her hair pulled back and she was dressed in jeans and a T-shirt. And she looked vulnerable. He took a step toward her before he stopped, reminding himself that he couldn't trust anything he thought or felt about her.

"Mr. Wainright?"

It was only then that he noticed the man standing behind her.

"Who are you?" he asked.

"I'm Detective Ramsey."

Lucas glanced at the badge the man produced.

"I just want to make sure that Dr. Lloyd is in good hands. She can't stay at her apartment tonight, and she shouldn't be alone."

Just seeing Mac had so many feelings tumbling through him. Guilt, desire, bitterness. He tried to hold on to the last one.

"I'm sorry about the wig," she said. "I had to wear it on the plane, and I just forgot to take it off."

"Why are you here?" he asked as he took another step

forward. For a moment he thought she would turn and run, but she held her ground.

He knew in that moment that he might not have let her run.

"I may know where Sophie is staying. Or was staying. And she may be in danger."

16

TAKING A LONG SWALLOW of the water that Lucas had poured for her, Mac tried to focus her attention on Detective Ramsey as he summarized what they'd discussed at her apartment. It hadn't been until she'd said the words out loud to Lucas that the fear had struck her full force. Sophie might be in real danger because of her. Setting her water on a low table, she saw her hand was shaking and curled her fingers into a fist.

"So, you believe that there's someone so desperate to get control of Dr. Lloyd's research that they would kidnap her?" Lucas said.

"More importantly, there are some higher-ups at the university who believe it," Detective Ramsey said. "According to them, there are a lot of pharmaceutical and biotech companies who've been showing some interest and offering money. Greed is a big motivator when it comes to crime. And someone has enough power to get my bosses to pay attention. Otherwise, I wouldn't be here. My usual job is to investigate robberies, murders and rapes—crimes that have already happened. In D.C., we don't have much time or manpower for prevention. I came over here at Dr. Lloyd's insistence. She seems much more concerned about Miss Wainright's safety than about her own. She says that your sister has been traveling as MacKenzie Lloyd, using that ID instead of her own, and now she's missing. She's afraid that Ms. Wainright's disappearance might be related to the incidents at her lab and her home. How long has your sister been missing?"

The detective's words had a new wave of fear settling in Mac's throat. If she'd been thinking more clearly, she could have warned Lucas before he'd left Key West. She should have figured out what Sophie was doing earlier. Maybe she could have prevented this, if she hadn't been so distracted by Lucas.

Lucas showed no emotion on his face as he glanced at his watch. "Sophie's been missing a little less than twenty-four hours. My security people traced her the same way that Dr. Lloyd did. Sophie went out last night and didn't come back to her hotel room, but I have a man in California checking the restaurant that the concierge recommended to her. We think she may have met a man there, someone she flew out there to be with. There's a possibility that she may be with him."

"No," Mac said.

Both men turned to look at her.

"She's not with him. She'd decided she didn't like him after all. She was going to cut her trip short."

Ramsey turned to Lucas. "Could be she's on her way back then. Do you have a way to check that out?"

Lucas nodded. "I'll have my security people check the flights out of San Francisco."

"Keep me posted. Here's my card. If you need me to contact the local law enforcement, just give me a call. I have to get back to the station." He met Lucas's eyes. "Now that I've warned Dr. Lloyd, there's not much else I can do."

Lucas nodded. "I'll take care of it."

As the two men moved toward the door of the office, Mac clasped her hands together in her lap. In a moment she'd be alone with Lucas. That had been the one thing she'd wanted to avoid. She could still leave. Even as the impulse moved through her to stand and run after Detective Ramsey, she heard the door click shut and her throat went dry. She was reaching for her glass when she saw the blond wig lying on the table where she'd tossed it. Quickly she dropped her hand to her side. If only she had refused to go along with Sophie's plan....

Rising, she steeled herself to meet Lucas's eyes, something she'd avoided since she'd first walked into the room. In that instant when she'd taken off the wig and he'd recognized her, she thought she'd seen...what? Relief? Pleasure? Or had it only been a fantasy, a projection of the feelings that had been running through her?

Pushing the hope down, she lifted her gaze to his...and saw nothing. His eyes were perfectly blank. She might have been a stranger he was meeting for the first time on the street. Drawing in a deep breath, she managed not to shiver. She told herself that she preferred blankness to the cold detachment she'd seen in the hotel room. "This is all my fault. All of it."

He took a step forward, then stopped. "Blame is beside the point right now, don't you think?" His tone was as neutral as his expression.

"Of course. Tell me what I can do."

"Do?" He took two more steps toward her and stopped again.

This close she could see that he wasn't as carefully controlled as she'd thought. For a moment the silence stretched between them, and her heart began to drum.

The ringing of the phone made them both start. Then Lucas moved to grab it.

"Yes, Ms. Burns?"

"Mr. Falcone on line two."

"Put him through."

"I HOPE YOUR FLIGHT from the Keys was uneventful, Lucas."

"To the point of being boring." Lucas was pleased to note that his voice was cool. Because he wasn't. He hadn't been since Mac had walked into the room. And it wasn't merely the news that his sister might have been kidnapped. Even now as he looked at Mac, she unlocked feelings in him that he couldn't seem to control. And what he'd feared most seemed to be true. In spite of everything, he still wanted her.

"You shouldn't have left your little playmate behind at the hotel. She could have amused you on the flight."

Fear was a copper taste in his mouth as several possibilities flooded his mind. He'd known that Falcone was monitoring his movements. How else would he have known to call him at the Wainright Casa Marina? And yet he'd left Mac there alone without any thought that Falcone might make a move on her. But she was here. She was safe even if it was no thanks to him.

Tearing his gaze away from Mac, he said, "I came to the same conclusion. That's why she's with me right now." Lucas sat on the edge of the desk and concentrated on relaxing every muscle in his body. He had to get some grip on his control or Falcone would believe he had the upper hand.

"Ah."

He hadn't known that, Lucas thought with some satisfaction.

"She seemed to be much different than your usual choice of companion. But I'm told she is very entertaining."

When his free hand tightened into a fist, Lucas relaxed it. "Surely you haven't called merely to comment on how I'm keeping myself entertained?"

Soft laughter rippled into his ear. "Of course not. I called to remind you of my party tomorrow at the vineyard. Bring your new little friend if you wish. For old times' sake, I'd like you to be there."

"The old times are over."

"Perhaps I can persuade you to create some new ones. Your sister has accepted my invitation."

"Sophie?" The surprise he heard in his voice was genuine. He hadn't expected Falcone to mention her. Had he already discovered that she was impersonating Mac? He felt the flutter of panic in his throat and swallowed it.

"She and Sonny have become very close over the past few weeks. He's persuaded her to come."

Falcone was choosing his words carefully. He was purposely creating the idea that his son and Sophie were intimate. Could Mac's theory be wrong? Was Tracker right and Sophie had merely spent the night with Sonny at the estate? Pushing the questions aside, Lucas concentrated on the one thing he could depend on. The old man wanted him frightened and angry. Therefore, he couldn't afford to be. "I'm sure you'll treat her as an honored guest. For old times' sake. Give Sophie my best."

There was a beat of silence, just long enough for Lucas to know he'd scored a point.

"There's another reason you should come. We have business to discuss."

Lucas waited a beat this time. "I don't think so."

"The pharmaceutical company you paid me off with, Lansing Biotech. We're about to get exclusive rights to some very promising research. You might be interested in buying back in. If not, I'll go directly to your board before the news hits the street."

Lucas said nothing, but his mind was racing. Lansing Biotech. Why hadn't he put it together sooner? Lansing Biotech gave Vincent Falcone the perfect motive to kidnap MacKenzie Lloyd.

Falcone's laugh was softer than before. "I'll see you tomorrow at…three, shall we say? I have a special bottle of wine I want to share with you."

For a moment after he hung up the phone, Lucas turned this new information over in his mind.

"Is Sophie safe?"

He glanced up at Mac's question. She had to have guessed that he'd been talking about her to Falcone, but all he could see was concern for Sophie in her eyes. "I don't know. I think I know who's got her. As far as I can tell, he thinks he's got both of you. He's an enemy of mine, and he says Sophie's going to be at his party tomorrow, and he's about to get exclusive rights to some exciting new research. How many pharmaceutical companies have been wooing you to come with them?''

''Three. It all started after I published that article last month. My results are preliminary, as I told you. But the enzymes I'm using are having very promising effects on rats.''

''What did you tell the companies?''

''That I wasn't interested. I was afraid that once I signed papers, they'd own me. That's why I prefer the university setting. There's much more freedom.''

Lucas's eyebrows shot up. ''Less money too.''

She shrugged. ''Money isn't everything.''

''Did anyone give you a hard time when you refused to sign?''

''One of them was hard to discourage. My fault, really. I dated the representative a few times. I thought he might be interested in me until he made his pitch. He wanted me to sign a contract that would give his company exclusive rights to manufacture the results of my research. He told me that I wouldn't have to come to work for them, that I could stay at the university. He was very upset when I didn't sign.''

''What was the name of the company?'' he asked.

''Lansing Biotech.''

''Bingo,'' Lucas said even as fear flooded through him, leaving a bitter taste in his mouth. ''How long ago was it when you gave the rep his walking papers?''

''Just a few days before Sophie's birthday.''

''That could explain why they went to plan B,'' he said. ''They broke into your lab that Sunday, which means they're desperate to get your signature on that contract.''

''But they must realize that if they kidnapped me and forced me to sign I could go to the police afterward, explain about the kidnapping and swear I signed the contract under duress.''

Lucas nodded. ''Sure, you could do that. But I'm betting

that Falcone has covered his tracks well. And that company rep you dated may have a different story. You wouldn't have any proof about when you signed the papers, and your signature would be authentic. It would take the courts a while to settle it. And if I'm right about what Falcone is planning to do, he'll only need to produce your signature to convince my board to invest in his company before the stock goes up. He'll make sure Wainright Enterprises makes a killing before the legal battles start. And if he could get his hands on your research notes, he wouldn't really need you anymore.''

"He won't get my research notes. They're safe. It's Sophie who's in trouble. What will happen when they find out she's not me?''

It was the question he hadn't wanted to ask himself.

Mac reached for his hands then. "We're going to find her before that happens.''

The words, just the fact that she said them out loud, stilled the fear that had been ripping through him. Before he could prevent himself, he linked his fingers with hers. There was comfort there, he thought, a kind he'd never hoped to have. He couldn't afford to trust it any more that he could prevent himself from clinging to it—for just a moment. "Mac...''

The phone on his desk rang again. Releasing her hands, Lucas reached for it and heard Tracker's voice in his ear.

"I'm at the Side Street Grill, the restaurant the concierge recommended to Sophie. Sonny Falcone was here for a short time last night. The bartender doesn't recall anyone who fits Sophie's description, but he remembers a redhead—someone he'd never seen before—talking to Sonny. Next thing he knows, she's gone. Sonny hung around until the place closed down.''

"Mac's here, and she says that Sophie told her she was bored with Sonny and planned on heading home.'' Quickly he summarized the rest of what he'd learned from Ramsey, Mac and his phone conversation with Vincent Falcone.

"Damn," Tracker said. "I'd like it a hell of a lot better if I knew who was who. You got any orders?"

"Any chance you could scout out Falcone's vineyard?"

"Can a duck swim? I was going to head out there anyway."

Lucas's lips curved slightly as he glanced at his watch. "I should be able to get there in five hours."

"What about Dr. Lloyd?"

Lucas glanced at Mac. "No. I'll make arrangements for her here. Just tell me who to call."

Lucas jotted down the instructions Tracker gave him, but he'd no sooner hung up when Mac said, "I'm going with you."

"It's not safe."

"You know who's got Sophie, don't you? Who is it?"

"I'm pretty sure it's an old enemy of mine by the name of Vincent Falcone. That's why I wanted Sophie with me down at my grandfather's cabin. I didn't foresee that he would go after you. I wasn't prepared for that at all." Lifting the phone, he punched in the numbers that Tracker had given him. "I'm going to leave you with someone who'll keep you safe."

"If I go with you, they'll know that they don't have the right person. They'll have to let her go."

Lucas frowned at her. "It's not that simple. Vincent Falcone is really after me. And I don't trust him." He filled her in on what Tracker had told him. "If he finds out that he's got the wrong woman, I don't think he'd hesitate to use Sophie to get what he wants."

"You still need me," Mac said. "He'll release her if I sign the papers he wants. I'll give him my research."

Lucas stared at her. "You can't do that. I couldn't allow it."

She moved to him then, until they were standing toe to toe. "You might be able to tell Sophie what to do, but not me. I can always do more research. I could never replace Sophie. If you don't take me with you, I'll go on my own."

Lucas studied her. She looked as fearless as he'd always imagined Joan of Arc would look as she was being led to the stake. And just as naive.

He didn't doubt for a minute that she would do what she said.

"If I agree to take you, there are some ground rules we'll have to set."

She leaned down to pick up her bag. "I can do rules. They're a scientist's way of life. Why don't we discuss them on the way?"

MAC LAY CURLED on the seat opposite him. As soon as his private plane had lifted into the air, she'd been out like a light.

Little wonder. Exhaustion bruised her eyes even in sleep. Sipping his wine, Lucas willed himself to relax. How much had either one of them slept in the past—what was it? Three days?

Was that all it had been? He felt as if he'd known her forever. Yet, as he watched her sleep, he wondered if he knew her at all.

Leaning back in his seat, he shifted his gaze out the small window at his elbow. Ever since they'd taken off from D.C., they'd been chasing the sunset. The light outside was soft and glowing. Focusing on it, he tried to think of other things. Tracker had called with information on the party, and the layout of Falcone's vineyard. They'd even mapped out a tentative plan for searching both the villa and the other buildings. But he didn't kid himself that Vincent Falcone wouldn't take excellent precautions. He might not even be keeping Sophie on the premises. They might not find her. He might not see her again.

Closing his eyes, he pressed two fingers against the bridge of his nose and dismissed the *might nots* from his mind. When he opened them, he found his gaze resting on Mac again, and he thought instead of another time he'd watched her sleep, little more than twelve hours ago. She'd been snuggled against him in bed, and he'd been making love to her, slowly, thoroughly. Even as he thought about it, an achy, edgy desire crawled through him anew.

That much hadn't changed. She'd looked fragile and defenseless then too. Someone a man should protect. And everything had been a lie.

Or had it?

Rising, he moved into the small galley and poured more wine into his glass. Ever since he'd learned about Sophie's deception, he'd convinced himself Mac had been playacting with him from start to finish. He'd told himself that nothing about her could be trusted. Nothing was real.

He'd been wrong. Her loyalty, her love for his sister was very real.

What else was? Turning, he moved back to settle himself in the seat opposite her.

Her dedication to her work. Her courage. She might think of herself as a coward, but she would risk her own safety, without a second thought, to save Sophie.

That was why he wasn't going to let her out of his sight until he'd settled things with Falcone. He couldn't forget the cold fear that had sliced through him when Falcone had revealed that he'd known Lucas had left Mac behind in Florida. What if Falcone had known she was MacKenzie Lloyd and gone after her then? He'd been careless about her safety. He couldn't forgive himself for that. And he wouldn't be careless again.

He lifted his glass of wine, then frowned and set it down. His determination to protect her wasn't the only reason he'd agreed to bring her along. He didn't like lies, and self-deception was the worst kind. He wanted MacKenzie Lloyd. It was just that simple. Just that vital.

Sitting here watching her sleep was enough to have his blood nearly boiling. He wanted to know everything about her, to discover what made her tick. He wanted to touch her, to discover what pleased her, to watch her come alive when he was inside her again.

He wanted all of her.

If he could make love to her—just once again without any kind of pretense between them—maybe then he could get her out of his system.

And if he couldn't? He'd just have to face that when he got to it.

He moved to her then, lifting her into his arms and carrying her into the small bedroom at the back of the plane.

SHE SHOT FROM deep sleep to half sleep with a swiftness that had her mind and senses reeling. Blood heating, pulse racing, she was trapped in a place where all she could feel was Lucas—his body pressed tightly against hers at every possible contact point, his hands holding her wrists. And his mouth, insatiable and possessive, moved over hers, drawing everything from her.

Freeing one of her hands, she ran it over his shoulder, testing the hard muscles, craving the warm smooth skin beneath the shirt. Hers. The word brought pleasure and a hint of panic. He was only hers for as long as she could hold on to the dream.

"Wake up. All the way now."

The voice was soft, seductive. She struggled against it.

His teeth nipped at her bottom lip. "C'mon, Mac. Wake up for me."

It was the sound of her name that had her eyes snapping open. All she could see was him, his mouth only inches from hers, his eyes dark and so hot.

"What?" She struggled to think. "Where?"

"Shh." He brushed his lips against hers. "We're on my private plane. Remember?"

Memories flooded back. They were flying to California to find Sophie. She was in danger. Mac tried to move and found she couldn't. His body truly was pressed against hers at every possible contact point. It hadn't been a dream.

"I figure we must be about forty thousand feet over Kansas right now."

"Lucas." The word sounded breathless.

"Shh." He continued to nibble at her lips. "We have to be very quiet. I don't think you want my pilot to know what we're doing."

She felt the rush of heat flood her face, felt the warmth of his chuckle at her ear.

"You're blushing, Mac. Did I ever tell you how much it excites me when you blush?" He spoke the words against her skin as he traced kisses along her jaw, down her neck. "And I don't think that Sally the hooker or Fiona the mermaid are genetically capable of being embarrassed. What's your expert opinion on that?"

"Stop," she managed to say. "If this is your way of punishing me..."

"Uh-oh. Now the doc is back. I don't think she blushes either. She's always so busy analyzing or planning." When he scraped his teeth along her throat, she moaned.

"Still want me to stop?"

Even as she struggled to form the word, he shifted his weight. For one moment she felt cold, bereft. Then his hands freed the snap of her jeans, pulling and tugging them down her legs.

"Yes," she breathed as his clever fingers began to move up her inner thighs. "Oh, yes." She no longer knew what question she was answering.

Pushing aside her panties, he slipped one finger inside her. "I'll stop anytime you say."

"Yes. Don't...stop." Pleasure streaked through her as she arched into his hand.

"I'm getting mixed signals here. Why don't you open your eyes and tell me exactly what you want me to do next?"

She saw his face above hers, his eyes so hot that she was sure they alone were causing the flames within her. Drawing in a deep breath, she tried to bank the fire, tried to find some shred of control. "We were going to lay down some rules."

She saw his lips curve just before he lowered them to hers. "I'm following the ones you laid down before. It's my turn, my fantasy."

He *was* punishing her, Mac thought as he withdrew his fingers and then slipped them inside again. But the pleasure was exquisite, irresistible. She moaned again when he did something with his thumb, and his fingers moved deeper.

"I never did admit to you what my fantasy was," he murmured as he trailed kisses from her temple to her jaw. "My fantasy is just you and me, Mac. Just the two of us alone with nothing to do but pleasure each other."

She should be able to resist. But she couldn't prevent her arms from going around him. She knew he didn't mean it. He couldn't mean it, not when he'd been so angry with her. He was just trying to get even. Still, she threaded her fingers through his hair. She couldn't, she wouldn't, push him away when she might never have this chance again.

"Just enjoy." The rhythm of his fingers increased, and suddenly her body grew taut. She lifted her hips from the bed, reaching. Very slowly, he withdrew his fingers.

"Not yet," he whispered as he kissed her forehead, her eyelids, her chin.

"Please," she whispered, gripping his shoulders.

His thumb teased her again. "Look at me."

When she did, she saw the heat in his and the reflection of herself.

"Tell me that you want me."

He was giving her a choice. She could say no. In some part of her mind she knew that. Her eyes never wavered from his when she said, "I want you."

He made a place for himself between her legs. "Look at me, Mac. Say my name."

"Lucas."

Even then he didn't enter her, not all the way. Instead, he leaned down and pressed his mouth to hers. The tenderness of the kiss shuddered through her, melting her. She was trembling, but her eyes were open and on his when he finally pushed into her.

This was the way he'd imagined her. This was exactly how he wanted her—pliant and warm beneath him, her muscles limber. But he hadn't anticipated the sweetness of her surrender. He hadn't realized how the piercing pleasure of it would pull at his control. Would it always be this way?

The moment that he began to move, she moved with him, absorbing and matching each stroke. She was his. He tried to keep the pace slow and easy because he wanted to spin out the moment. He wanted to remember the way she looked, her cheeks flushed, her eyes dark with desire.

But each time he sank into her, he was losing a part of himself. He should have been able to slow down or pull back. All he could so was move faster. And still she moved with him. When she ran one possessive hand down his back, he knew he was lost.

"Come with me." His voice was raspy, raw as he increased his rhythm and they began to race together to the finish. He felt the climax move through her, then heard his name mingle with hers as he held her tight and surged within her.

FOR A WHILE, Mac let herself drift, absorbing the sensations. His head was still buried in her hair, her hand was still tangled in his. She could feel the rapid beat of his heart. Or was it her own?

She'd never been taken so completely by anyone. She'd never even imagined anything like it. In a minute she was sure she would start to form a list in her mind of all the reasons why she shouldn't have let Lucas Wainright seduce her.

Right now she didn't care. She didn't want to think, to analyze, to plan. Outside the window, the light had softened to a glow. Day was teetering on the brink of tumbling into night. And it would. No one could hold off tomorrow. All one could do was cling to the present.

A sudden, enormous thump shook the cabin.

Lucas raised his head. "What the...?

The plane lurched suddenly and they tumbled off the narrow bed to the floor. Another lurch sent them rolling, and her head rapped smartly against the wall.

"Are you all right?" Lucas asked, holding tight as the plane banked sharply. This time he managed to keep them from rolling, but they still slid into the bed.

Mac made a strangled sound.

"You're hurt," he said.

"No."

When she lifted her head, he saw that her eyes were filled with laughter. She clamped a quick hand over her mouth and turned a giggle into a gurgle.

Relief nearly made him giddy.

"Sorry about that." Jill Roberts's voice poured out of the speaker. "The turbulence was a little rougher than predicted or I would have warned you. I hope you had your seat belts fastened."

"We're fine."

Mac buried her head against his chest to muffle a fresh wave of giggles.

"I'm climbing out of it now, but there may be a few more bumps. Keep your belts fastened."

"Thanks, Jill," Lucas said. The moment he heard the intercom click off, he gave Mac a shake. "You want to tell me what's so funny."

When she lifted her head, her hand was still clamped over her mouth. Lowering it, she took a deep breath, then paused to swallow a giggle. "I just remembered when we fell off the bed. Doing it on a plane—it's one of the top ten fantasies of men. They even have a club you can join. You must have heard of it."

"The mile-high club? I still don't see what's tickling your funny bone."

The plane banked again and they rolled into the wall so

that he held her pinned against it as laughter moved through her.

"Some men even charter a plane so that they can join the club. My question is why? So they can roll around and nearly kill themselves?"

She had a point. He was willing to bet that they'd both have bruises. "On a commercial jet, there'd be the challenge, the added excitement of not getting caught. That seems to be a big factor in your research."

"Yeah, but it seems to me that the chances of coitus interruptus are greatly increased."

He laughed then and held her tight. "I don't think I'm ever going to figure out how your mind works. But I'm going to try. How's this?" He shifted so that she was beneath him.

She read his intent immediately. "Stop."

"Just a little experiment, Doc. This is step number one," he murmured as he slipped into her.

"Ohhh."

The hitch in her breath sent the heat shooting through him. "Ready for step number two?"

"We shouldn't," she managed to say.

"I thought scientists always wanted to find out answers. Why is having sex at forty thousand feet one of the top ten fantasies? Wasn't that your question? Ahhh," he sighed as her sleek softness pulsed around him, pulling him deeper. "There you go, Doc. You're already ahead of me on step number two."

Her fingers pressed into his hips.

"And three," he murmured as he began to move.

17

TRACKER MET THEM at a little all-night diner where the Golden Gate Bridge could just be seen glimmering in the distance.

"Dr. Lloyd, I presume," he said, shaking her hand with a perfectly straight face. But his eyes were filled with humor.

Mac decided she liked him on the spot. "And you, I'll bet, are the Shadow."

His eyebrows snapped together. "The what?"

"That's what Sophie calls you, because you're always slipping into them," she explained. "You frustrate her."

"Yeah, well I guess you could say that the feeling is mutual."

"But I think she admires you."

"That's mutual too."

Mac wasn't even aware that Tracker hadn't released her hand until Lucas took her arm and nudged her into a nearby booth.

"Were you followed?" Tracker asked as Lucas slid in beside her.

"No. We checked into the St. Francis, then slipped out by way of the delivery dock. We came the rest of the way on foot."

And her feet were still complaining, Mac thought, wincing. Not to mention her shins. They'd run up a very steep hill before they'd angled their way down again toward the water.

"What? You're not having fun yet?" Tracker winked at her.

Fun. It only took the mention of the word to have her thoughts flying back to the plane trip and what they'd done in the small bedroom at the back of the aircraft. Heat flooded her cheeks. She'd never thought that lovemaking could be fun. But it had been. Lucas had shown her that. When this was over, when they found Sophie and she went back to her work, she would still have that.

She risked giving Lucas a sideways glance and found that he was looking at her. He ran a finger down the side of her cheek before he shifted his gaze back to Tracker.

"You're awfully cheerful," Lucas said dryly.

"I could say the same about you. I guess we both got lucky after I talked to you last."

"You found out where Sophie is?"

"I hung around the Side Street Grill after I talked to the bartender. Couple of valets came on duty around six-thirty. One of them saw a woman pass out in the parking lot last night, just about the time the bartender says that the redhead disappeared. The kid says it was dark, and he didn't get a good look at the woman. He wouldn't have thought much about it. Figured she was drunk. But he had his eye on the car these two guys helped her into, thinking you never know when something could be not quite right. It was a silver RV and he gave me a detailed description of it, including its performance capabilities *and* a license-plate number. After a little research, guess who I found out it belongs to?"

"Falcone?" Lucas asked.

"Sonny."

"He stayed at the bar after she left."

Tracker nodded. "That gives him an alibi. Might have been a perfect plan if he hadn't used one of his family's cars to drive her off in."

"No one said he was Einstein."

"Can we go after her?" Mac asked.

"We will," Tracker assured her. And this time there wasn't a trace of laughter in his eyes. Then he shifted his gaze back to Lucas. "My question is who Sonny thought he was kidnapping? She was wearing a wig and using Mac's credit card last night. But she wasn't wearing any kind of disguise when she went out with Sonny in D.C. And my man definitely saw him eat lunch with a blonde on Thursday.''

"Sophie might not have given him her real name," Mac said, and the two men turned to stare at her. "Last weekend, when we were talking in the tree house, she told me that she wasn't going to tell the next man she dated that she was Sophie Wainright. Her experience with Bradley Davis had really gotten her down. Then she got a call on her cell phone, and I had the feeling it was from someone she was already seeing. Could it have been Sonny?''

Lucas and Tracker exchanged glances.

"Could she have told this man that she was you?" Lucas asked.

Mac thought for a minute. "No, I don't think that Sophie would have done that. I mean, she might have pretended to be someone else. But I don't think…'' She let the sentence trail off as she met Lucas's eyes. "But then I figured she was really at that spa. And I can't explain why she was wearing the wig and pretending to be me last night. I wish we'd never bought those foolish wigs. If we hadn't, none of this would have happened.''

For a moment Lucas said nothing. He merely looked at her with an unreadable expression on his face.

"Look," Tracker said. "None of this makes sense right now. All we know for sure is that someone snatched Sophie out of that parking lot last night.''

"Can't we go to the police with that much?" Mac asked.

"Right now it would be tricky," Tracker said. "Sonny stayed at the Side Street Grill until well after midnight. He can always claim that his RV was stolen.''

"And while he's shielding himself behind his father's legal team, something could happen to Sophie," Lucas said. "You think she's on the estate?''

Tracker waited until the waitress, a woman named Leona,

had slapped down mugs of coffee and taken their orders. The moment she waddled back to the kitchen, he pulled out a hand-drawn map and spread it on the table.

"I took a little tour of the Falcone Vineyards this afternoon, along with thirty or so other tourists. Of course, I kind of got lost. Falcone's security is pretty good, and they weren't happy when they caught up with me. Before they did, I found the silver RV safe and sound in the garage along with six other cars."

Pausing, he pointed to one of the boxes he'd drawn on the map. "This is the garage. The main house right next to it has three stories with decks on each level. There seem to be several guests staying there already and all have access to the cars."

"Do you think Sophie is being kept at the house?" Mac asked.

Tracker shrugged. "I'm not ruling it out, but it'd be tricky with all the people around. What if she cries for help?"

Mac found Lucas's hand and gripped it.

"The outbuildings where the actual wine is made are nestled together over here." Tracker tapped a finger on the map closer to the highway.

"That's even riskier," Lucas said.

"Yeah." Tracker took a quick swallow of coffee. "Too many people in and out on the tours. But there are places they don't let the tourists into. The tents for the party this weekend are being built here." He moved his finger in a straight line to a point halfway between the winery and the main house. "There's going to be a lot of traffic to and from this point tomorrow and Sunday. But the house won't be open to the public, only to a few invited guests."

"And we'll be among them," Lucas said.

Both men stopped talking as the waitress placed heaping platters onto the table. Mac glanced down at the mountain of eggs, bacon and home fries and wondered where to begin. Lucas and Tracker reached simultaneously for the saltshaker. When their hands collided, Lucas settled for the pepper, and then they switched. Their movements were so smooth that Mac was sure they'd done this before. How similar they were, it occurred to as she watched them sample their eggs, then reach for the ketchup.

"You've worked together before, haven't you?" she asked.

Both men shot her a look of surprise.

"How do you know that?" Tracker asked.

Mac shrugged. "You've shared meals before, and you can practically finish each other's sentences."

Lucas looked at Tracker. "The doc has a sharp, analytical mind."

"Welcome aboard, Dr. Lloyd," Tracker said as he poured more salt on his home fries. "We're going to need all the help we can get."

They even looked alike, she thought as she watched them attack the mountain of food. Each had the dark good looks of a Brontë hero. Tracker's edges were rugged, Lucas's more polished. But both had a capacity for stillness, and both of them exuded that hint of danger. In Lucas, that threat of danger might be hidden under a more civilized veneer, but it was there, and it had never been more apparent than now when she saw him with Tracker.

Lucas Wainright certainly didn't fit the profile of the man she'd thought she would fall in love with. She should be afraid of him, but she wasn't. Perhaps because he had that other side too—that streak of boyish mischief that lay hidden beneath the surface. It was something that he didn't share very often. She was sure he shared it with his friend Tracker. And he'd shared it with her. In spite of his harsh words, he must still trust her a little. She hugged the knowledge to her.

Tracker shoveled in a final mouthful of scrambled eggs, chewed and swallowed. "I'm betting that Sophie's somewhere on the estate. There are apartments over the garage that I didn't get a chance to check. Falcone's security is top of the line. Electronic surveillance as well as human. The two who helped Sophie into the RV were probably part of his crew.''

"It might help if we knew who they thought they snatched in the parking lot last night," Lucas said.

"Tell me about it," Tracker said.

"The D.C. police think that there have been two attempts to snatch Mac here because of her research. So it's probable that whoever took Sophie last night thinks they have Mac. When she wasn't in her apartment on Thursday morning, they could have traced her eventually the same way we did."

"Yeah. And they have every right to think they have Dr. Lloyd," Tracker pointed out. "Sophie was registered as the doc and she was dressed up impersonating the doc. Plus she was using the doc's credit card at the bar."

"But if Sonny dated Sophie in D.C., he might have seen through her disguise last night," Mac said. "In those wigs, we do look a lot alike. But if I was wearing the blond wig right now, you'd still know it was me."

Lucas turned to her. "What are you saying?"

"Only that if Sonny thought he was dating me and had an inside track to my research, and he suddenly found out that Sophie wasn't me…"

"He could have snatched her in the heat of the moment, so to speak, and he could be using her as a pawn," Tracker said. "She's got a point."

"Looking at it objectively as possible, there's only one fact we can be sure of. Sophie was taken last night in that silver van," Mac said. "The rest is just theory. We won't know if it's true until we test it. Therefore, it's only logical that you take me along to the party because that will give you so much more flexibility in solving the problem. If I have to, I can sign papers on the spot, give them what they want, and we can walk out of there with Sophie."

Lucas stared at her. "But you don't want to sign those papers."

She met his gaze steadily. "Sophie wouldn't be in this situation if it weren't for me. Everything you said to me in

Florida was true. I did lie to you. I didn't tell you the whole truth. If I had, she wouldn't be where she is right now."

"Mac—" Lucas began.

"She's my best friend and I love her."

There was a beat of silence. Mac thought she saw something in his eyes, but then it was gone.

"You can't fault her logic," Tracker said.

"Thank you." Mac sent him a crooked smile.

"Anytime," Tracker said. "You gonna finish your home fries?"

Mac pushed her plate toward him.

"You hardly ate anything," Lucas said with a frown.

"I ate a lot," Mac said. "I knocked at least two inches off the top of this mountain."

"No bickering, kids," Tracker managed to say around a mouthful. "Whoever they think they've got, the way I see it, our job is to get in there and get her out."

"The question is how to do that," Lucas said.

Tracker sighed. "You always ask the tough questions."

"There ought to be a lot of confusion when I show up as the real Dr. MacKenzie Lloyd."

"No." Tracker and Lucas spoke in unison.

"You can make your move then, while I'm distracting them," Mac insisted.

"You can't show up as yourself. It's too risky. And it could put Sophie in even more danger," Lucas said.

"Then I'll come as Sally."

"Sally?"

"Sally made quite an impression on the staff at the Wainright Casa Marina. Lucas even introduced me as his wife," Mac said. "I bet Mr. Falcone won't be surprised if you bring me. And I can help."

"She could be right," Tracker said.

Lucas hesitated for a moment, then said, "We'll have to lay down some ground rules."

18

_____

IT WAS NEARLY DAWN when Lucas rose and slipped from the bed. Moving quietly, he went into the living room of the suite at the St. Francis. Through the wide expanse of window, he could see the lights winking on the Golden Gate Bridge.

A quick glance at his watch told him that it would be at least four hours before Tracker would arrive, and the time could best be utilized by sleeping.

But sleep did not seem to be a possibility as long as he was in the same bed with Mac. He couldn't seem to be anywhere near her and not make love to her. It hadn't even mattered that she'd been asleep when he'd finally lost the battle he'd been waging with himself and crawled in next to her. Immediately she'd snuggled her backside into him so that they were lying side by side, nestled like spoons in a drawer. And immediately, his body had responded, growing hard.

It had been the same trusting way she'd slept with him in Florida, except, this time, he hadn't been gentleman enough to just watch her. Just thinking of how he'd slipped his arms around her and eased his hand beneath the elastic of her panties was enough to have his body hardening all over again.

She'd been so soft and warm, as if she'd been waiting just for him. She'd hadn't awakened right away, moving only slightly as he'd eased her panties off. She'd stirred again as he'd probed her from behind and then entered her. But she'd only fully surfaced when he'd begun to thrust into her with long, slow strokes. Even now he could hear her soft cries, urging him, pleading with him to go faster.

He hadn't.

Instead, he'd touched her, brushing his fingers under her breasts and lightly over her nipples, then down her torso and lower. Then he would begin the whole process again. He'd purposely kept the pace slow, building the pleasure and then retreating until it had become so intense that neither one of them could bear it. Only then had he allowed her to climax. When she'd cried out his name, he'd finally sought his own release.

Afterward, she hadn't been able to stop trembling. He'd held her close until she'd drifted off to sleep again. It had occurred to him that he could have gone on holding her just that way for a very long time.

The problem was that while his mind had found some kind of contentment, his body hadn't. She'd barely dozed off when he'd wanted to wake her again.

Lucas made his way to the couch. He couldn't stay in the same bed with her and not want to take her again. And again. At least if he stayed on the couch, one of them could get some sleep. He frowned down at the cramped space thoughtfully. Maybe if he hung his feet over one edge, and his head over the other...

Settling himself on the sofa, he twisted one way, turned the other, then tucked one arm beneath his head.

In his mind, he tried to focus on the plan that Tracker had outlined before they'd left the diner—where Mac had barely touched her food, he recalled with a frown. Of course, the food there hadn't been the best introduction to San Francisco cuisine, he thought ruefully. He could think of several restaurants he wanted to take her to the next time they visited.

The next time?

The two words had him rising again and pacing to the window. Oh, there was going to be a next time, all right. He was going to make it happen.

Because he was almost sure he was falling in love with her.

Slowly, he lowered himself to the arm of a chair. If it hadn't been directly behind him, he might have sat down right on the floor. He hadn't planned on falling in love. In fact, he'd spent most of his life making sure that it would never happen.

Hadn't his father always said that it was more fun when it sort of sneaked up on you and blindsided you? He'd always thought his father a fool for letting it just happen—for not building up a sort of protective armor against it.

His own armor hadn't been able to stand up against Mac.

And just how did she feel about him? Oh, she was enjoying the sex part. There wasn't enough dishonesty in her to be faking that. And, after all, that had been what her whole little experiment had been about—acquiring the skill that it would take to keep a man's eye from wandering.

But he hadn't been thinking about contributing to her research on the plane or just now in the bedroom.

All he'd been thinking about was Mac. There were so many women inside her. Not only was she Dr. Lloyd, the focused, serious-minded scientist, but she was also Mac, who wouldn't be left behind when her best friend was in danger. She had the loyal, nurturing nature of Lania, yet there was a very passionately playful and reckless side to her that was very much like Sally.

His gaze shifted to the bedroom door. And there was also a part of her who was Fiona—a part that desperately needed to be loved, without restraint, without inhibitions.

And heaven help him, he was in love with all of them.

Rising, he moved back to the sofa and stretched out on it again. He would do something about that once he made sure that both Sophie and Mac were safe. Twisting, he settled himself into the cushions. He had an idea that rescuing his sister was going to be an easier task than getting a restful night's sleep on a piece of furniture that seemed to be designed for children.

VOICES PIERCED the dream Sophie was having.

"She's got to be awake. It's been over twenty-four hours."

Instantly, she tried to clear her mind. How long had she slept? It was hotter now than the last time she'd awakened. In her earlier investigation, she'd figured out that she was lying on burlap bags filled with sand. And the place where she was being held was isolated. All she'd heard besides the voices of her captors was the sound of birds and the buzz of insects.

The floor beneath her shook.

"The drug we gave her was more powerful than we thought."

The man who'd spoken was so close she could smell his breath. Strong hands gripped her shoulders and drew her into a sitting position.

"She's faking."

Sophie couldn't prevent the wince when the blow struck her cheek.

"C'mon, lady. Wake up." The hands on her shoulders shook her roughly.

"I need her signature on the papers."

She hadn't heard that voice before; it didn't belong to either of her captors. Suddenly, Sophie frowned. Or had she? There was something familiar...

Hands shook her again until her head snapped. She felt the wig being pulled off.

"You fools."

She knew that voice. Where had she heard it before?

"You've got the wrong woman."

"HOW LOVELY," Mac said as the limo Lucas had hired wound its way along a drive banked on either side by multicolored flowers. Even as she said the words, she knew they were inadequate. Lavish was closer to the mark. And the place was certainly well guarded. They'd been stopped at a set of heavy iron gates, and a uniformed security guard had verified their invitation by calling the main house.

The buildings where the wine was made were just as Tracker had described them, sleek and modern in structure, their tall gray windows glinting in the afternoon sun. But it was the villa itself that had sparked her comment. The modern, three-story structure of gray wood and glass was large enough to be a small hotel.

"Falcone has some very lucrative business interests," Lucas said.

Mac blinked. It was the first sentence Lucas had addressed directly to her since they'd been in the diner the night before. He hadn't even spoken when he'd come to her bed and made love to her.

Made love to her. That's what it had felt like. Everything he'd done to her on the plane and in the hotel last night had *felt* as if he was making love. Last night he'd been so tender, so gentle that she'd thought it was a dream at first. And it had been so erotic. No one had ever done anything like that to her. Just thinking about it had her blood heating and her body melting again.

Then he'd left—without a word.

When she'd awakened, the bed had been empty. But his scent was still on her skin and on the pillow next to hers. She'd found him in the suite devouring another huge breakfast with Tracker.

It was then that she'd made herself face facts—a scientist wasn't worth her weight in salt unless she did that. Whatever they'd shared in the past few days had been just sex to him. He'd agreed to help her with her research, and he desired her. That did not equal love. She'd learned from her research that emotions didn't have to play much of a role when it came to men and sex.

Of course, she'd made it equally clear at the outset that she neither wanted nor expected anything more than to experiment on him like a guinea pig.

She hadn't wanted and she hadn't expected to fall in love with him.

"You know what to do?" Tracker asked from where he sat in the limo.

"Hmm?" Dragging her eyes away from Lucas, she turned to him.

"You know what to do?" he repeated.

"Yes," she said. A moron could have played the part they'd created for her. She was to be "Sally Maxwell," a woman Lucas was currently too infatuated with to leave behind at his hotel. Her dress was more conservative than what the Key West "Sally" might have worn. And she wasn't supposed to do anything to draw attention to herself. But since Falcone had invited her, it wouldn't cause much speculation if "Sally" was to appear as Lucas's guest.

And Tracker's role was to play her brother, Jerry. Turning, Mac checked out Tracker's disguise again. In her opinion, it was perfect. She barely recognized the man who'd sat across from her in the diner last night. "Jerry" was slighter in build. She would have sworn to it in court. His hair was long enough to be pulled back in a ponytail and he wore a diamond stud in his left ear. She would have guessed he was gay. Not Tracker, but this man who was supposed to be her brother was definitely effeminate in the way he talked and walked.

"At some point, Falcone will want to see me alone," Lucas said.

"And that's my cue to mix with the crowd. I'll introduce myself to men. That's the kind of friendly girl Sally is," Mac said.

"While you keep yourself highly visible among the guests, I sneak off to the upper floors and investigate," Tracker finished as the limo pulled to a stop in front of the house. "The moment I find Sophie, I'll take her out. Once we're clear of the estate, I'll call Lucas."

Lucas turned to Mac. "I don't like leaving you alone. As soon as Falcone and I finish our business, I'll come for you. Until then, stay with the other guests. There's always the chance that he'll guess who you really are. The man's smart. I'm banking on the fact that he's not likely to try anything where there are witnesses.''

"I don't see why I can't slip away to look for Sophie too. We'd have a better chance of finding her."

"We've been over that," Lucas said. "Falcone will have someone watching all of us. It will be difficult enough for Tracker to—"

Whatever else Lucas would have said was cut off when the driver of the limo opened the door. Tracker slid out first. Mac had one foot on the ground when she caught a glimpse of a tall man with a mane of white hair walking down a shallow set of steps to greet them. She could feel Lucas stiffen behind her just before his arms gripped her shoulders and turned her back toward him.

"Follow orders," he warned in a low voice. Then without warning, his mouth covered hers. The kiss was hard and thorough. And her response was immediate. Her thoughts seemed to explode, then fade into nothing, drowned out by the beat of her heart. She had to get closer. Her hands moved to his shoulders and into his hair. There was no one, nothing but him.

He released her so suddenly that she blinked. Then he was urging her out of the car. As the man she'd spotted earlier reached them and Lucas made the introductions, she concentrated on breathing and keeping her balance.

"Lucas. Welcome, my dear boy." Vincent Falcone enveloped Lucas in a hug. "And I completely understand why you brought Ms. Maxwell. I wouldn't have left her behind at a hotel either."

"I knew you'd understand, and since you mentioned her…" Lucas ran his hand down her arm in a lingering, possessive stroke.

He'd only kissed her for show. Everything he was doing was an act to impress Falcone. Pushing the hurt and the anger down, Mac concentrated on Sophie.

"Anyone you wish to bring is welcome. I want you to think of my home as yours." Turning to Mac, he extended his arm, then waited for her to place her hand on it. "First, Ms. Maxwell, I want you to meet some of my guests. Then while Lucas and I discuss a little business, perhaps you and your brother can enjoy the party?"

She gave him her best "Sally" smile. The sooner he pried Lucas loose from her, the sooner she could look for Sophie. "We'd be delighted."

"Lucas is a very lucky man," Falcone said as he led them into the house.

LUCAS HELD HIS GLASS up to the light pouring through the glass windows of Vincent Falcone's office. From here, he could see the multicolored tents on the lawn, the rows upon rows of vines fanning out beyond and the winery buildings to his far right.

He took a sip of the pale, gold-green liquid.

"What do you think?" Vincent asked.

"It's quite nice, but I think you didn't ask me in here to solicit my opinion on your prize-winning chardonnay."

Vincent sighed. "Do you ever take a break from business?"

Lucas raised his eyebrows. "Isn't that what you invited me in here to discuss? I'd like to conclude it as quickly as possible."

"Ah, yes. You wish to return to your Sally. A charming girl. Perhaps this will ease your concerns." Moving to a wall, he pushed a button and the panel of a Renoir print slipped silently out of sight. The clear glass that remained offered a view of the main room of the house.

Tracker was talking to a tall blond woman, Falcone's hostess for the party. It took him a second longer to find Mac who was laughing at something an older gentleman was saying, her hand on his arm. He could almost hear the sound of her laughter in his ear. When the man leaned down to whisper in hers, he felt a sharp stab in his gut.

"She's not your usual type," Vincent said.

Lucas set his glass down with a snap. "That is not the topic of our business either."

"Your grandfather would have liked her," Vincent said.

"What would you know—" Lucas caught himself. What was the matter with him? Mac was flirting with that old man because that was what she was supposed to do. This was the second time that he'd let her distract him. He never should have grabbed and kissed her like that in the limo. It was out of character for him, and it was just the thing that would put Falcone on the alert. He'd better keep his mind on what he had to do. Shifting his gaze to Falcone, he said, "I didn't come in here with you to discuss my grandfather either."

"That's where you're wrong. Our business begins and ends with him." Moving to another painting on the wall, he pushed it aside and began to turn the knob on a small safe. When it was open, he extracted an envelope and held it out to Lucas. "Read this first and then we'll talk."

"Tiny Morelli's the name, and you are?"

Mac felt her hand gripped in a vise. When she glanced up, her first thought was that the name was a misnomer. Tiny Morelli was huge. He towered at least a foot above her and his hand was easily the length of her forearm.

"Sally Maxwell."

"Ever been to the Napa Valley before?"

"No." Tiny was the third man who'd gravitated to her since Lucas had disappeared with Vincent Falcone. This one was younger than the other two. But it didn't seem to matter. "Sally" was a definite man magnet. There didn't seem to be a male in the room who was immune to a woman in a short skirt, a top that showed cleavage and very high heels.

Added to that, she was a stranger. If she'd doubted the validity of her male-fantasy research before, she certainly didn't now. A week ago, this verification would have thrilled her.

"How about a dance, sugar?"

"I can't leave. My fiancé made me promise to stay here."

"Then we'll dance right here."

Mac blinked and stared. The only music in the room came from a string quartet. "It's a little hard to dance to Mozart."

"We'll improvise," Tiny said, placing his wineglass on the tray of a passing waiter. "I got some moves we'll both enjoy."

She just bet he did. Out of the corner of her eye, she noticed that Tracker had worked his way to the archway that led to the hall. He was nearly home free. Trying to ignore the quick stab of envy, she turned up the wattage on her smile and flicked her gaze back to the man whose fingers were now sliding up the inside of her arm. The one thing she wasn't supposed to do was call attention to herself.

"I shouldn't really," she pointed out. "My fiancé wouldn't like it."

"Who cares?" he murmured as he leaned a little closer. Then to her astonishment, she felt the backs of his fingers brush very deliberately along the side of her breast. She took a quick step back into a waiter. Wineglasses clinked and jiggled on his tray, and one dropped to the floor. In the midst of the confusion, Mac upended the contents of hers down the front of Tiny's shirt.

"I'm so sorry," she said.

"Why, you little..." Tiny paused to glare at her as he searched for a word. "You did that on purpose."

Mac lifted her chin. "That's not a very nice thing to accuse a lady of."

"Sally, my dear, is there a problem?"

Mac turned to find Tracker pushing through a circle of people. "I spilled my wine."

"She poured it over me on purpose," Tiny maintained.

Whipping out a hankie, Tracker began to brush it down the front of Tiny's shirt. "You're so lucky it was white wine. Red wine stains are so difficult to take out." Pausing, he ran his finger down the cloth. "Oh my. This is silk. And chardonnays have been known to leave a mark."

The man slapped Tracker's hand away. "Leave it, will you?"

Tracker made a tsking sound. "Just to be sure, you should rinse it immediately with cold water." He gave the shirt one last brush with his hankie. "I can show you where the men's room is."

"Never mind," Tiny said, backing away. "I can find it on my own."

"You weren't supposed to create a scene," Tracker said under his breath as he took her arm and parted a way for them through the little crowd that had gathered.

"I don't like to be fondled in public," she said. Then it occurred to her that she'd just told an outright lie. Hadn't Lucas touched her almost as intimately in front of Vincent Falcone? "At least not by strangers."

"C'mon, let's get you a breath of fresh air." Taking her arm, Tracker guided her through a glass door to a redwood deck.

"I'm sorry."

"The boss has you rattled, doesn't he?"

She sighed as she turned to him. "Yes. But I shouldn't be letting it interfere. I should be able to put it out of my mind until we find—" Cutting herself off, she glanced quickly around. They were alone on one of the wide decks she'd spotted from the limo. Beyond Tracker's shoulder, she could see the flight of steps that led to the upper levels. Shifting her eyes back to Tracker, she said, "In the lab, I never lose my focus."

"He's rattled too, if that helps. As far as making my escape goes, I think we've just found a better way to get to the upper levels of this little hotel. C'mon."

"I'm supposed to keep myself visible," Mac said. The stairs looked steeper and steeper as they drew closer to them.

"Been there. Done that," Tracker said as he began to climb. "And since you've called a little too much attention to yourself, it's time for plan B. Besides, I think you're safer with me right now than you are with Tiny."

"But we can be seen by anyone who glances this way." Drawing in a deep breath, she took the first step, then the second. This was what she wanted, wasn't it? She wanted to help find Sophie.

"It's the best kind of cover," he explained in a low tone as he turned to draw her up the last steps. "If someone asks, we're just trying to get a better view of the whole estate." He guided her toward the railing and raised his voice. "Mr. Falcone wanted us to make ourselves at home. And the view is so much better from here. Look, there's even a telescope we can use."

Mac was sure that the view was incredible, but it was hard to enjoy it with the way her stomach had started to pitch and roll. She gripped the edge of the railing.

Tracker leaned close and whispered, "One of the glass doors behind us is ajar. I'm going to wander in, then check out the room and the floor. You stay here and keep watch. Any trouble, you head down to the party. Okay?"

"Sure." Mac managed a nod. She wasn't sure she could get back down the stairs, but she wasn't going to keep Tracker from doing his job.

In a louder voice, he said, "Nature is calling, sweetie. Be right back."

Mac kept her eyes directly in front of her as Tracker slipped away. The view was spectacular. If she kept her attention focused on that, the dizziness would fade. From this level, she could see the neat patterns that the rows of vines made as they crisscrossed in the distance. She let her gaze follow one pattern into the next as she drew in deep breaths and let them out. Any minute now, the queasiness would pass. Out of the corner of her eye, she caught a flash of color.

Turning, she saw just the edge of a colored cloth spread across the grass. She inched her way along the railing as it curved around the side of the house until she spotted the baskets and the splashes of colored silk. Deflated hot-air balloons.

Sophie had mentioned taking a ride in one—how long ago? Two days? Mac recalled the excitement in her friend's voice, and now she wondered if Sophie would ever...

No, she wasn't going to let herself think that way. They were going to find Sophie. She was going to be all right. Tracker could be finding her right now.

Suddenly, she narrowed her eyes. She'd just seen it again, that flash of color. Something had caused one of the swatches of red and green silk spread along the ground to ripple a little. That was what must have caught her eye a few moments ago.

What was causing it? There wasn't any wind, but she was sure she'd seen the cloth move. She waited and watched.

"What in hell am I supposed to do now?"

The sudden break in the silence made Mac jump. It was coming from the section of the deck below her where she and Tracker had been standing only moments before. And the voice was familiar.

"I promised my father that I would have exclusive rights to MacKenzie Lloyd's research by today. You promised me that I would."

"Look. I was sure that you would have it too. But you know how difficult she is to deal with."

Mac's hands tightened on the railing. The second voice was more than familiar; she recognized it instantly. Leaning over the railing, she confirmed what she already knew. The second man was Professor Gil Stafford, her department chair at the university. And the first was Vincent Smith, the representative from Lansing Biotech who'd dated her in the hopes that she'd sign with his company.

"You assured me it was a done deal," Vincent said.

"It's just a minor glitch. She left town unexpectedly. Once I can get her out here, she'll sign the papers. I guarantee it." Gil Stafford's voice was as smooth as an oil slick, and just as dangerous.

"You've been wrong about her before. You told me that all I would have to do was get her to fall in love with me and she would sign everything over to Lansing Biotech. That didn't work. And I've guaranteed my father that he can make this announcement today."

"Calm down, Sonny."

Another wave of dizziness hit at the same instant that everything clicked in Mac's mind. She pulled her head up slowly and focused on the colorful balloon silk in the distance. The man who had introduced himself to her and romanced her as Vincent Smith of Lansing Biotech had to be none other than Sonny Falcone. She took a deep breath and let it out.

What name had he used when he'd been dating Sophie? she wondered. Then she clamped down ruthlessly on the hysterical bubble of laughter that threatened to erupt. There would be time to laugh with Sophie later. Right now she had to listen and think.

"I admit I misjudged Dr. Lloyd at first. When she turned down the money you were offering, I thought she might be persuaded by romance. She's such a little mouse. But everyone has a price." Gil's tone was soothing, his laugh soft. "I now have something that she wants—something that she will do anything to get back. I guarantee it."

"Then why isn't she here, signing the papers right now?"

"I told you. I have to get her out here first."

For the first time, Mac heard a hint of anger and frustration in Gil Stafford's voice.

"The important thing is not to let your father know that

there's a problem, right?'' Gil said. ''No need in getting him all upset when everything will work out in the end.''

''As long as you're sure...''

''When he calls you into his office, just tell him that the paperwork will be here shortly. Dr. Lloyd is sending it by special messenger.''

Mac heard footsteps then. They were taking the outside stairs to the lower level. As the voices faded, she focused her eyes on the bright silk cloth. This time it wasn't the thoughts spinning around in her head or even the height of the deck that was making her dizzy. It was the fear blooming inside her. If Gil Stafford had something she wanted, it must mean that he had Sophie—and he knew it was her.

Just then the silk rippled. And this time she saw what was causing it. One of the baskets had swayed, tipping one way and then righting itself.

Moving quickly to the telescope, she focused it on the balloon. Someone had to be in it, making it move. Then she caught a glimpse of a head with blond hair. Sophie?

Whirling, she made her way to the stairs. Two flights. The moment she glanced down, the panic slammed into her and stopped her short. Closing her eyes, she gripped the railing and took a steadying breath. But it didn't seem to help.

There was a sliding glass door behind her. She could go back into the house and find Tracker. But that would take time. And Sophie—if it had been Sophie that she'd seen— needed her help now.

I've been promised a balloon ride. The words slipped into her mind as clearly as if Sophie had spoken them aloud. She'd said them the first time she'd called from the spa. Except she'd been here in California.

Keeping her eyes closed, Mac took another deep breath and let it out. This time she wasn't going to let the fear stop her. All she had to do was take the stairs one step at a time. Gripping the railing, she placed her foot on the first one.

19

LUCAS COULD HEAR the ticking of the clock on Vincent Falcone's desk as he read the letter for the second time.

My dear Ham,
  If you are reading this, it means that my friend Vince is calling in an old debt. Since I owe him my life, I hope you will find it possible to grant him his request.

All my love,
Green Eggs

The words hadn't changed since the first time he'd read them. As always his grandfather had been brief. Lucas Wainright believed that brevity was one of the cardinal virtues. But the conciseness of the letter wasn't the only detail convincing him that it was authentic. The signature, too, was his grandfather's. Of course, Falcone was resourceful enough to hire an excellent forger. But as far as Lucas knew, no one else had ever known the secret code name his grandfather and he had used whenever they had gone on one of their private vacations to the cabin.

So this had been the source of the slow, sinking certainty in his gut he'd been experiencing ever since Falcone had walked out of his office that day—the one that always told him when his opponent had something up his sleeve. At least it was good to know that his instincts weren't failing him.

Raising his eyes from the letter, Lucas looked at the older

man. He was standing at the drawn curtain, gazing at the group of people he'd gathered together to celebrate the fifth anniversary of the vineyard. The ruler surveying his happy subjects. That was what he should have looked like in his moment of triumph. But to Lucas, Vincent Falcone suddenly seemed older and more frail. He was reminded of the way his grandfather had looked shortly before he'd died.

Shaking the impression off, he said, ''My grandfather owed you his life.''

Falcone threw back his head and laughed, and a sound of genuine amusement filled the room as he turned to face Lucas. ''You are so very much like him. You accept the facts and cut right to the heart of the matter. No quibbling. Your father would have argued forever, questioning the authenticity of the letter, arguing that he wasn't bound by it.''

Lucas shrugged. ''I'm pretty certain my grandfather wrote it.''

Falcone moved toward him and took the seat behind his desk. The negotiations were about to begin, Lucas thought.

''I could give you some time. If you check, you'll find his prints on both the note and the envelope, along with your own. I've always used gloves when I've touched it. And the handwriting will also check out.''

When Lucas said nothing, the older man said, ''And, yes, I did save your grandfather's life. We fought in the same unit in France. We were very young, barely eighteen. I have no proof of that, by the way. Only the two of us knew about it.''

Lucas's eyes narrowed. ''What happened?''

''We were the last two left in a bunker. Everyone else in our unit had been shot or had made a run for it. The shelling was heavy and the hits were getting closer.'' Vincent Falcone leaned back in his chair, a half smile of remembrance on his face. ''I knew we were just sitting ducks and I wanted to get out. Your grandfather felt it was safer to stay. We had a fight. Luckily, I knocked him out, then carried him with me to safety. The bunker was leveled about ten minutes after we cleared out.''

Lucas nodded. His grandfather had told him the story more than once—about the man who hadn't been afraid to take a risk. He'd credited the man, not only with saving his life, but with showing him how to live it.

And that man was Vincent Falcone, a man he'd viewed as an enemy for the past five years. ''Did my father receive one of the letters too? Is that how he came to get mixed up with you?''

Falcone shook his head. ''Your grandfather wrote only one letter. He sent it to me shortly before he died. It wasn't long after that your father came to me and asked for money.''

''Which you were only too happy to lend him.''

''It served my interests well. I won't mince words. Your father was a weak man.'' He turned a hand over, palm upward. ''The strong will always take advantage of the weak.''

Lucas folded his grandfather's letter and put it back into the envelope. ''What do you want?''

Falcone's lips curved. ''You might as well be your grandfather's clone.''

''Then you know that I will not let you back into Wainright Enterprises.'' He placed the envelope between them on the desk. ''My grandfather would not have asked me to do that.''

''No, he wouldn't.''

''So?'' Lucas asked. ''Play your hole card.''

For a moment, Falcone studied him, eyes narrowing. Then once again, Lucas thought he caught a glimpse of frailty. Finally, the older man said, ''I have a favor I want to ask you. No, it's a favor I want to collect from you. My doctors tell me that I am going to die within the year.''

Lucas managed to keep his astonishment masked. Whatever he'd expected to hear when he'd followed Falcone into the office, it hadn't been this. What kind of game was the old man playing?

"I've been making certain preparations. One step is that I've sold off all my business interests that are not what you might refer to as legitimate."

Lucas said nothing.

"Your grandfather and I never associated publicly after we came home from the war, but we kept in touch over the years. I took a few vacations with him on that island of his. He used to talk about how he was disappointed in his son, your father. He said that the future of Wainright Enterprises would depend on you. I have come to accept that the future of the Falcone fortunes will depend on my grandchild."

Lucas's eyes narrowed. "Sonny is…?"

The older man rose from his desk and moved toward the one-way glass. "No, my grandchild hasn't been conceived yet. I won't live to see him. Or her. I had hopes that perhaps Sonny and your sister would hit it off. He's a nice enough looking young man."

Lucas followed the direction of Falcone's gaze and saw that Sonny had joined the gathering in the other room.

"He didn't have any more luck with her than he seems to be having at Lansing Biotech. I thought for a while he was on the right track there. He hired a research scientist as a consultant. It's what I would have done. That's him, the tall blond man right there next to my son. According to Sonny, they're very close to getting exclusive rights to some very important research."

"What kind of research?" Lucas asked. But it was beginning to take some effort to remain patient and play the dupe.

Falcone waved a hand. "Something on slowing down the aging process. I had it checked into, and the research was indeed legitimate and very promising. It's also on the up-and-up to have these scientists sign these contracts. Lansing Biotech finances some of the cost of the research in return for exclusive rights to manufacture any results in the future. Sonny was supposed to have all the papers signed so that I could make the announcement today.''

''But he doesn't.''

''We wouldn't be having this conversation if he did.''

''What exactly is it that you want me to do?'' Lucas asked.

Vincent Falcone met his eyes, and there was no trace of the frailty he'd glimpsed earlier. ''I want you to take Sonny under your wing and make sure that my two remaining businesses prosper until one of my grandchildren can take over. Sonny swore he'd prove to me that he was capable of running both business's, but he's made a mess of it. I advanced him some money—told him to show me what he could do with it to increase profits here at the vineyard. He bought hot-air balloons.''

''Balloons?'' Lucas asked.

''My reaction exactly. He could have used the money for research, he could have imported some old vines from France or Italy. Instead, he bought hot-air balloons so that he could offer the tourists who stop by an aerial tour of the valley.'' Falcone sighed. ''But that's not the worst of it. To be perfectly honest, he's gotten himself into a bit of a scrape.''

Finally, Lucas thought. We're getting to the hole card.

''The simplest way to put it is that I believe he's kidnapped that young scientist who was at your house party last weekend, and I need your help.''

Lucas studied the older man for a moment, trying to come to a decision. Vincent Falcone was a consummate actor, but the request seemed to be costing him. In the end he decided to trust the man who had saved his grandfather's life. ''Do you know where she is now?''

Falcone shook his head. ''I had some men keeping an eye on her, but they lost her last night. She met my son at a restaurant, the Side Street Grill. One minute she was talking to him, then she went to the ladies' room and never came back. She hasn't been back to her hotel either.''

"And you think your son is involved?" Lucas asked.

"He told me he was going to have her signature on a contract by today. He also told me that he would be bringing your sister to this party. Neither event has come to pass yet. In his effort to prove himself to me, he may have panicked. Look at him. Does he look like he has good news to tell me?''

Lucas did just that. Sonny didn't look happy. Neither did the man standing next to him as he stopped a passing waiter to exchange an empty glass for a full one.

Lucas scanned the room. There was no sign of Tracker or Mac. "Tell me everything else you know."

As SHE NEARED the end of the row of vines she'd been following, Mac paused to catch her breath. The clearing with the balloons had been a lot farther away than it had appeared to be from the deck, and Sally's shoes were not made for running.

During the time it had taken her to get there, all four balloons had become bright balls of color in the air.

Keeping her head down, Mac inched her way to the edge of the row. Her stomach sank. The four balloon baskets floated about fifteen feet in the air. A rope ladder hung from each one, and other ropes anchored each to the ground.

Her gaze lingered on the red-and-green one. There was no way to tell if the person she'd spotted from the deck was still in there.

"What the hell were you thinking?"

The deep voice had Mac ducking low and flattening herself against the nearest grapevine.

"They said they had orders from Sonny Falcone to get the balloons in the air. There were two of them and only one of me. What was I supposed to do?"

"You didn't have to help them."

"At least I kept them from discovering the girl. And I

convinced them to take a break and get some beers in the kitchen.''

There were a few beats of silence. Mac waited, hardly daring to breathe.

''They'll discover her soon enough once they start offering the party guests rides.''

''I'm getting out of here.''

''You can't. All we have to do is get her out of there. Stash her someplace else.''

''You want to hang around and have somebody catch you? Fine. But I've got a feeling that this whole job is going south. First, he tells us we've kidnapped the wrong girl. Then he wants us to keep her here in this damn basket until the right one comes calling. I'm hitting the road.''

Mac held her breath while she counted the receding footsteps of the man who'd just spoken.

''Hell, wait up… Wait up, I said.''

Mac waited, counting to ten as the sound of the footsteps faded. In the distance, she could hear the music of the band. Closer, she could hear the drone of insects. Just to make sure, she counted to ten again. Then she straightened and raced across the clearing to the red-and-green balloon.

It appeared to be even higher off the ground than she'd first thought.

''Sophie,'' she called.

There was no answer.

She tried again. ''Sophie.''

There was still no answer.

20

"SHE WASN'T SUPPOSED to leave the room," Lucas said, more to himself than to Tracker. "All she had to do was mingle. She wasn't supposed to call attention to herself. She sure as hell wasn't supposed to dump a glass of wine over one of Falcone's guests."

"It was my fault she left the room," Tracker said as he pulled on the steering wheel and took the jeep Vincent Falcone had lent them into a two-wheeled turn. Once the vehicle had stabilized, he continued, "But I told her to stay put on that deck until I got back."

"She never does anything you tell her. She can't even do what you expect her to do. She's..." It occurred to Lucas that he didn't have a word that would describe Mac. He might never have one.

"She'll be fine," Tracker said.

Lucas wished he could believe that. It was Tracker who'd spotted her through the telescope from the upper deck of the villa. The quick surge of relief had given way to a sharp stab of fear as he'd watched her start up one of the rope ladders attached to a balloon.

"She's found Sophie," Tracker had said.

It made sense, Lucas thought. She'd no doubt spotted something through the telescope and taken off. Thank God Tracker was thinking clearly, because he wasn't. He couldn't rid his mind of the image of Mac climbing up that rope ladder.

"How much farther?"

Tracker merely grunted as he dragged the Jeep into another two-wheeled turn that shot them off in another direction. Vincent Falcone had given them directions to the clearing, but the dirt road zigged and zagged, slowing their progress.

They didn't seem to be getting any closer. Fear ate like acid in the back of Lucas's throat.

"She was alone," Tracker said. "There was no one else in the clearing."

Lucas tightened his grip on the side of the Jeep. "We saw her. Someone else could have seen her too."

"Falcone's got Sonny in his study."

What Tracker didn't say, what neither of them had spoken aloud, was that Sonny had denied everything hotly. Oh, he'd admitted to wining and dining both women—the doctor because he wanted her name on a contract and Sophie to please his father. That much Tracker had intimidated out of him. He'd even confessed that he'd talked to a redhead at the Side Street Grill. But it hadn't been MacKenzie Lloyd. On that point he'd been adamant.

"You think Sonny's behind this?" Lucas asked as Tracker eased up on the gas.

"That boy's as dumb as a rock," Tracker said.

Under other circumstances Lucas might have grinned. "We're on the same page there."

"Beats me that he had the business savvy to want to sign Mac in the first place."

"My thought exactly," Lucas said.

The Jeep careened around another curve. Dust spewed up, tires spun, then gripped the dirt again.

"You're thinking little Sonny might have a silent partner that he doesn't want to talk about in front of Daddy."

"Bingo. Pull over here. We'll go the rest of the way on foot."

CLOSING HER EYES, Mac wiped one damp hand on her skirt, then gripped the next rung of the rope ladder. Her heart was beating so loudly that she could hear it above the sound of the band in the distance. She had no idea how high she'd climbed, and she wasn't sure she could go any farther.

Running back to the villa for help just hadn't been an option. There was no time. Sophie might be hurt.

Reaching up, Mac wrapped her hands around the rope. Every instinct she had told her that Sophie was here, and she had to get her out. *One step at a time. Just one.* This was the easy part. She wasn't even going to think about climbing down. Drawing in a deep breath, she moved her hands and her feet to the next rung. The moment the swaying stopped and the rope steadied, she made herself repeat the process.

"You can stop right where you are."

Mac recognized Gil Stafford's voice immediately. And this time she felt what she hadn't allowed herself to feel before—anger.

"Turn around."

She clamped down on her anger just as she had on her fear. Then she made herself face Gil. The gun in his hand was pointed at her. When the nausea hit, she pushed it away and concentrated on his face. If her disguise worked, she might have a chance.

"MacKenzie, I've been waiting for you."

His voice was soft, the tone falsely welcoming. It was the look of hatred in Gil Stafford's eyes more than the gun in his hand that sent an icy shiver sliding up her spine.

"Gil. What are you doing here?"

"I think you know. I saw you climb down from the upper level of the deck." His lips curved in a smile that never made it to his eyes. "Oh, the disguise is quite good. It might have fooled even me, but I saw the way you hesitated on the stairs, the way you gripped the railing. I remembered your telling me about how frightened you were of heights. You should have worked that through with a therapist long ago. It's a dead giveaway."

Mac's chin lifted, but she clamped her lips tight on the

words that wanted to tumble out. It wouldn't do her any good to provoke a man with a gun in his hand.

"As it is, you're going to have a very scary ride ahead of you."

Mac's heart leaped to her throat as she watched him move to one of the ropes that anchored the balloon to the ground and pull it free. "What are you—"

The basket above her lurched, and she clung tightly to the ladder as it swayed crazily, swinging her back and forth.

"We're going away—you, me and your friend Sophie Wainright."

"No," Mac managed to say. Then she forced herself to open her eyes. "Gil, you have to let Sophie go. She has nothing to do with this."

Gil grabbed the bottom rung of the rope ladder and gave it a shake. "She was pretending to be you. And she ruined everything."

Sweat, cold and clammy, broke out on her skin. Mac couldn't move. For a moment, she couldn't even think. Clinging to the rope, she lifted her gaze from the ground, tried to focus on something else. Her vision grayed, the edges blurring with fear, but a movement at the edge of the vineyard registered. She made herself blink hard and saw Lucas at the edge of one of the rows of vines. If she could just stall Gil... Slowly, she lowered her eyes to his. "Why are you doing this?"

"Because your research is going to make you rich one day, and part of that money belongs to me. The school promised me time and money for my research. Then they hired you and decided to pour their money into your project. They even installed you in the lab they'd promised me."

Mac let out the breath she was holding and drew another in. She couldn't let herself look to see where Lucas was. She had to keep Gil's attention focused on her. "If you'd let me know, I would have done something."

"What?" Gil's laugh was bitter. "What would you have

done? Would you have told me you were sorry? Or given up your work, moved somewhere else?"

She stared at him. The hatred she saw in his eyes was hot and lethal. Then he moved to the second anchor rope and began to twist it free. Mac fought against a fresh wave of dizziness as the ladder swung out and in.

"Lansing Biotech was going to pay me a half-million dollars for getting your signature on a contract. But you couldn't even do that."

"If you let Sophie go, I'll sign anything you want."

Gil twisted the freed anchor rope around his wrist, then grabbed the bottom rung of the ladder. Closing her eyes, Mac held on for dear life.

"No, I have a much better plan. I think that Lucas Wainright might pay handsomely for the safety of his sister, don't you?"

"No, I won't. Drop the gun."

Gil whirled around, one hand on the rope ladder, a gun in the other. He aimed it at Lucas. "Drop yours or I'll free the balloon, and your sister and Dr. Lloyd will go for a little ride all by themselves."

Lucas stopped dead in his tracks. "All right. I'm putting it down." Bending over, he placed his weapon on the ground. "We should talk about this. You're not going to accomplish anything by letting that balloon go."

Mac felt the balloon already struggling to rise, saw the anchor rope slipping free of Gil's wrist. Frozen with fear, she watched Gil place one foot on the bottom rung of the ladder. He was going to climb up. The moment his other foot left the ground, they would be airborne.

"No," Lucas said as he moved forward.

A shot rang out.

The sound had the fear streaming through her, but Lucas didn't fall. Instead, he took another step forward.

"This time, I won't miss," Gil said as he steadied his aim.

Mac let go of the rope and jumped. She felt her body

slam into Gil's, heard another shot ring out as they both tumbled to the ground. Then the blackness enveloped her.

SOPHIE SAT on a crowded counter in Mac's kitchen, swinging her feet back and forth. "It's nice to see that everything's back to normal."

Mac looked up from the carrot she was shredding for Wilbur, then glanced around the room. It was perfectly back in order. When she'd thanked her landlord, he'd told her that someone from Wainright Enterprises had arranged to have it cleaned. Lucas.

Quickly, she pushed the name and all the images that came with it away and focused her gaze on Sophie. "Yes, everything's fine."

It was such a lie Mac wondered that her nose didn't grow three inches. Or that Sophie didn't hoot right out loud.

But all Sophie did was nod as she grabbed one of the carrots Mac was shredding. "Absolutely. Wilbur's happy you're back, you have that extra space in your lab you've always wanted, your hair's back in that unattractive bun, and you're wearing your old drab clothes. And, as a bonus, you're going to be in the *Guinness Book of World Records* for shredding five pounds of carrots in ten minutes flat."

Mac's gaze sharpened. She had a good idea where the conversation was leading, and she was going to head it off. "We agreed that we're not going to discuss your brother."

Sophie raised both hands, palms out. "I never mentioned him. Did I say his name or refer to him in anyway?"

"You said I was back in my drab clothes. The before—" She caught herself before she said his name. It hurt too much to say it out loud. *The before Lucas clothes.*

It was bad enough to think his name. She hadn't seen him since she'd taken that flying leap onto Gil Stafford. When she'd woken up in one of the guest rooms at the Falcone villa, she'd been sure that Lucas had been shot. Sophie had assured her that he was fine and dandy. And later, when Sophie had left, Tracker had stopped by to fill her in on everything that had happened. Gil Stafford had been arrested along with the two men who'd kidnapped Sophie. Even Sonny Falcone and his father had dropped in to apologize and to tell her that Lansing Biotech wouldn't pressure her anymore.

But Lucas hadn't stopped by even once. He had some loose ends to tie up, Tracker had said. That had been a week ago—seven whole days. Sophie had spent the first five badgering her to call Lucas.

But she hadn't. She couldn't. They'd agreed that when her research was over, they'd go back to their own lives. No strings.

Her whole body ached from missing him. She couldn't fall asleep without dreaming about him, without reliving every moment that they'd spent together.

"So now I can't even mention your clothes." Whipping a notebook from her purse, Sophie plucked a pen out of a nearby cup and began to scribble. "Don't mention her dreary, drab clothes even if they make you wretch. There." She glanced up at Mac. "Anything else that's off-limits?"

Mac frowned. "Don't be ridiculous. I'm sorry. I…you can talk to me about my clothes. You always have. This…" She raised her hands and dropped them. "I wish I'd never gone to that island. It's ruined everything."

"The person whose name we're not mentioning has a way of doing that. I'm annoyed with him myself." Sophie bit into a carrot and chewed. When Mac continued to shred in silence, she said, "I still don't know what was really going on down there in California. Why wasn't Sonny Falcone arrested?"

"He didn't have anything to do with the kidnapping. As I understand it, Sonny was trying desperately to prove to his father that he has the wherewithal to run both Lansing Biotech and the vineyard."

"Sonny? He didn't impress me as having a lot going for him upstairs. Well, maybe at first he did, " Sophie said. "But I was in a rebellious mood. I don't know what I was thinking when I agreed to go out there to California—except that it would be a good way to defy Lucas. Whoops!'' She slapped a hand over her mouth, then mumbled, ''Sorry. It just slipped out.'' Dropping her hand, she shot an apologetic glance at Mac. ''Anyway, to get back to Sonny. I can see him being duped by someone else. But I still don't understand what Gil Stafford hoped to gain by kidnapping me. I mean you. Your signature on a Lansing Biotech contract wouldn't have been worth anything once you explained how you were forced to sign the contract.''

''The way I understand it—and I was sworn to secrecy on this—Gil knew that the Falcone family has...I guess you'd have to say *connections* to organized crime, and he was assuming that once Sonny had my name on the contract, I would be strongly *encouraged* to cooperate.''

Sophie stared at her. ''*Encouraged* as in broken kneecaps?''

Mac shrugged. ''Something like that.''

Sophie let out a low whistle. ''I never would have figured that a man with his education and intelligence would get himself involved in something like that.''

''At first, I think his plan was just to cash in on my research. He approached Sonny and convinced him to offer me a contract on behalf of Lansing Biotech. Gil was the one who introduced me to Vincent Smith, a.k.a. Sonny, and he did everything he could to get me to sign. When his plan didn't work, Gil got desperate.''

''So he hired those two goons who kidnapped me to break into the safe at the lab?''

Mac nodded. ''He thought the formulas were in the safe. Of course, he had the combination, but he had to make it look as if someone else had done it. But the formula wasn't in the safe.''

''Why not?'' Sophie asked.

''It's the first place a thief would look, so I've always kept it at the bottom of Wilbur's cage. I can't think of anybody who'd want to look there.''

"And they searched your house too."

"Yes. And when they came up empty there, they got desperate. That's when Gil decided to hire someone to kidnap me. He figured that was the way that the Falcones would handle things. Only he figured wrong. Whatever shady connections the Falcones have had in the past, Lansing Biotech and the vineyard are one-hundred-percent legitimate businesses and Sonny's going to testify against Gil."

Sophie narrowed her eyes as she studied Mac for a moment. "You are a lot more well informed about this whole thing than I am. It sounds to me like you *have* been talking to my brother."

"No." Mac set down a nub of carrot and chose another from the plate. "Tracker told me."

Sophie's eyes widened. "Tracker McGuire? You mean you've actually been in contact with the Shadow?"

"Several times. I think he's been told to keep an eye on me. He's stopped by here and the lab almost every day." Mac felt a little band of pain tighten around her heart even as she said the words.

"Well!" The word came out on an annoyed huff of breath. "Do you think he'll be stopping by tonight?"

Mac concentrated hard on rubbing the carrot back and forth on the grater. If she just concentrated on small details, just one step, then the next, she was going to survive. Tracker's continuous visits over the past week was just one of the signs that told her she would never see Lucas again. Of course, he would want to tie up any loose ends. That was what Tracker had said he was doing in California. But she knew Lucas was distancing himself, using Tracker as his go-between. "I told him it's not necessary. I'm not in any danger. But it's very kind of…your brother to want to make sure. But everything's fine."

"Mac!"

She looked down and realized she'd grated right down to her knuckle and was now bleeding all over the grater.

"Here, let me." Sophie took Mac's hand and drew it under running water. When she was satisfied that the wounds were clean, she reached into a nearby cupboard.

"Did I ever tell you how much I hate people who are stupid?" Sophie asked as she applied disinfectant and bandages to Mac's fingers.

"Several times." Mac felt her lips curve slightly.

Sophie turned to face her. "I'm going to say this just once. You and my brother are being very stupid." At Mac's frown, she hurried on. "That's it. I don't intend to elaborate or lecture. My experience with stupid people is that you can't ever get them to change their minds. So, I've merely stated a fact."

Mac was saved from replying by the ringing of a cell phone. Both women moved toward their purses. Sophie dragged hers out on the third ring. "Yes? Okay." A frown appeared on her forehead as she listened. "Tell him I'll be there."

When she turned back to Mac, she had a smile on her face, but her shoulders were tense. "The person whose name I can't mention is arriving in D.C. this evening and wants to see me in his office tomorrow. He was too busy to lecture me in California. But that was his secretary. It turns out he had me penciled in for tomorrow, and she's just calling to confirm his calendar."

"Sophie, he loves you."

"But he's going to play big brother. That's why he isn't calling himself." She sighed. "Not that I don't deserve the lecture. My little rebellion got me kidnapped. And I don't want to think about what might have happened if Gil Stafford had let go of that rope. It seems that whatever I do, I just can't measure up to what Lucas wants."

Moving forward, Mac took Sophie's hands. "That's the way I've felt about my family my whole life—that I could never measure up. But they never really loved me. Not the way Lucas loves you."

Sophie managed a smile as she hugged Mac. "I know that. And on that note, I'm leaving."

In the doorway to the kitchen, she turned back. "But before I go, I do have a suggestion."

Mac frowned.

"Don't give me that look. It doesn't have anything to do with the person whose name I promised not to mention. I'm just going to say that since you did give your research a little field test down in the Keys, you should be ready to put it into action for real, right?"

Mac blinked. She hadn't given any thought to her fantasy research for the past week—other than reliving every single thing she'd tried out on Lucas. Without saying a word, she studied her friend. Oh, Sophie's face wore an innocent enough expression, but Mac didn't trust her. She trusted her even less as she saw puzzlement fill Sophie's eyes.

"The whole plan was geared to keep hold of a husband once you found him, wasn't it?"

"Yes." It seemed like a lifetime ago, Mac thought.

"Step one, as I recall, was to test the research."

"Yes," Mac repeated, wondering why she felt as if she was being led down the garden path.

"Then it's time for step two—finding the husband."

"Sophie, I—"

"I'll be happy to come along with you. Come on, Mac. Wilbur's got enough carrots there to keep him going for a month. It's high time you got dressed up in some of your fantasy clothes from Madame Gervaise and we did a little manhunting in Georgetown."

"Soph—"

Sophie cut her off with a raised hand. "I'm not taking no for an answer. The best way to get over a man is to move on to the next one. We've both been through a rough time, and we need to do this for ourselves."

Mac might have said no, but she could see that Sophie needed it too. "Okay."

"Good. I'll be back in an hour."

21

"THIS ISN'T THE OFFICE," Lucas said.

"No," Tracker said.

He'd been so lost in thought that he hadn't even noticed where they were until Tracker had parked at the curb. The sun had set, but in the thin light of dusk he could see the tree-lined street, the small but carefully tended lawns. Georgetown.

"Mind telling me why we're here?" Lucas asked.

"*She's* here. You asked about the doc twice when you called from the plane and two more times since I picked you up at the airport. Obviously, you have some doubts about my ability to keep an eye on her, so I figured you wanted to take over."

"No. I'm not...I—" It was one of the only times in his thirty-two years that Lucas found himself at a loss for words. He had a plan for handling MacKenzie Lloyd. He'd come up with it during the seven nights he'd spent at Vincent Falcone's villa. Seven sleepless nights. Without Mac. He'd shared a bed with her...what? Only twice. And now he couldn't seem to sleep without her. Even on the plane ride home, he hadn't been able to concentrate. All he could think about was her.

"You're not what?" Tracker asked. "Worried about her? Head over heels in love with her?"

"She doesn't...I don't... We...."

"See. You can't even finish a sentence. She's not in much better shape herself."

Lucas whirled on him then and grabbed the front of his shirt. "You said she was all right."

"She's fine, except for the fact that she asks about you just about as often as you ask about her. The two of you are gaga over each other."

"I'm just tired." Lucas relaxed his grip, knowing that he hadn't told the truth. For the first time in his life, he was truly afraid. It was the same cold deadly fear that had bit into him when he'd seen her hanging from the balloon while Gil Stafford pointed a gun at her heart.

He couldn't lose her. The words had screamed through his mind. After that, he wasn't sure of the exact sequence of events. Mac had jumped and landed on Stafford, a gun had gone off, he'd felt the heat of a bullet pass by his cheek. Later, they'd told him that while he was breaking Stafford's jaw, Tracker had climbed the rope ladder and landed the balloon and Sophie safely. But his only clear memory was of what Mac had looked like, lying on the ground, so pale, so still. For one moment, until he'd felt the pulse at her throat, he was sure she was gone.

Lucas rubbed the heels of his hands over his eyes. That heart-stopping moment had been what had prevented him from contacting Mac over the past seven days. The mind-numbing, body-aching, out-of-control fear that had ripped through him had scared him. He'd never been someone to lose control and Mac had a way of making him do just that on a continual basis.

"You can think of this as an intervention, if you want. But I can't see you getting anything accomplished at the office until you settle things with the doc. That deal you made with Falcone—promising to mentor Sonny until his heir can take over—that was not something a sane man does. You're not making any money for Wainright Enterprises on that one."

"It's an old debt," Lucas said. "A personal one."

Tracker paused for a moment as he digested that. "Okay. But I still say the office isn't the place for you right now.

You can either go in there and settle things with the doc or you and I are going to get rip-roaring drunk.''

Lucas nearly smiled. ''Do you remember the last time?''

''Small town near Trinidad.''

''Istanbul. I'll never forget carrying you back to the hotel.''

''It was Trinidad and I carried you. You never could hold your booze.''

''You passed out first.''

For a few moments, silence settled over the car.

''You're right,'' Lucas finally said. ''I love her.''

''You got a plan?''

''I don't have a clue.'' Lucas opened the door and stepped out.

STEPPING OUT of her shower, Mac grabbed a towel and wrapped herself in it. She had barely ten minutes until Sophie would be back, and she hadn't yet decided what to wear. Every time she looked at one of the outfits she'd shopped for with Madame Gervaise, she began to imagine wearing it with Lucas.

Lucas. As sadness bloomed within her, she reached to rub the steam off the mirror so that she could see her image clearly.

She was a mess. And she was going to stay that way until she got a grip.

As a scientist, she knew that it was essential to face the facts. Number one, she had fallen in love with Lucas Wainright. Number two, he did not love her back. So what was she going to do about that?

Tightening the towel around her, she began to pace back and forth in the small bathroom. There had to be a solution. She could always find one in the lab. Frowning, she began to pace faster. What she had on her hands was a man who didn't want her.

Stopping short, she stared at herself in the mirror. *A man who didn't want her!* Her father hadn't wanted her either. He'd walked away, and she hadn't been able to stop him.

But she wasn't a child anymore. And wasn't the whole point of her research to make sure that her future husband never walked away from her?

Striding into the bedroom, she studied her clothes. She was going to go manhunting all right. And she wasn't going to give up until she had tried every single bit of her research on Lucas Wainright III.

She was reaching for a short red leather skirt when the doorbell rang. Sophie. Tightening the knot on her towel, she raced down the hall and opened the door.

For one moment she couldn't speak. The joy was sharp and bright, the panic racing behind it fast and fierce.

"What the hell do you think you're doing?" Lucas asked as he stepped into the room and slammed the door behind him. "You couldn't know who was knocking. You just threw open the door, dressed in practically nothing."

He was angry, she noted as he began to pace. Furious. She watched his legs eat up the length of her living-room floor in four paces. She sensed the same leashed violence in him that she'd felt that morning at the Wainright Casa Marina when he'd discovered she'd lied to him about Sophie. Her stomach sank as he whirled to face her.

It was only then that she noticed how tired he looked.

Nerves jumping, she said, "Would you like something to drink? Wine? Coffee? I have a very nice brandy that Sophie gave me for my birthday."

She was babbling. She had to stop and think.

"Brandy."

She had to move past him—close enough to catch his scent, feel his heat. It was enough to make her knees weak, so weak that she wasn't sure how she made it to the kitchen. It didn't help one bit that he dogged her steps.

"I came to clear up some matters between us."

Her stomach sank to her feet. He was tying up loose

ends. She didn't feel it at all when the brandy snifter slipped out of her hand and splintered on the floor.

"Don't move. Where do you keep your broom?"

She didn't say a word as he opened a closet and found what he was looking for. Instead, she drew in a deep breath, unfastened the towel she was wearing, and let it slip to the floor.

The moment Lucas turned around, he felt as if he'd been poleaxed. Her skin had the milky, translucent look of fine porcelain, and the glass shards at her feet glinted like diamonds. But it was her eyes that drew him. In them he saw the same mixture of hope and fear that he was feeling. In them he saw his future.

"Don't move," he said again as he dropped the broom and moved toward her. Gripping her hips, he lifted her onto the counter.

But she didn't obey. Even as his hands moved over her, she was busy, pulling at his belt, loosening his slacks. Then her mouth moved on his, teeth nipping, tongue probing, as her fingers closed around him.

"Now," she murmured, inching closer and wrapping her legs around him. "Right now."

It took him only seconds, an eternity, to free himself and push into her, to feel her flesh part then pulse and tighten around him. For a moment he was sure his heart stopped. It was like coming home.

Then she arched against him.

"No, don't," he managed to say as he gripped her hips and held her still. His voice sounded hoarse, strange. His whole body was straining to move, to drive himself into her. "Do you know how long I've been waiting to do this?"

"Seven days, three hours, and… If you'd let me move, I could check my watch and tell you the minutes. Not that I've been keeping track."

Lucas grinned. And though he didn't know how in the world it was possible in his present position, he felt some of his tension ease. It was the first time he'd smiled in seven days too. She never said what he expected. She never did what he expected. Was he ever going to get used to that? He used one hand to tip back her head so that he could see her eyes. "I wasn't talking about the sex. I've waited all my life for you."

He watched her eyes widen.

"I just didn't know what I was waiting for. I didn't even fully realize how empty my life was until…" No, he wasn't going to spoil this by thinking of what might have been. "I love you, Mac."

Her eyes went even wider. "Lucas—"

"No, let me finish. I know that it's too soon. I know what we agreed on. No strings. I had a strategy all mapped out. I was going to call you tomorrow and ask you out on a traditional date—flowers, champagne, dancing under the stars. I figured after a month, I'd propose."

"Propose?"

The stunned look on her face sent a bolt of panic shooting through him.

"Lucas, you don't even know me. I'm just beginning to know myself."

"We'll work on it together, over a lifetime. I'm not going to take no for an answer. I'll hound you until—"

"Yes."

Feelings tumbled through him. Joy. Relief. He barely had time to absorb them before she was tightening her grip on him with her arms and legs and the hot, moist inner part of her.

"There's just one condition."

His eyes narrowed. "And that would be?"

Her lips curved. "That I get to start moving now."

He felt the laughter bubble up. It might have broken free, but she wasn't waiting for his permission. Her mouth was on his again, her body arching. He thought his brain might just evaporate into steam.

"Now," she murmured over and over until it became a

chant in his blood. Not that he needed any encouragement. Still, he struggled to keep his rhythm under control so that the pleasure could stretch out and build. Each time he sank into her and felt that slick, wet grip pull him deeper, he knew that he was losing part of himself, gaining part of her.

"Quick. Now." Her voice was breathless, her body agile.

He started to move then, hard and fast. He felt the moment that her climax tore through her; it was more than enough to draw him with her into a dark vortex of pleasure.

Afterward, they clung, trying to catch their breaths. He could feel hers, tickling his neck. "I love you, MacKenzie Lloyd."

"I love you too."

He didn't know until she said it how much he'd wanted to hear the words from her.

"I have a secret to tell you."

She drew back then to look at him. "I hope you're not going to tell me that you have a crazy wife hidden away in the attic."

With a quick chuckle, he rested his head against her forehead. "No. Not that. This is something that you can add to your research. I've just discovered what my favorite sexual fantasy is."

Her eyebrows arched. "And that would be?"

"Coming home from work to find a naked woman in my kitchen."

"No problem," she said as he lifted her and started down the hall in search of the bedroom. "But I'm going to change that."

"You think?"

"I *know*," she assured him. "You're going to love being wrapped in plastic wrap."

They were both laughing when they tumbled together onto the bed.

Epilogue

LUCAS LET HIMSELF into his house, smiling at the spicy scent of cinnamon and…apples? It had to mean Mac was cooking. In his bachelor days, he'd rarely used the kitchen, preferring instead to eat out or order food brought in. Since their wedding three months ago, Mac had insisted on fixing dinner at least three times a week.

Wives should know how to cook, she'd insisted. After all, how hard could it be? Surely not more difficult than one of her experiments in the lab.

His smile widening, Lucas set down his briefcase and began to loosen his tie as he strode down the hall. "Mac the chef" was just one more delightful personality that was part of MacKenzie Lloyd. She cooked with the same total focus and precision that she did everything else. The food was…getting better. Coming home to find his wife elbow deep in pots and bowls and finding a way to lure her off task, well, that was quite simply the best.

His wife. Just thinking the word sent a wave of joy through him. And this was the first night she'd cooked all week because she hadn't been feeling up to par. Each night they'd ordered in from a different restaurant, but nothing had tempted her. She must be feeling better.

Perhaps well enough to create his favorite fantasy? He quickened his stride, but when he entered the kitchen, there was no naked woman waiting for him.

There was no sign of Mac either. The room was pristine clean except for the items lined up on one counter. The moment his gaze swept over them, he began to smile again.

A bowl of thick whipped cream, a tall squeeze bottle of chocolate syrup, a large economy-size roll of plastic wrap and a string of pearls.

A very long string of pears. Lifting it, he drew it out to its full length—nearly three feet. Lucas felt himself grow hard just imagining…

The bell on the microwave dinged. Opening it, he discovered a glass mug with a cinnamon stick in it. Hot spiced apple cider?

He knew the moment she entered the kitchen, and he slowly turned to face her. Three months of marriage and he still wasn't used to the shock of pleasure that moved through him when he saw her in his house and realized that she was his to keep, to cherish. "You're not naked."

And she wasn't. She was wearing one of his shirts, opened just enough to let him know that she was wearing nothing underneath it, and she'd knotted a black tie loosely around her neck. Her hair was mussed and her feet were bare, the toenails painted a pale shade of pink. Desire speared through him.

"I thought I would dress for dinner tonight."

He glanced at the counter, surprised at the effort it took not to go to her and to take her where she stood. But three months of marriage had taught him that sometimes it was better to give over control and go along for the ride.

"New pearls?" he asked.

"Do you like them?

"I don't think I want to eat them."

She smiled then, and he realized that it was the first time she had. And she hadn't moved toward him yet.

"What would you like to start off with?" she asked.

"My choice?"

"The first one is. Then it will be my turn."

He wanted to laugh then. But there was something in her eyes beneath the excitement…apprehension?

He glanced again at the selection lined up on the counter.

"It's quite a feast. Why don't you come here and help me select?"

He noticed the slight hesitation before she moved toward him. Once he had her hand tucked safely in his, he said, "I'm kind of leaning toward the whipped cream and chocolate syrup myself."

"Good choice. If we top that off with the hot apple cider, I figure we've hit at least two-thirds of the food pyramid—fruit, dairy and protein."

"I'm lucky to have a scientist keeping my diet on track."

"Want to know what I have in mind for the cider?" Mac asked.

"I always want to know what you have in mind," he said as he tucked a strand of flyaway hair behind her ear. The apprehension hadn't vanished yet from her eyes.

"I melted those little red-hot cinnamon pieces in it, so it's doubly hot. I'm going to drink it and then taste you." Her hand unerringly found the part of him that she was thinking of tasting.

With a sigh that ended on a moan, he rested his head against her forehead. "You're going to be the death of me." Then he carefully removed her hand from his erection. "Before we get to that, why don't you tell me the reason for the feast. Are we celebrating a special occasion?"

"Yes."

Now it was his turn to be apprehensive. Had he forgotten an anniversary of some sort?

Licking her lips, she continued, "I did a little experiment today. And then I reran it five times. I wanted to make sure."

He smiled at her. "You had a breakthrough at the lab. Don't tell me—let me guess. Wilbur is going to live to be a hundred."

"Not exactly. I mean, I didn't do it at the lab. I did it here."

"Here?"

"It came out positive. All five times. And the pharmacist told me the test has a very high accuracy rating. I'm…we're…pregnant."

"Pregnant?" Even as he said the word aloud, he struggled to take it in.

"Yes. That's why I have to get started, using my research, I mean. I'm going to get fat. I can't afford to let you get bored."

"Pregnant." He was beginning to absorb it. He could tell by the joy that was zinging through him. "You're pregnant." Lifting her off her feet, he swung her around and around, then abruptly stopped and set her on the counter. "I shouldn't be doing that. Are you all right?"

"I'm fine." Eye to eye, she studied him for a moment. "You're happy?"

He grinned at her. "Very."

Her expression remained serious. "I don't want to bore you. I don't want to lose you…ever."

He kissed her softly, coaxing her into it, pouring everything he felt into it until they were both nearly drowning. Finally, he drew away. "You're not going to lose me. Ever. And I don't know how I'm supposed to get bored. There are so many parts of you that I love. So many parts that I'm still discovering. I can't wait to meet Mac the mother."

She hugged him then, and he felt her lips curve against his chest. Her sigh moved through him. "Let's get started on dinner. You grab the chocolate and whipped cream. I'll bring the cider and the other stuff."

"Appetizers first," he said as he quickly wrapped her legs around him and pulled down his zipper.

"Appetizers?" Her breath hitched as she took him in.

"I'm very hungry."

"You are?"

"Oh, yes. And the appetizer is always the first step to enjoying a great meal. You do like to take everything one step at a time, right?"

"Absolutely," Mac managed.

The laughter, the overwhelming joy welled up between them as they began to move together in a steady and familiar rhythm.

"We'll take it slowly," Lucas promised as he struggled to do just that. But already he could feel her climax begin to move through her. As always, his own control began to slip away. Drawing her closer, he spoke softly. "And when you reach the heights, I'll be right there...with you. Always."

And he was.

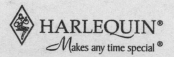

HINTBB

Back by popular request...
those amazing Buckhorn Brothers!

*Once
and Again*

Containing two full-length novels by
the Queen of Sizzle,

USA Today bestselling author

LORI
FOSTER

They're all gorgeous, all sexy and all single...at least for now!
This special volume brings you the sassy and seductive
stories of Sawyer and Morgan Buckhorn—offering you
hours of *hot, hot* reading!

Available in June 2002 wherever books are sold.

And in September 2002 look for FOREVER AND ALWAYS,
containing the stories of Gabe and Jordan Buckhorn!

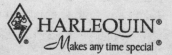

HARLEQUIN®
Makes any time special ®

Visit us at www.eHarlequin.com

PHLF-1R